BY
ALEXANDER GORDON SMITH

THE FURY

ESCAPE FROM FURNACE

LOCKDOWN

SOLITARY

DEATH SENTENCE

FUGITIVES

EXECUTION

THE NIGHT CHILDREN:
AN ESCAPE FROM FURNACE STORY

ALEXANDER GORDON SMITH

FUGITIVES

ESCAPE FROM FURNACE 4

SQUARE
FISH

FARRAR STRAUS GIROUX
NEW YORK

SQUARE
FISH

An Imprint of Macmillan

Library of Congress Cataloging-in-Publication Data
Smith, Alexander Gordon.
    Fugitives / Alexander Gordon Smith.
        p.   cm. — (Escape from Furnace ; 4)
    Summary: After achieving the impossible by escaping the laboratories and
cells of Furnace Penitentiary, Alex, injected with superhuman abilities, must
uncover the last of Furnace's secrets—the truth about the man who built the
prison.
    ISBN 978-1-250-00339-3
    [1. Prisons—Fiction.   2. Fugitives from justice—Fiction.   3. Science
fiction.   4. Horror stories.]   I. Title.
PZ7.S6423Fu 2012   [Fic]—dc23   2011022981

First published in Great Britain by Faber and Faber Limited.
Originally published in the United States by Farrar Straus Giroux
First Square Fish Edition: September 2012
Square Fish logo designed by Filomena Tuosto
Book designed by Jay Colvin
macteenbooks.com

6   8   10   9   7

AR: 6.5 / LEXILE: 950L

TO GRAN BAIRD

Thanks for everything

AND TO GRANDDAD BAIRD

I wish we could have shared our stories

I'm grateful that there's so much of both of you in me

FUGITIVES

BENEATH HEAVEN IS HELL.
BENEATH HELL IS FURNACE.

ESCAPE FROM FURNACE 4

HAPPY EVER AFTER

I WISH I COULD TELL YOU that my story ended here.

I wish I could tell you that this was my happy ever after.

Because it should have been, right? I mean, we were out. We'd been to hell and back but the important thing was that we *had* made it back. We'd slit open the belly of Furnace Penitentiary, spilled its guts all over the streets. It was dead, and we'd been born again, taking our first steps in a world we thought we'd lost forever. It had to be over. This had to be the end of it. All we had to do was run for the hills and live out the rest of our lives on fresh air and freedom.

But can a story like mine ever have a happy ending?

Does somebody like me ever deserve one?

There wasn't much time for looking back as we ran from the broken gates, ushered on by the blinding brightness of the rising sun. But I couldn't help it. Even as the sound of the siren faded into birdsong my mind replayed everything that had happened. I don't know why, exactly. All I wanted to do was forget it, put everything behind me, pretend that it had never happened. But Furnace wasn't going to let me. I may have found a way out of the prison but the prison was still buried deep inside my head, locked in every thought, every memory.

I pictured myself as a kid, walking streets just like these a life-time ago, so obsessed with money that I didn't care that I was a thief, a bully. I saw myself and Toby—a friend whose face I could no longer picture but who I would never forget—breaking into a house, hoping that we'd strike it rich. I saw us being cornered by the blacksuits, Furnace's hulking guards with their cruel silver eyes. I watched them shoot Toby in the head, the same way I'd watched it a hundred times before; a thousand. I saw myself framed for his murder and sentenced to life without possibility of parole in Furnace Penitentiary. I saw it all in shades of black and gray and red that seemed so much brighter than the world through which I was running.

The flashbacks kept coming, bleeding into my vision like some kind of hemorrhage. It felt as though I relived every single second of my incarceration—the early days where I thought the only escape I'd make was jumping off the eighth level; my cellmate Donovan and my best friend, Zee, the only ones keeping me sane; lying in bed at night waiting for the blood watch to come, for the wheezers to drag me into the tunnels below; then discovering that crack in the chipping-room floor and blowing our way to freedom—only to find ourselves recaptured and snared by the darkness of solitary confinement.

There, with the weight of the world on our shoulders, we un-covered the truth about Furnace—the experiments that the war-den and the wheezers were doing on the kids. They were pumped full of nectar, a black liquid full of tiny golden flecks, like distant stars. Then the wheezers cut them open and stitched them back together into something completely different. I still don't know exactly how the nectar worked. If it was successful, then it turned its child victim into a superhuman blacksuit, packed tight with muscle and able to survive an injury that would kill a mortal. You had no memory of who you were, your past life. You became one of the warden's soldiers. That's what had happened to Donovan, but I'd killed him—I'd *freed* him—before he could turn completely.

The nectar didn't work with everybody, though. Sometimes it had no effect at all, and other times it would go wrong, poisoning its victim's soul, reducing him to a mindless, razor-clawed freak that stalked the corridors feasting on blood. A *rat*.

But that wasn't the worst of it. Some prisoners didn't turn into blacksuits or rats. They became something else, something that shouldn't be possible. The nectar *chose* them, flooding their bodies and causing them to mutate into immense beasts of unimaginable fury, killing machines known as berserkers.

There was no telling what you'd become with nectar inside you. It was the warden's poison that decided your fate.

Zee and I had been down there, in solitary, for what seemed like forever, rescued by a kid called Simon who'd managed to escape the wheezers' knives. He'd been halfway to becoming a blacksuit, his torso and one arm packed with muscle, his eyes turned silver, but he'd been discarded before the procedure could be finished. Once again we'd made a bid for freedom—climbing the incinerator chimney—and once again we'd failed. This time we'd fallen right into the warden's lap.

The warden. I could see his face now: every time I blinked he flashed up before me, his mouth twisted into that soulless smile, his eyes black pits that promised nothing but pain. He had let his wheezers cut me open with their filthy tools and pump me full of their poison. He had let them stuff me with someone else's muscles, someone else's flesh. He had turned me into one of them. He'd given me silver eyes and a black suit and for a moment—for a single, horrific second—I'd almost given myself to him, I'd almost called him Father and myself a Soldier of Furnace . . .

But something had stopped me. Something had kept me human. And instead of making me one of them the warden had given me the strength I needed to make a final bid for freedom. Zee, Simon, and I, we fought our way up from the tunnels back into the main prison. The blacksuits hadn't been able to stop us, the mutant, skinless dogs had cowered with their tails between their legs, the wheezers had been powerless, even the warden had run out of tricks.

No, only one person had come close to ending our dream of freedom. Alfred Furnace himself, the mysterious man behind the prison's darkest secrets. He had sent two berserkers to stop us, and only by injecting myself with more of the warden's poison, the nectar, had I been able to stop them. The battle may not have cost me my life, but it stripped away all but the last remnants of my sanity. Now the nectar is the only thing keeping me alive, but it's also trying to turn me into one of them. It's what drives the freaks of Furnace—and freaks like me.

WITH THE HELP OF THE INMATES we cracked the gates and stormed out into the world, hundreds of us, shouting and screaming as we flooded the streets, bleeding the prison dry. We were out. We were free.

That should have been it, shouldn't it? That should have been the end of my story. But how could it be? Even now I can hear the sound of gunfire as the police start to round us up, the *whump-whump-whump* of helicopter blades overhead. Soon the entire city will be in lockdown. We haven't escaped from our prison, we've just moved into a new one. And although there are countless places to hide, there's still nowhere to run.

And that's not all. Alfred Furnace is coming, and he's bringing his army. I can hear his voice in my head, carried by the nectar, and his fury is almost enough to crack my soul in two. Yes, Furnace is coming. He will find us.

And when he does there will be all hell to pay.

Some happy ending.

FREEDOM

WHEN YOU'VE BEEN LOCKED up for too long, freedom can kill you.

It's overwhelming, like a dam bursting, a trillion gallons of icy water surging into your head, threatening to demolish or short-circuit all that remains of your sanity. I can't think of any other way to describe it. The moment I began to run from the ruined gates of Furnace my brain started to overload, my vision flickering, my limbs surrendering, my speech failing. All that existed was that sudden rush, a moment of blind emotion—half panic, half euphoria—that felt powerful enough to stop my heart dead.

Great, I thought as I struggled to stay upright, my heart misfiring like a clogged engine, each desperate beat sending a bolt of pain through my chest. *I went through all that to get out, and the second I do my mind decides it's had enough.*

I stumbled, felt hands grab my arms. I stared to my side, but I couldn't make out who was there, my vision had become an ocean of dirty white flecked with sparks. I scrunched my eyes shut, forced myself to take in a breath. It was hard, as though my body had forgotten how to perform its most basic functions, but as soon as the air hit my lungs the whiteout began to clear.

"Jesus, Alex," came a voice, the fingers on my arm squeezing hard. "I thought you'd be fitter than this, what with all that running away you did inside."

I let my head drop to my chest, took a second deep breath that steadied my pulse and another that seemed to put the bones back into my limbs. This time when I looked, I could see that Zee was standing next to me, his face shiny with sweat and his eyes on fire. Somebody tugged from the other side and I turned to see Simon, his grossly muscled arm wrapped around mine.

"We gotta keep moving if we don't want to end up back down there," Simon said. He stamped on the sidewalk and I suddenly pictured the labyrinth of Furnace Penitentiary deep beneath the concrete, the vast complex like some razor-toothed behemoth rising up through the depths, its mouth open wide to swallow the city whole. I shook the image from my head, the motion making the world spin.

A blurred shape sped past us down the road, the slap of paper shoes echoing off the buildings on either side. Two more inmates were racing along the sidewalk opposite. It was pretty clear what they were running from: the air behind us was alive with sirens, so many of them that the sound they made had lost its undulating pitch and was now a constant, tuneless wail. In the copper-colored skies above, three helicopters scoured the shrinking shadows, their spotlights silver streaks against the sun as it unfolded itself from the horizon.

"Ready?" asked Zee. "I know you've been through a lot, but if we don't move . . ." He seemed to choke at the thought of what might happen.

I started running again, Zee's hand on my arm for the first few steps. Been through a lot? He wasn't kidding. My body—my new body, the one that the warden had given me—was a patchwork of scars. Every time I moved they threatened to split, and I pictured the poisoned flesh escaping from beneath my skin, the muscles uncoiling. It was an unpleasant thought. Or was it? I would have given anything to be able to undo the warden's work so easily.

But it was this mutated body that had gotten us all out of Furnace alive. Without it, I wouldn't have stood a chance against the berserkers. Those monsters would have torn everybody in Furnace to shreds, every last living soul. I may have hated having the body of a blacksuit, but without it I'd have had no body at all.

"Anyone know where we are?" Simon said as he sprinted. "Do either of you two know the city? I lived over in Carlton Heights; never been up this way before."

I took my eyes off the road to look around, still squinting into the pale light. To our left was a warehouse of some sort, emblazoned with a massive sign shaped like a cardboard box. Similar buildings lined the street on both sides. There were dark alleyways between them, and corrugated-iron fences that promised hiding places beyond. But if we took cover this close to Furnace we'd be found in minutes.

"I didn't live in the city," Zee wheezed. "Our house was miles away, sorry. What about you, Alex?"

"Yeah, I lived here," I said, trying to get my bearings. "But on the other side of town, over the river in the suburbs. I don't think I've ever been this far south."

We reached a junction, the red traffic light reflecting in the puddles below, making it look as if the street was about to erupt like a volcano. Just to get off the main road we swung right onto a narrow side street, our pace slowing as we all fought to breathe. The buildings here were smaller, mainly shops locked up for the night. One stood out from the rest, however, a hulking lump of plastic and concrete that nudged up against the pinkening skies like a massive headstone. My breath caught with the shock of recognition.

"I know this place," I sputtered. "It's Edwards Mall, isn't it?"

"Yeah," said Simon, wiping a hand across his brow. "I think you're right. I came here when I was a kid, all the time. Had no idea this was a stone's throw from Furnace."

I'd come here with my parents too, once a month or so. It had been like a family day out. The memories hit me like a punch to the gut, the smell of Subway sandwiches and pretzels, the hum of people, the promise of presents. I mentally slapped myself. Reminiscing would get me killed. That life, my old life, was long gone.

Something popped, a gunshot from maybe a couple of streets away. We slowed down, scampering into the shadows that pooled against the shops and crouching to a halt. It had only been a few minutes since we'd gotten out, but already the new day was drawing a blanket of light over the city. At first the sight had been the best thing I'd ever witnessed—I never thought I'd see a sunrise again. But now it seemed as if nature was conspiring with Furnace, and with the police. If the sun can see you, so can everybody else.

"We should get inside," Zee whispered, nodding toward the mall.

"You kidding?" Simon replied. "In ten minutes or so that place is gonna be crawling with police. We gotta move, head up to the river. If we can get into the city we can disappear, get on a train, hot-wire a car or something, anything to get us as far away from Furnace as possible. I ain't gonna get caught hiding out in some shopping center just around the corner."

"Simon's got a point," I said, wanting nothing more than to rest but desperate to put as much distance as I could between us and the prison. "We should break now; run for it, before they get organized."

"No, you're wrong," Zee said. "We really need to—"

He broke off as one of the sirens rose up from the chorus. We froze against one another as a squad car blazed across the junction we had just crossed, vanishing as quickly as it had appeared. It had probably been following the inmates we'd seen earlier, but more would follow, countless more.

"We need to get off the streets and come up with a plan," Zee went on. "In there we can grab some food and water, and we can get out of these prison uniforms. If we're walking down the street in Furnace rags then we're definitely going to get picked up. It'll only take five minutes. Besides . . ."

Zee looked me up and down and I followed his gaze. My overalls, which had been falling apart to begin with, were ripped in a dozen places, my tortured skin visible beneath.

"Besides what?" I muttered.

"You're practically indecent," Zee said with a glint of a smile in his eyes. "Any minute now that thing's gonna fall right off you and you'll be running down the street naked."

Both Simon and I began to laugh and I had to pinch my nose to make it stop. It didn't want to, the emotion bubbling up inside me so hard that my shoulders were shaking and my ribs were singing. Even when another wailing police car roared over the intersection, taking it so fast that when it hit a bump in the road it almost took off, I was snorting into my hand. Freedom will do that to you, though, like I was saying. You could laugh yourself right into the grave.

Simon wiped a tear from his eye and turned toward the mall. After a second or two he nodded decisively.

"Okay," he said. "But we're in and out, right? I'm not spending all day looking around the bloody shops."

His words could have come from my dad—he'd said something similar every time Mom had dragged him into the city—and that made me laugh until I cried. I felt Zee's hand clamp over my own and gradually the moment of insanity passed. I shrugged him away and got to my feet, leading the way toward the huge building and whispering over my shoulder.

"Okay, people, let's go shopping."

DAYBREAK

THE HUGE MAIN DOORS of Edwards Mall were still shuttered so we walked farther down the street and turned left at the next junction, walking along the side of the mall until we came to the loading-bay entranceways. They opened up into nothing but darkness, and the way they sloped tunnel-like beneath the ground made my skin crawl.

"Déjà vu, anyone?" Zee said with a nervous laugh.

"Come on, it's just a mall," I replied, leading the way. My silver eyes penetrated the shadows as though I was holding a flashlight, peeling away layers of gloom to reveal an empty service road that curled down and to the left. If we carried straight on we'd get to the parking lot, but we swung around the bend to find ourselves in an enormous underground loading dock. I let my eyes drift up to see three sets of double doors in the far wall. It was then that I noticed the blinking red lights studded into the ceiling.

"We're being watched," I said, pointing. "Security cameras."

"Forget them," Simon said, making his way cautiously toward the doors. He reached the low wall of one of the bays and began to haul himself up. "They're just recording; won't nobody see that footage till we're long gone."

As if to prove his point he flicked his middle finger at the ceiling, waving it around for a second before crouching down and offering Zee his hand. Zee took it, letting himself be pulled up. I followed with a graceless leap, my muscles crying out as they propelled me onto the platform. Simon made his way to the nearest door, pressing gently on its handle.

"It won't be—" was as far as I got before the door clicked open, flooding the bay with light. Simon turned and flashed me a lopsided smile.

"My brother used to work in a mall, over by Carlton," he said. "We'd sneak in sometimes after dark. Same thing everywhere—shops are all locked, front and back, but the access areas are always open." He pushed through. "Great for playing manhunt."

Beyond was a wide corridor of cinder block and concrete, lined with metal doors and lit by just about the brightest bulbs in existence. I had to squint as we jogged along it.

"Computer games?" Simon said, reading the names of the shops stenciled on the back of the doors. "Nope. How about some books? Yeah, right. Alex, you remember if there was a department store in here?"

There had been. Another vivid memory flashed up—a vast shop occupying one corner of the mall, filled with just about every item imaginable. My parents had let me spend ten minutes in the toy department each time they visited, but they had rarely bought me anything. I let myself get lost in the past, realizing with sadness that I could picture every inch of that toy shop—the stuffed bears around the cash register, the magic sets stacked on the shelf opposite the elevator, the vast tree they always put up on the top floor every Christmas—but I couldn't remember what my parents looked like. In my head they were faceless mannequins that stood in the corner of my vision, moving every time I moved so I could never see them clearly.

"Yo, Alex!" said Simon, giving me a gentle tap on the shoulder. The memory flew, but left behind a dull throb of heartache. "You still with us? Department store? Remember?"

"Yeah," I said. "Yeah, there is one. No idea where, though, sorry. Coming in this way, everything's all back to front."

Simon muttered something and carried on, the doors flashing past us on either side—furniture, phones, music and DVDs, underwear, pharmaceuticals, sweets. It was five minutes later, so deep into the warren of passageways that I didn't think I'd ever be able to navigate my way back, that we reached a double door marked HARVEY'S.

"That's it!" I blurted. "Harvey's, like the rabbit."

Simon stopped and began to run his fingers along the edge of the right-hand door, eventually pulling free a thick cable. He peeled it away from the wall, splinters of paint fluttering earthward.

"This won't take a second," he said, frowning in concentration. He used a long fingernail to split the insulation lengthways, then he clamped one of the wires in his broken teeth and bit down.

"Whoa!" said Zee. "You crazy?"

Simon shook his head, chowing down on the wire like a rabid dog until it finally surrendered. He carefully folded the split ends away from each other then let it fall back against the wall.

"Stand back," he said. We did as we were told, and Simon threw himself at the doors. They were solid, and with a wheeze he rebounded onto his backside. Zee's laughter tinkled down the corridor, the sound like wind chimes. Simon clambered to his feet and looked at me. "You wanna do the honors?"

I tensed my upper body and ran at the doors, hitting them

square in the middle. With a squeal that sounded almost human, the lock sprang and both sides flapped open. I stumbled forward into shadow, skidding across the smooth floor and almost losing my balance. By the time I turned around Zee and Simon had followed me in and closed the doors behind them. Simon slapped the wall a few times before hitting a bank of switches, flipping them all. Gradually the lights blinked to life, revealing another narrow corridor, this one lined with clothes racks, stacked pallets, and various loose ends. Limbless store dummies eyeballed us.

"How'd you know how to get in?" asked Zee, collapsing onto a shrink-wrapped sofa. He lifted his foot and I noticed it was bare aside from a covering of blood. Paper shoes weren't much use on the outside. I flexed my toes inside the boots the warden had given me, happy that I hadn't thrown them on the fire the same way I'd thrown my black suit.

"Piece of piss," Simon replied. "Done it countless times. I weren't no angel on the outside, remember?" He looked at me knowingly. "Hell, none of us was, right?"

"Right," I replied. "Come on."

I made my way to the end of the corridor, past a stockroom that was too similar to the ones in Furnace for my liking. I peered inside, half expecting a rat to bound from the darkness and lock its teeth into my throat, and I turned away before I could think the creature into existence.

"Oh God, I'm not getting in that," came Zee's voice. I followed his line of sight to the elevator at the end of the hallway, the doors open as if inviting us in. It was about the same size as the one in Furnace, not the main elevator but the smaller one that linked the bottom of general population to the blood-drenched tunnels below. I was with Zee on this one. I had no desire ever to ride in an elevator again. I just wouldn't trust it not to carry us to the bowels of hell.

Fortunately there was another door beside it, the round glass panel revealing a staircase beyond. We bounded through and started upward. Every step felt like my last. I could have happily curled up right there and then on the cold concrete and slept for a thousand years. I could barely even remember the last time I had rested, an age ago in a bed deep beneath the surface. I had just completed the warden's test, he had welcomed me into his family and called me his son. And I had slept better than I had ever done in my life.

The thought sent a chill scurrying up my spine, and I forced it from my mind. I'd have all the time in the world to sleep when we were out of the city. Right now I had to stay sharp. But still tiredness gripped me like a funeral shroud, numbing my body and my mind, making the world seem dream-like. And behind the exhaustion something else, a feeling that I was hollow, empty. It was almost like hunger, but deeper, as though it came from the very core of my being, as though my soul was starving.

I realized my thoughts were bordering on delusional, tried to switch them off in order to concentrate on putting one foot in front of the other. We climbed three flights before coming to a door, and Zee pushed it open.

"Women's clothing," he said. "Anybody fancy it?"

Simon nudged his way past Zee and through the door, holding it open for us. I staggered in to see that the store was alive, the lights on, the elevators running, and the gentle buzz of mall music giving the scene a surreal atmosphere. I shrank back, half expecting to see shoppers milling about between the racks of clothing, then realized that Simon must have switched everything on when we first arrived. There was no sign of a clock anywhere and I had no idea what the time was, but given that the sun had barely risen, we probably still had a few hours before the mall opened for business.

Not that it would be opening today, I thought, given the fact that the entire neighborhood was crawling with escaped convicts and armed police.

"Come on," said Simon, setting off across the shop floor. Harvey's was huge, each level a seemingly endless expanse broken up by various displays and cash register stations. Simon made his way toward the nearest escalator, where a directory listed the various departments. He pressed an oversize finger against MENSWEAR.

"Let's get some kit first," he said, hopping onto the moving steps.

"I don't know, but I think this might be the best thing for you, Alex." I turned to see Zee holding up a pair of huge blue maternity dungarees covered with friendly-faced sunflowers. He pressed them up against me and murmured approvingly. "They're probably the only thing in here that will fit you. And besides, the denim really brings out the color of your bruises."

I brushed them away with a halfhearted scowl.

"You'll be wearing them on your head if you're not careful," I grumbled, stepping onto the escalator. It carried us up to the second level. To the left was an ocean of blacks and grays that stretched to the distant far wall. To the right was a small collection of sporting goods and behind that a bank of televisions. Framing it all was a huge glass wall that looked out over the rest of the mall.

Simon dashed into menswear with a cheerful whoop but Zee angled off toward the window. I followed Zee, walking into a small café and peering through the thick glass. Two levels of shops were laid out before us, lit by the dim glow of the mall's night security lights. On the ground floor I could make out a collection of cars and half expected to see police clambering out of them. But they were as still and as silent as the rest of the displays and I realized they were there on show.

"Looks like we're not alone," Zee said. I cupped my hand against the glare, peering through my own reflection to see a group of inmates strolling out of the shattered glass of a hardware store window on the level beneath us. They were too far away to recognize, but they were all holding what looked like shotguns. I didn't remember there being a gun shop in the mall, but then things had changed a lot since I was a kid.

"Maybe we should have thought of that," Zee said.

"Yeah, right," I replied, my breath clouding the view. "I haven't forgotten the last time you tried to use a gun. You almost killed us!"

"Shut up!" he replied with a grin. He turned, sniffing the air like a dog until he was facing a cabinet full of cakes. With a cry of delight he leaped behind the café's counter, picked up a chocolate cupcake, and stuffed the entire thing in his mouth. He started to move, then doubled back and picked up another one before setting off in the direction of the electronics department.

"This is great," he chirruped through a mouthful of cake. "I feel like we're in *Dawn of the Dead* or something. You ever see that? Y'know, when there are zombies all over the world and these people lock themselves up inside a mall."

I kind of remembered watching the remake but Zee was spouting off again before I could reply.

"Yeah, it was like the perfect place to hide out. You got food, supplies, water, everything you need. Loads of films and stuff, TVs like these ones. You'd never get bored." He had reached the televisions and began turning them on one by one. Most showed nothing but static, others blank blue screens that made Zee's face look even grayer than usual. "Man, it would be so cool if that's what was happening."

"I hate to break it to you, Zee," I said. "But what's after us is a lot worse than zombies. And we really don't have time to watch a film."

Zee had finished with the televisions and was busy switching on the various DVD players and satellite boxes beneath them. Three of the huge screens burst into life, the sudden flare of volume making my heart miss a beat. Zee stood back to admire his handiwork, tucking into his second cupcake. He didn't offer me any and I knew why—the last time I'd tried to eat anything I'd spewed up everywhere. Another gift of the warden's poison. I'd never eat chocolate again.

"Does that look like a film?" he said, pointing at the nearest screen. I looked to see a broadcaster sitting at a desk, her face a mask of seriousness. Behind her on the studio screen was live aerial footage of Furnace Penitentiary. In the short time since we had escaped, the Black Fort—the building that formed the only entrance to the prison—had been gripped by fire. One entire side was now bathed in liquid flame, the smoke masking the cruel sculptures mounted beneath its cathedral-like spire. I wasn't sure if the destruction inside had spread, or whether one of the inmates had started the inferno on his way out, but I found myself grinning. Nothing could make me happier than watching that hellhole burn.

Especially knowing that the warden, the blacksuits, and the

wheezers, and the rats too, were still down there, trapped. I offered a silent prayer that they'd all die screaming.

Except I knew that sooner or later the creeps would get out. The warden and his army, his sick force of freaks, would hit the streets. And Alfred Furnace too. I could still hear his laughter buried deep in the black poison that circulated through my veins. He was on his way, and he was bringing his berserkers with him. They were all heading to the city, they were heading here right now, and I knew deep down that they weren't coming just to round up a bunch of escapees.

"Man, we totally trashed that place," Zee said softly, another peal of laughter spilling from his grin.

I stared at the screen, too mesmerized by the pixelated flames to reply. It was the prison that was on fire now, but when Furnace reached the city the chaos would spread. It would spread far and wide.

I couldn't help thinking that when he arrived, the whole world would burn.

TELEVISION

THE BREACH OCCURRED *shortly after five o'clock this morning.*

The broadcaster's clipped accent was the perfect contrast to the scenes of carnage behind her. Zee and I had collapsed against a pillar, our eyes flicking between the various reports. There didn't seem to be anything on any channel but breaking news of our escape.

Authorities have cordoned off the prison and the surrounding area and have reportedly petitioned the government for help from the army to contain the breakout. There is as yet no word from Furnace Penitentiary itself as to exactly how the prison's security was breached and how many inmates have escaped.

On the bottom of the screen was a digital clock that read 05.43, and indicated the date. It was March the twenty-third. I couldn't believe how much time had passed, how much of my life had been stolen. Beneath that was a rolling text bar. I followed it as I listened.

PEOPLE IN THE CITY ARE BEING URGED TO STAY AT HOME, LOCK THEIR DOORS, AND IF POSSIBLE KEEP LIGHTS OFF AND CURTAINS

**CLOSED. DO NOT APPROACH OR CONFRONT
INMATES OR STRANGERS UNDER ANY CIRCUM-
STANCES. IF YOU SEE A PRISONER, OR SOME-
BODY YOU SUSPECT TO BE A PRISONER,
PLEASE CALL THE DESIGNATED PHONE LINE
BELOW. WE WILL UPDATE YOU AS SOON AS WE
HAVE FURTHER INFORMATION.**

Zee looked as if he was about to fall asleep—his eyelids almost
shut and his chocolate-streaked mouth drooping. I didn't blame
him. We weren't exactly safe in here, but for the first time in a
long time we weren't running for our lives or fighting tooth and
nail to stay alive. This mall was the closest thing we had to a
home, and the stillness that hung over the place—the quiet almost
church-like despite the chatter of the TVs and the constant drone
of music—was disarming. It was tempting to believe that we could
close our eyes here and wake up free men. And it was easy to forget that the events on-screen were happening half a dozen streets
away.

I turned my attention back to the television. A middle-aged
reporter was standing in the center of a street, trying and failing
not to look nervous, the burning prison visible behind him.
There were cops everywhere, and I thought I caught a glimpse of
a bunch of inmates being bundled into a van. The thick smoke,
flecked with sparkling reds and blues, meant that I couldn't be
sure.

*. . . supposed to have been the most secure prison in the world, but the
big question today is just how a group of teenage inmates managed to
crack security at Furnace Penitentiary. With memories of what has been*

dubbed the Summer of Slaughter still fresh in the minds of the nation, it's no surprise that people here are reacting with anger and distress to the news.

"This reminds me of being at home," Zee said, his voice slurred.

"You lived in a mall?" I joked. Zee raised a hand and batted me gently on the leg.

"No, you doofus. The news. I used to sit with my folks after dinner and watch it. They'd always stick a documentary or something on afterward." He paused, and for a moment I thought he might have dropped off. On-screen the reporter was being jostled to one side by an armed policeman, a gloved hand raised to block the shot. I tried to watch but my vision was swimming in and out of focus. For a fraction of a second the reporter and the policeman seemed to appear out of the screen, standing right in front of me wearing flowery maternity dresses, and I realized I'd fallen asleep. I snapped my head up, my entire body jolting.

"Do you think we'll be able to go home?" Zee asked. The question took me by surprise, waking me up a little.

"Seriously?" I asked. He nodded, and the sheer desperation in his expression was almost enough to force a lie from my lips. But there was no denying the truth. "Come on, Zee. As soon as they've finished searching the area, the police will be checking out our addresses. If you head home they'll catch you before the day is up, I guarantee it."

"Not if my parents hide me," he said. "Or if we all go away together. They'd do that, I know they would. They'd just get in the car and we could all drive somewhere nice, somewhere out of the way. Yours would do the same. We're their kids."

I spluttered, the noise half laugh and half sob. I may not have been able to remember my parents' faces but I had never forgotten the way they had condemned me, the way my mom had turned away after the court hearing, the way they had forgotten me. I had no doubt that if I stepped through my kitchen door they'd welcome me with tight smiles and a hushed call to the police. Zee seemed to read my mind.

"Well, mine would. You could come too; they'd like you."

The last few words were so quiet they were almost unrecognizable. Zee's chin slowly dropped until it hit his chest, his breathing growing heavier and steadier.

"Dream on, Zee," I said gently. "We're on our own now."

I lifted a hand and rested it on his shoulder, shaking him gently. We couldn't afford to sleep. The moment we let down our guard was the moment we put ourselves back in the warden's hands.

"Zee," I said more loudly. "Zee, stay awake."

I gripped him harder, feeling the jutting ridge of his shoulder blade beneath the skin. It was rising and falling with each breath, but after three or four it stopped, trembling weakly for a second before lying still. I waited for him to inhale, my heart in my throat, but he sat there scrunched against the pillar as still and silent as a corpse. I rolled onto my knees before him, both of my hands on his shoulders, shaking hard enough to make his teeth rattle.

"Zee!" I was shouting now. "Jesus, wake up! Zee? What's wrong."

His head lurched up like a puppet's, eyes locked onto mine. Only they weren't Zee's eyes, they were empty sockets in his head. No, not empty . . . They were full of darkness, not just shadow but something heavy and substantial that thrashed and spilled inside them like they were two cups of oil. I looked at Zee and felt as though all the goodness in the world had been extinguished. It was like meeting the warden's gaze, only infinitely worse. No, these eyes belonged to someone else. Some*thing* else. Something unspeakably evil. I don't know how I could be sure, but I was.

These eyes belonged to Alfred Furnace.

"Alex," the thing that was once Zee screamed, words blasted from the red-raw tunnel of its throat, "I AM COMING FOR YOU!"

Then it was grabbing me, shaking me relentlessly, my head banging against the wall, my teeth clacking together, screaming my name over and over and over—

"Alex! Alex, wake up!"

My eyes opened and for a moment all I could see was those oil-slick eyes gaping at me. I blinked, and the two versions of Zee's face overlapped, as though he was wearing a cheap Halloween mask that had slipped. One more blink and he snapped back to normal, his expression one of concern. His hands were around my collar and he was shaking me, hard enough to bounce my head off the pillar. When he saw that I'd come to he let go, rocking back on his heels.

"Thought we'd lost you for a minute there," he said.

I staggered to my feet, trying to rub some of the confusion from my head. I could have just fallen asleep, the vision a nightmare. But I knew better. Furnace had been inside my head. Somehow he had peeled open my mind with filthy fingers and seeded his thoughts there. I slapped my cheek a couple of times, then yawned twice, the rush of oxygen to my brain brightening the room.

"Where's Simon?" I said, knowing that the only way I was going to stay awake was by keeping upright. "We'd better get moving."

I didn't wait for a response, shuffling across the smooth floor toward menswear. Simon was lost in the middle of it, almost buried by a pile of clothes. He was smoothing down the front of a black designer hoodie.

"Fatties' department is just over there," he said, peeking out of the cotton folds and nodding to one side.

"Thanks," I muttered, squeezing between the overstuffed racks. My mind must still have been pretty fragile, because it almost shattered when I crossed an aisle and saw a shape loom up beside me. I turned to see a blacksuit there, decked in torn overalls and his cold silver eyes glinting. I fell back against a table laden with jeans, my hands darting up defensively. The blacksuit's did the same, and it was only when I waved at it, the hulking brute imitating my actions, that I recognized my reflection.

It was the first time I had seen myself properly since my surgery. Of course deep down I'd known what the warden had done to me. I knew that he'd torn me open and stuffed me with somebody else's flesh, making me bigger, stronger, faster. But when I saw myself in my own imagination I still saw *me*, the skinny kid I'd been when I entered the prison.

That . . . that *thing* in the mirror—its torso massive, its limbs bulging so much they looked like they would burst, its skin lined with black veins, and those eyes . . . It was a monster. It was Frankenstein's repulsive creation, bruises and blemishes beaten into every square inch, scars crisscrossing like roads on a map. It couldn't be me. It just couldn't.

But it was.

I groaned, the noise boiling up from my stomach. I held my

giant hands up in front of my face so I wouldn't see the tears, then I scurried shamefully away from the mirror.

Focus, I told myself. *You have to focus or you're not getting out of here.*

Ahead was a shelf full of carefully folded tracksuit trousers and I rummaged through them, wiping my blurred eyes until I could make out the size. I pulled out an XXXL, sending the rest crumpling to the floor. They were tight but comfortable enough. A minute or so later and I was also wearing a massive black hooded sweatshirt and a brand-new pair of size-14 Nikes. I felt a little better being free of my Furnace stripes, but I still avoided the full-length mirrors as I made my way back to the electronics department.

Simon was leaning against the same pillar as I had been earlier, trying on a gold watch he had found. Zee had also gotten himself some new kit—a pair of dark blue jeans and a brown T-shirt. He had a black beanie on his head and a parka draped over his shoulders. He looked over when he heard me coming and smiled at my hoodie.

"Nice touch," he said. I frowned, looking down to see a bright yellow smiley face plastered across my chest. I wasn't quite sure how I had failed to notice it when I'd plucked the thing off the shelf. I thought about taking it off but I just couldn't be bothered. Besides, if a guy couldn't wear a smiley when he'd just gotten out of prison, then when could he?

"How are things out there?" I asked, nodding at the televisions.

"Bad," said Zee. "Looks like the army is on the way, the coast guard too. They're bringing in everyone they can to round us up. Take a look at this, though." He pointed at a smaller television which was showing CNN. "Wait for it, hang on . . . There."

Just to recap on this latest story, said the anchorman, his finger pressed to his ear. *There have been reports of some kind of . . . animal loose in the city. This footage from close to the prison shows what looks like a large dog . . .* The picture on the screen flicked to a CCTV clip of something huge and beetle-black darting down an alleyway. It was on-screen for less than a second, the image too grainy to make out any detail other than four long legs. I knew what it was, though, and it was no dog, not even one of the warden's skinless beasts.

"The berserker," I whispered to myself, my injuries seeming to throb even more painfully as I remembered the battle I'd had with it, a fight that had almost killed me. If that thing was loose, then we needed to be careful; there was no way I could face it again, even with its injuries.

I studied the array of screens in front of me to see whether there was anything else about the berserker, but the other channels only wanted to talk about the breakout. On one they were interviewing a politician, the man half asleep. On another they were showing a blueprint of Furnace that I knew from just glancing at it was completely wrong. I turned to the next, the largest television in the display. It was another aerial shot, obviously being filmed live from one of the choppers. There was no prison in view, just a bunch of narrow streets and shops, plus another building that looked much larger than the rest. There was a round glass dome in the roof and a shaft of light beamed up from it like an emergency flare.

The helicopter was so low that we could see through the dome to the shop beyond, and a bank of flickering television screens against which three hunched forms were silhouetted. I watched one of those figures turn and wave, a slight delay between Zee's action and its digital echo.

"We're on the telly," he said as we all stared in disbelief at the vast dome over our heads.

Then the glass exploded, armed police dropping on ropes like spiders scuttling in for the kill.

FOUND

THERE WERE FOUR OF THEM, SWAT plastered over their body armor, and they had landed in a heartbeat.

"Lighting up!"

One of the cops pulled a grenade from his belt and lobbed it toward us. It rolled across the floor like a baseball, rebounding off one of the television stands and coming to rest less than a meter from my feet. I closed my eyes, waiting for it to explode, to blow me into smithereens. For a ludicrous second my heart lifted as I realized I didn't have to run anymore, I didn't have to hide. I could just let life slip away, drop into a comforting nothingness where there were no police, no monsters, no me.

But it didn't explode. There was a rush of light so bright that it seared through my eyelids and burned into the flesh of my brain. At the same time a sharp crack of noise seemed to reduce my eardrums to pulp. The world disintegrated, spinning furiously as my senses were ravaged. I tried to move but it was like running inside a spinning globe—every step cartwheeling me into oblivion. Before I knew it I felt myself thump into something, sprawling onto the ground.

All around me, barely audible over the ringing in my ears, were voices. I recognized Zee and Simon's cries, their desperate shouts. Past them were the barked orders of the descending SWAT team—"Show yourselves now! Move to the center of the floor! Keep your hands visible at all times! We *will* use deadly force!"— and the sound of guns being cocked. If I didn't do something fast, then in less than a minute we'd be cuffed and carted back behind bars.

And even if we weren't taken back to the burning ruins of Furnace, we'd still be the warden's prisoners again. And I'd rather die than have to face his fury.

I forced myself to open my eyes and saw a world smudged with smears of dirty light. I pushed myself off the floor, discovering that I had landed on one of the flat-screens. Incredibly, it was still working, the picture an aerial shot that made me feel as if I was flying over the city. Without thinking, I hefted the heavy TV set in both hands as I stood, swinging it like a massive Frisbee.

I didn't have time to aim, but luck was on my side. The cops were out of menswear and moving purposefully toward electronics. Each was wearing some sort of protective goggles, the green-tipped lenses making them look like robots. They saw my makeshift missile too late. It sailed through sportswear, hitting one of the cops in the chest and sending him somersaulting back the way he'd come.

In the split second it took for the rest of the team to respond I had grabbed another television, hurling this one in the same direction. The cops scattered, one firing a wild burst from his submachine gun that reduced a nearby mannequin to plastic splinters. I threw another one for good measure, the screen shattering

into a million pieces as it thumped into a shelf, then I turned and
fled.

There was no sign of Simon, but Zee was taking shelter behind
the remaining televisions. I hefted him up like a parent would a
child, gripping him tight under my arm. He clutched me as hard
as his skinny arms were able, trying not to scream as we charged
toward the window overlooking the main concourse. Behind me
I heard the dull pop of silenced guns, like somebody playing with
bubble wrap. Something whispered past my ear, so hot that it felt
ice cold, and up ahead I saw ragged holes punch themselves into
the window.

"Take him down!" somebody yelled, and suddenly the air was
alive with bullets as the SWAT team unleashed their full force.
But I was running too fast for them to get a bead on me, the world
a blur as I zigzagged among the café tables and lunged at the glass.
At the last minute I did my best to curl myself over, using a hand
to shield my face and my body to protect Zee.

"Alex, you can't—!" was all he had time to say before we hit.
The glass detonated outward as we crashed through it. My stomach lurched as we dropped, surrounded by multicolored glinting
shards that would have been pretty if they hadn't been so lethal.
The window was only a single story above the first-floor walkway
but I staggered as I landed, Zee slipping from my grip and falling
into the pool of glass that had formed around us. I grabbed him by
the collar, hoisting him up before he could start complaining and
dragging him out into the mall. There was no sign of the inmates
we'd seen earlier.

"What now?" he yelled, finding his feet and shrugging off my
grip. "Where's Simon?"

I glanced back up at the window, now nothing but a vast mouth filled with broken teeth of glass. A figure popped up, silhouetted by the harsh store lights, and I thought at first it might be him. Then the shape rested its gun on the ledge and began to fire. It was joined a second later by another, the floor around us suddenly shredded by bullets. I retreated against the grilles that covered Harvey's entrance, directly beneath the window, Zee on my tail. The SWAT team didn't have a direct line on us here, but it didn't stop them trying, a curtain of lead dropping down in front of us like a waterfall.

"We need to get down there," Zee shouted over the thunder. He wasn't stupid enough to try to point—he'd have lost his finger in seconds—but he nodded over the balcony to the ground floor of the mall below.

"Yeah," I said. One of the bullets ricocheted off a chunk of stone and smashed through the window beside me, leaving a hole the size of a large coin. Zee looked as if he was about to speak when something big and heavy landed beside us with a crack. To my surprise it was one of the SWAT team. The man looked as though he had hit headfirst and he wasn't moving.

The sound of gunfire continued, but the cops had switched their attention to something inside the building. A machine gun clattered to the floor, still smoking, followed by a pair of goggles.

"What the hell?" Zee asked. "Come on, let's go while we can."

I didn't argue, leaping out across the walkway. The floor beneath me was broken, bullet casings everywhere, as treacherous as ball bearings. But I kept my balance and ran to the balcony rail.

Behind us the shooting had stopped, and I peeked over my shoulder to see two shadowed figures wrestling in the window. One had a huge arm locked around the other's throat, his body bent, and the way it was framed in the arch made me think of the Hunchback of Notre-Dame. Simon gave the cop a shove, the man's body twisting through the air and landing next to that of its teammate. Then he clambered through the broken glass and jumped to the floor, brushing his hands with satisfaction.

"Thanks for the help, guys," he said. I noticed that there was black blood dripping from a wound in his shoulder and pointed it out to him. He just shrugged. "One of the pigs got me but I showed 'em."

"What happened?" Zee asked, reaching out with a curious finger and prodding Simon's wound. The bigger boy flinched and brushed Zee's hand away.

"They were so busy chasing you they never even saw me coming," he explained, looking at the scarred and stretched skin of his mutated arm. "They aren't ready for us, you know. These guys haven't seen anything like us before. We're bigger than them and faster too. I guess sometimes it pays to be a freak."

He dashed over to where the machine gun lay, lifting it up and fumbling with it until the magazine popped out. He peered at the bullets inside, then slapped the cartridge clumsily back in, holding the weapon to his chest.

"Come on," he said. "We should get back into the service corridors before they send reinforcements; they won't be able to find us down there. We can sneak out around the back."

"Uh-uh," Zee said, shaking his head. "There's a better way."

He ran along the walkway toward an escalator, bounding down the motionless steps. I couldn't be bothered with the extra walk and grabbed the balcony rail, vaulting it with as much grace as I could manage, landing on the ground floor. There was a muffled grunt as Simon dropped next to me, his smaller hand massaging the wound in his shoulder. Zee propelled himself off the bottom step and sprinted to the display of cars in the large plaza that formed the center of the mall. They were arranged around a flower-shaped fountain, the water reflecting the quiet light onto their shiny silver skins and making them look like fish.

"Nice," said Simon, running his hand over the hood of the nearest car—a squat, square SUV. "Now all we need is a driving instructor."

"Speak for yourself," Zee said. He walked to a display stand on the other side of the fountain, and I followed to see him kicking out at a padlock. He looked up at me imploringly and I grabbed the bolted doors, bending them open as though they were made of tinfoil. Behind them was a series of pegs on which hung dozens of keys. Zee selected one and aimed it behind him, pushing the remote-locking button. A small hatchback came alive, beeping softly and flashing its indicators. He began to walk toward it, but I stopped him.

"That thing won't get us five feet if they start firing on it," I said. I pointed toward a massive 4x4 that sat close by, its ribbed hood mounted with bull bars and promising a monstrous engine beneath. "We should take the Humvee."

"Amen to that," added Simon. "And I call shotgun."

"No way," I moaned as Zee flicked through the keys, the air alive with artificial birdsong.

"Sorry, Alex, the shotgun rule is solid—right, Zee?"

Zee selected a key fob and pressed it, bringing the Humvee to life with an unsubtle grunt of its horn. He looked at me and nodded.

"Afraid so," he said. "There are few rules in life that can't be broken, but shotgun is one of them. You're in the back."

I grumbled my way to the car, yanking open the rear door and pulling myself up onto the leather. Zee hopped into the driver's seat and Simon clambered next to him with a smug grin. I don't know why we were acting like kids. I mean, the mall was surrounded by armed police and we were now officially cop killers. But we were still alive, and now we had wheels. In the grand scheme of life, things weren't nearly as bad as they could have been.

Zee pressed the ignition button and the car roared. The beast was automatic, and Zee wiggled the stick until it slotted into Drive. Then he gripped the wheel so tightly that his knuckles turned white, sitting up straight in order to see over the enormous dashboard. It didn't exactly fill me with confidence.

"You sure you can drive this?" I asked as he gunned the engine, the car lurching forward. Instinctively I pulled on my seat belt.

"It's cool," he said. "Trust me. It's why I was in Furnace, remember?"

"Yeah, but you said they framed you for killing that old bird," Simon said.

"They did," Zee replied as the car began to move, stopping and starting as he got the hang of the accelerator. "I never killed nobody. But I'd been done a couple of times for twocking. That's how they got the case to stick." He looked at my puzzled expression in the rearview mirror. "Twocking, TWOC, taking without consent. I'd boosted a few cars. Nothing serious, just here and there. We'd take them for a spin around the park near my house, after dark."

"And here's me thinking you were one of the good guys," I said, the idea of Zee committing any sort of crime throwing me. He just grinned.

"Like Simon said, none of us were angels."

He slammed his foot on the gas, the tires skidding on the smooth floor, then finding grip as we accelerated toward the mall doors, and toward the army of police that waited outside.

THE CHASE

ZEE'S FOOT NEVER let up on the accelerator, and by the time we'd reached the end of the plaza the dial was reading over sixty. I felt myself pressed back into the pungent leather like I was on a roller coaster, my stomach doing loop-the-loops and making me wish I'd had time to use the facilities in Harvey's. The shops flashed past so quickly I couldn't make out their names, the window displays blurring into one long line of smudged mannequins and colored banners. This wasn't the biggest mall in the world, and I knew that at this speed we were going to run out of road, fast.

"You know where you're going?" I asked, but my words were lost beneath the growl of the engine and Simon's enthusiastic whoops. He hadn't even bothered to put on his seat belt, and was leaning forward banging the dashboard to urge Zee on. The machine gun was still clamped tightly in his hand and I hoped he wouldn't accidentally pull the trigger in his excitement.

I peered between them to see the wide walkway that rose toward the mall's main entrance. The glass doors were shuttered, the metal slats glowing red and blue from God knows how many cop cars parked outside. But Zee showed no sign of noticing the flashing warning. His face in the mirror was a mask of determination, and as we hit the rise I felt the car speed up.

"Zee! Slow down!" I screamed as the gates loomed in the windshield, snapping down on us like a bear trap. "Holy shi—"

We hit them doing seventy-seven miles per hour and the result was catastrophic. The shutters weren't designed for anything more than deterring burglars, and the sheer velocity of the Humvee drove it through them like a fist through wet paper. The entire frame was ripped from the brickwork, riding on the hood as we punched through the glass doors out onto the street. Both of the front air bags deployed, filling the interior with white powder. Simon bounced off his, blood spiraling from his nose, but Zee's belt kept him from harm. He patted the bag down, never taking his foot off the accelerator even though he couldn't see a thing through the windshield.

"Left!" I shouted, remembering the layout of the street. "Turn left."

Zee spun the wheel, hard enough to make the car tilt to one side. For a moment I thought it was going over, then he twitched his hands and it slammed back down. The shutters were still plastered across the hood and they were sparking furiously as the police outside began to fire. I ducked down, more prayers streaming from my lips as the side windows shattered and cold air flooded in.

We hit something and I was thrown against the seat in front. More gunfire, shouts, the sound of sirens booting up. Then Zee was accelerating again, a dull rumble from beneath me letting me know a tire had blown. Bullets smashed the rear window, making noises like angry wasps as they thudded into the upholstery and through the roof. The car swung alarmingly then settled, pulling away so fast I thought I'd left my guts back there by the mall. Only when the gunfire had faded did I dare sit up.

"Everyone okay?" I asked. The boys in front were both moving, Zee with his head out of the window trying to see past the shutters and Simon kicking at the windshield trying to dislodge it. With a dull groan the bullet-ridden glass finally gave way, Simon's sneaker-clad foot shattering it into large chunks before knocking loose the grille. It resisted for a moment, then the wind caught it and it clattered over the roof of the car, landing in the road behind us. Zee pulled his head back in, his hair wild and his cheeks blazing from the wind, then turned and grinned at us both.

"That . . ." was all he seemed able to manage. He swiveled back to the road, reaching a junction and heading left.

"Was insane," I finished for him. I risked a look behind to see the glow of red and blue getting closer. "We've got company. Why the hell are they sending the whole damn police force after us?"

"Because we were the only inmates stupid enough to advertise our hiding place to the world," Simon said.

Zee looked up at the rearview mirror but it had been reduced to shreds by a bullet. He looked over his shoulder but Simon pushed his head away.

"You just keep those eyeballs on the road, Dastardly," he said, peering past me out of the back window. "Me and Muttley'll watch the rear."

Simon clambered between the front seats until he was next to me, kneeling on the leather and resting the machine gun on the ledge. Behind us a cop car was catching up fast, siren blazing and two grimacing faces just visible behind the glare. The Humvee lurched again and our pursuers disappeared as we swung around a corner. We turned again, so hard that I almost flattened Simon. He brushed me away, never taking his eyes off the road.

"Go navigate," he barked.

I did as I was told, unclipping my belt and squeezing between the seats until I was sitting next to Zee. It was so windy up front that I had to squinch my eyes shut to stop them from watering. I peered through the blur to see an empty street just like the one we'd left.

"Know where we're going?" I asked.

"Nope," Zee replied through clenched teeth. "Just got to lose them. Hang on."

He steered the massive car down an alley without slowing, sparks flying from the doors as they scraped the brickwork. Ahead was a chain-link fence but the car smashed through it as if it wasn't there, bumping out onto a wider road beyond. Zee slammed on the brakes and wrenched the wheel to avoid a parked milk truck but he was too slow, clipping the back and spinning the truck in a double helix of semi-skimmed. It skidded across the road on its side, hitting a lamppost with a crunch.

"Whoops," said Zee, accelerating down the wrong side of the road. There was more traffic here, mainly delivery vans that honked their horns and pulled wildly onto the sidewalk to avoid being hit. One bin lorry didn't want to move and Zee swore at it, cutting over the flowered divide onto the other side of the street. "Any sign of the—"

He didn't need to finish because a cop car bulleted out of a side street in front of us, sending wheelie bins full of garbage flying as it screeched onto the road. Its windows were rolled down and through one poked a shotgun, the barrel flaming as it fired. The three of us ducked in unison, the shot tinkling almost musically as it struck the car.

"Get rid of them!" Zee yelled, but Simon was already firing through the back window. There was a second police car on our tail, and a third sliding out behind it. They were backing off to avoid the unfriendly fire, but they weren't going to let us go.

"Bandits at twelve o'clock," said Zee, and I heard another shotgun blast ahead. Zee drove the Hummer into the cop car, sending it spiraling across the divide. The engine groaned, coughing alarmingly before settling down. I'd played enough video games to know that cars could only take so much punishment before they caught fire and blew up.

"Punch it!" I yelled. "Get us somewhere safe. We need to lose them and ditch this thing."

"What do you think I'm trying to do, genius?" he retorted, steering around a station wagon hard enough to rock it on its wheels before taking us up to eighty. "Can't escape the eye in the sky, though."

I stared through the broken windshield to see a chopper above us, hovering so close that I could make out the police logo on its side. I almost laughed, remembering the times I'd seen car chases like this on the television, the idiots who thought they could hide from a helicopter equipped with infrared cameras. I was probably on television right now, plastered over the news. Not that anyone would recognize me with my new face and my silver eyes.

"Anyone got any bright ideas?" Zee asked.

We thundered over an intersection, and down the road to our left I caught a glimpse of the river. Even with the sun fully over the horizon it sat on the city like a dark scar, thrown into permanent shadow by the high-rise office blocks on either side. It vanished behind a building after a split second but left its trace on my vision.

"We could swim for it," I said. "Or find a boat. How far is it to the coast? We could make it."

Zee shook his head, slamming through a red light and causing a chorus of car tires to rise up behind us. The two cop cars still gripped us like shadows, and I hadn't heard Simon fire another shot. Chances were he was out of ammo, and sooner or later the police would realize it.

"We'd freeze out there," he said. "This time of day the water's not much above zero. Jesus!"

Three more squad cars roared out from behind a tower block and squealed to a halt dead ahead, the cops scrambling out and firing at us from behind the opened doors. Something burned through my neck and I cried out as I ducked down, feeling the car tip as Zee swung a left. Plastic exploded, sparks bursting from the dashboard. I realized I could see the street through several holes in the car's side, a dozen furious faces flashing by as we left the cops behind.

I closed my eyes, trying to think back to the times I'd come here with my parents—another world, another life. We'd never driven, the traffic across the bridge had always been bad, especially at the weekends. A couple of times we'd traveled by bus, but the way I'd always loved best had been . . .

"The underground," I blurted out. "There's a Metro station near here, I'm sure of it."

Zee was shaking his head again, desperately looking for a way to go, the car slower as he steered it down a narrow street. The river was closer now, the city visible on the other side, its vast skyscrapers glinting in the newborn sun. He whipped the car to the right, bumping up onto the sidewalk and driving through a courtyard. Behind us the cop cars were just turning the corner, painting the world around them red and blue.

"There won't be any trains running with all us cons on the loose," Zee said, steering the 4x4 gently down a set of steps then flooring it along a pedestrian walkway. As soon as the cops were out of sight he swung left, barely squeezing the vehicle down another alley. We were closed in here, the buildings rising on either side of us shielding us from the helicopter. It was quiet too, deceptively so. I wanted Zee to switch off the engine. Maybe the cops would miss us, drive right past. But he kept the speed up, heading for the light at the end of the alley.

"We can hide down there," I went on. "In the tunnels. If the trains aren't running we might be able to walk it."

"Alex is right," Simon said. He'd thrown the gun onto the seat beside him and had a hand pressed up against the wound in his shoulder. "We gotta get off the streets."

Zee looked as if he was about to argue, but he obviously didn't have any better ideas. "Okay, it's better than nothing. You know where the nearest stop is?"

"Down by the river there's one," I said. "Find the bridge and you'll see it."

Zee nodded then floored it, the car tearing out of the alleyway onto the wide avenue that ran parallel to the water. There were vehicles here but they looked deserted, doors left open and engines still running. A truck had been driven into the side of a small office building, a fire raging inside and spreading fast. I turned my attention to the street, seeing the bridge up ahead. There were at least a dozen crossing the river at various points in the city, but

I recognized this one by the untidy white and red paint that decorated the arches. This far out from the center of the city, everything was shabby.

A wailing rose up as the squad cars bombed out behind us, but their sirens were drowned by a sudden roar that flooded the 4x4. The vehicle rocked, buffeted by wind, and through the broken windshield I saw a helicopter pull itself up from behind the stalls and small shops that lined the water's edge. It wasn't the police chopper, it was a bright orange coast guard bird. The main door was open, and through it I could see a .50 caliber cannon that was probably used to scupper smuggling boats. It was aimed right at us.

"Oh no," I groaned, feeling my blood turn to ice. With a bark the gun fired, a breath of flame bursting from the muzzle. Zee swerved but he was too slow, the shells carving their way through the front of the car and sending the engine hood flying overhead. Smoke began to spew from the mangled guts inside. "Go faster!"

"It's on the floor!" he yelled back. "Damn engine is screwed."

The car was slowing, coughing and spluttering like an old man. Zee pumped the pedal but it wasn't doing anything except making us lurch. I watched the speedometer sink from sixty to fifty-five to fifty, all the time the cop cars behind us getting closer.

"Isn't that it?" Simon yelled, his mouth so close to my ear that it made me jump. He was leaning between us, his huge hand pointing at a signpost visible maybe a hundred meters away. I squinted into the dawn to make out a set of stairs leading belowground. My eyes strayed back to the dial. Forty now and slowing fast, but we might just make it.

"Stop your vehicle immediately or we will fire again," came an amplified voice from the helicopter. I ignored it. With the car in

the state it was I doubted the brakes would work even if Zee tried
to use them. He was steering in the direction of the subway entrance, nudging forward in his seat as if attempting to push the
car himself. We were doing thirty, the flat tires trying their best
to slow us down, but the station entrance was in spitting distance.
Zee swung out over the centerline so that he could steer us in
straight, and that's when the engine gave one last mechanical cry
and conked out completely.

"Get ready to run for it," he said, one hand on the door handle.
The car hit the curb, and I thought for a second that its momentum would carry us over, but then it rocked back to a halt. I got
ready to open my door, but Simon cried out and I looked back to
see the squad cars tearing toward us. Two stopped, but one kept
on coming, accelerating all the way. Behind the windshield I could
make out a face bent and twisted by fury. It hit us hard from behind, bouncing the Hummer up over the sidewalk.

I was thrown into the dashboard, the deflated air bag hanging
uselessly by my feet. But Zee was quick, pulling on the wheel and
steering us through the posts of the station entrance and down
the steps. Everything tilted forward, Simon's body pinning me
against the glove box. Behind us I heard the bark of the coast
guard cannon again. This time we all reacted instantly, terror
ejecting us from those seats through the windshield and over the
steaming hood as a hail of bullets shredded the wreck of the car.

We started running, making it maybe twenty paces before the
Hummer exploded. The heat was channeled down the walkway, a
hand of flame that slapped us hard, sending us sprawling onto the
tiles, but it petered out after a second or two. And it wasn't as if
we'd never been in an explosion before. My eyebrows still hadn't
grown back after the last one.

I didn't get up straightaway, just rolled onto my back and peered at the burning shell. It filled the subway stairs perfectly, a gate that would keep the police out for as long as it took them to bring in a fire engine. I let my head drop to the cool floor, staring at a poster for Coke for what seemed like forever. Eventually I felt Zee's hand tugging at my hoodie and saw that both he and Simon were on their feet. I let them help me up; then, with the raging heat of the burning car still clawing our backs, we set off into the station.

UNDERGROUND

IT WAS HARD TO BELIEVE IT, but here we were again: underground.

We walked along the passageway that led into the Metro station, the floor gradually descending, leading down toward the guts of the earth. It was deserted, our only company the gentle echo of our feet and the frozen stares from the faded posters that lined the walls. I knew we were free—for now, anyway—but with each step we took away from the gates, away from the surface, I found myself thinking we were being led toward Furnace.

It was like being underwater, deep inside a black pool, and trying to reach the surface. Every time we thought we could see daylight we ended up being pulled back under, unable to take a breath. I looked down the tunnel, into the shadows that clustered there, and the coiling of my guts screamed at me to turn around, to stay in the light.

Of course, the logical part of my mind knew that the train lines wouldn't pass anywhere near the bowels of Furnace. The prison was too deep, still a mile or so beneath us. But I could feel its touch on my skin, filthy fingers pawing at me, pulling at me. And as we trod our weary way deeper into the darkness it felt as though we were throwing ourselves back through the gates of hell.

We rounded a bend into the ticket office foyer. Every other time I'd been here the place had been heaving, people everywhere bustling and shoving and swearing at each other. Now it stood empty, the quiet unnerving, weighted, as though we'd caught it doing something it shouldn't have been. Ticket machines blinked at us, startled, and overhead one of the fluorescents shimmered on and off.

Devoid of life, the station felt artificial, as if it was nothing but stage props, and another insane thought crossed my mind. What if this *was* a stage? What if this was just one of the warden's jokes, his sadistic tests? Letting us think we'd gotten out, letting us think we'd made it, only to reveal that this world was his creation, that it was a giant theater of evil buried deep in Furnace. Any minute now he would jump out of the shadows with his blacksuits and his dogs, howling with laughter as he tossed us back to the wheezers. Had we really just been outside? Had that really been the sun? Right now my mind was too ravaged to be able to give a straight answer.

"Anyone got enough to buy a travel card?" Zee said, his whisper almost deafening in the silence. It shivered around the hall, bouncing off the tiled walls and the concrete floor before ebbing away, leaving goose bumps on my arms. He was patting the empty pockets of his jeans. "I'm a bit short right now."

We walked across the middle of the room toward the gates, Zee stopping by a vending machine. He kicked out at it repeatedly, and on his fifth attempt the glass smashed. Reaching inside, he pulled out a handful of Kit Kats and a bottle of Coke. Then he grabbed a carbonated mineral water and handed it to me. I hadn't realized how thirsty I was until I unscrewed the cap and let the cool water flow into my mouth. It fizzed down my throat, seeming to strip some of the tiredness, some of the fear, along with it. I threw the empty bottle aside and grabbed another one, downing four in a row then unleashing the longest, loudest belch I had ever done in my life—so impressive that Simon almost jumped right out of his skin.

"Easy there, tiger," he said. "You'll burp yourself inside out."

I laughed. The water was good, had spun my energy levels back up, but it hadn't done anything about the gaping hole in my stomach, that unbearable, impossible hunger that made me feel like a hollow man. I remembered what Simon had told me, back in the prison, about my appetites. I was hungry because my body was running out of nectar. If it didn't find a way to function without the warden's poison then I was doomed either to die, or to become a bloodthirsty beast killing anything that got in my way.

It wasn't exactly the future I'd been hoping for.

"You all right?" Simon said.

"Yeah, fine." I nodded.

Zee had walked ahead to a route map. He ran his hand over the mess of tangled, colored lines, stopping at one marked WHITE-SMITH LANE—the same name detailed in mosaics all over the station. We were near the bottom edge of the map, five more southbound stops to the end of the line.

"If we head in that direction we could make it all the way to Hollenbeck," Zee said, running his finger along the blue string until it popped off the edge of the board. I doubted if our escape would be as easy as that, but it was nice to imagine. He used the same finger to scratch his nose before plopping it back where it had started. "Trouble is, that's what they'll be expecting. They'll know anybody down here will be making a break for the edge of the city, so I'm guessing those stations will be rammed."

To the side of the map was an electronic board listing the status of each line. To my surprise every single route but this one was running, albeit with a warning: SEVERE DELAYS.

"So what do we do?" asked Simon. "Head for the city?"

"Yeah," Zee replied, nodding. "I'm guessing—and this really is just a guess, guys—that they won't be expecting us to head north. It's too risky, there are too many people. We're escaped cons, we need shadows and darkness, at least that's what they'll be thinking. If we head into town then there will be cops everywhere, but there will also be crowds, thousands of people."

"We can lose ourselves," I said.

"We can lose ourselves," Zee confirmed. "Nowhere better to do that than the city." He turned his attention back to the map. "So, we head north on the tracks, two stops, that's a couple of miles I should think. We hit Twofields and get on Line 11; should take us all the way through the city and out the other side."

"That's a whole lotta stations to get through," said Simon. "What if they search the trains."

"As soon as we see police we change trains," Zee said. "If they're all running then we'll be able to hop between them. So long as we keep moving we'll get out of the city eventually. If we leave at one of the stops up there," he nodded at the top of the map, "we're home and dry. Won't be many police on the northern ring, they won't be expecting anyone to make it that far."

"And if there are . . ." Simon slapped his huge fist against his smaller one, then winced, clutching his shoulder.

"You'll moan and groan at them and they'll feel so sorry for us

they'll let us go?" I finished. He grunted something indecipherable at me, pulling his hand away to investigate the smear of black
blood on his palm. My expression grew serious. "You sure you're
okay?"

"I'll live," he answered with a weak smile. "I'll treat myself to a
bandage when we're out of the city. Now come on."

He jogged to the nearest gate and bounded over it, Zee and I
close behind. We traipsed along another passageway then reached
the escalators. I started to run down one but Simon clambered
onto the middle section that separated the moving stairs and cautiously began to skid down it, looking like a surfer in the middle of
a wave. He giggled as he slid, losing his balance somewhere near
the bottom and skittering onto the tiles below.

"I've always wanted to do that!" he shouted up at us once he'd
found his feet. I skipped off the bottom of the escalator and made
my way toward one of two arched openings in the walls. The sign
beside it read NORTHBOUND and showed a map of the stops. We
strolled through to find ourselves on an empty platform. It was
freezing down here, a cold wind ripping through one side of the
tunnel and out the other, and it felt good. This was nothing like
the hot stench of Furnace's breath. This was a fresh current that
would carry us to freedom.

The electronic board above us read NO TRAINS, but we didn't
need one. Zee checked both ways before lowering himself over
the edge of the platform into the pit.

"Don't go anywhere near that rail," he said, pointing at the
third rail of four. It was different from the rest, higher and with
yellow supports. Simon and I sat on the platform and jumped
down together, doing our best to ignore the smell of oil and urine
that clawed at our throats. "If you touch it, just once, then you'll

be blown right out of those shiny new shoes. I watched a program about it, about all the people that had been killed down here. Nasty stuff."

I could feel the buzz in the air, the low whine in my ears, and the slightly metallic taste you get when you're near something with a huge electrical charge. The last time I'd sensed it was on my first day in Furnace, standing in the wire compound they called the Barbecue. It wasn't a pleasant memory.

"And whatever you do," Zee said as he started making his way up the track, keeping one hand against the wall to steady himself. "And I'm talking to you, Alex, since you've just drank about a gallon of water, don't take a piss. There was one guy in that program who tried that and, well, I don't need to tell you that wouldn't be a pleasant way to die." He made a gruesome exploding sound and I was glad that I couldn't see where his hands were.

WE PICKED UP THE PACE, entering the tunnel to the right-hand side of the station. It was dark in here, but my improved vision did what it was supposed to, picking apart the shadows to see the line stretching out to the vanishing point. Mine weren't the only silver eyes in the tunnel—tiny, glinting spots glared at us from beneath the tracks, desperate squeaks like fingernails on a blackboard.

Rats, I thought to myself, the word chilling me to the bone. I didn't mind these furry ones—the worst that could happen down here was getting rodent crap on our shoes—but the sight of those demonic eyes up ahead made me think of the tunnels beneath Furnace, the warden's horrific creations with the same name, the ones that had gone wrong, the creatures that had once been kids but that were now mindless freaks with ragged claws and razored teeth, that wanted to feast on blood . . .

"Maybe you should take the lead, Alex," said Zee, interrupting my thoughts. "Can't see squat in here."

"Sure," I said, squeezing past Simon then Zee, my heart pounding as I tripped over a foot and nearly sprawled into the death rail. I swore, the noise bouncing off the walls like the tunnel was mocking me. Then I set off again, walking as fast as I dared, the end of the tunnel always the same distance ahead.

Eventually the light from the platform grew dim, then faded altogether. We were all used to darkness, keeping our breathing hushed and our mouths closed so we could let our ears guide us. There were noises down here, not just the click of clawed feet on concrete but the rise and fall of the wind as it gusted past us, and distant squeals that sounded like monsters but which I knew were the trains. Every time I heard those brakes I just about died, imagining lights blazing up in front of us as twenty tons of solid steel bulldozed this way. If that happened, if this line started working again, then we were history.

And after having seen the sun again, the worst thing I could think of was being a ghost trapped in these tunnels, so close to daylight and yet back underground. I gritted my teeth together so hard it hurt, increasing my pace. We had to have walked half a mile, at least. The next station couldn't be far.

It was. I counted my heartbeats, three for every second, reaching a thousand, then two, and nearly five before I caught a glimmer of something at the end of the tunnel. We all stumbled toward it, blinking as the light became stronger. We peeked up over the platform—COLLIER'S POINT stenciled on the walls—and at first I thought it was deserted. Then I noticed the bodies, maybe five or six of them. Two were wearing body armor, two were in prison uniforms, and the last had been stripped down to his underwear, revealing the bullet holes in his pale flesh.

There were noises too. The patter of distant footsteps echoing out from the archway to our side, and a hiss of dry laughter, too close for comfort.

We continued along the lines, crouching below the level of the platform in case there was anybody else nearby. But as we drew level with the corpses I risked another look to see that the blood pooled beneath them was sticky and almost dry. Whatever had happened here had happened a while back.

"We obviously weren't the first to think of doing this," Zee whispered.

We scampered along the length of the platform and into the tunnel at the other end. Even my supercharged vision struggled to make sense of the shadows, and I kept my hand firmly against the wall so I didn't stray to my death. Tiny objects kept popping beneath my feet and it took me a while to realize they were probably rat skulls, weakened by time. The smell too was age-old and rotten. It reminded me, more than anything, of the warden's breath; of decay, of bodies pulverized and putrefied. And it was difficult not to picture ourselves strolling down his throat.

"You hear that?" Simon said, his words turning my bones to ice water. I tried to calm my heart, cocking my head to see if I could make out what he'd heard. There was still a distant, banshee-like squeal of brakes, along with the echo of our steps and the constant whine of the electrified rail. But other than that I couldn't make out anything new. "Thought I heard shouting," he went on. "Probably my—"

He stopped, and this time I heard it too, a dull voice that could have been a pipe clanging. It was too far away to tell. We moved as stealthily as we could, marching in time until once again the gloom of the tunnel began to peel away, the distant glow rising like daybreak, a semicircle of tired yellow light breaking free from the night. It grew as we approached, as did the noises. Simon had been right, they were shouts.

"What should we do?" asked Zee as we crept toward the Twofields platform. It was deserted, but there were definitely voices filtering through the doors, echoing off the cold, clean tiles and making it sound like they were right there in front of us. Like they were ghosts.

"Leave them," Simon said. "Keep moving to the next station."

"But this is the one we need," Zee replied. "It's a junction stop. The Elizabeth Line is through those doors. If we keep going then it's five or six more stops to the next junction, and then we only get on . . . I can't remember which line is up there but it will take us in the wrong direction, I'm sure of it."

Another noise tore through the arched opening of the tunnel, this one somehow far more unnerving than the rest. It was a laugh, high-pitched and lunatic. I looked at Simon, then at Zee, meeting each boy's gaze with the same reluctance.

"It might be even worse if we carry on," I said.

"Okay, that settles it," Zee said, putting his hands on the platform and clumsily hauling himself up. He stood, brushing his hands on his jeans. "We watch each other's backs, same as always."

"Same as always," I said, waiting for Simon to clamber up reluctantly before leaping onto the platform. The noises may have been even louder up here but it was good to be back in the light. We cautiously made our way toward the nearest exit, peering through the archway to see a sight that might have belonged in a war movie.

The first thing I noticed was the color. The pristine white tiles had been splashed with so much red that it looked like a hospital morgue. It was so vivid that it didn't seem real. There were more bodies, slumped and broken, dead eyes staring at the rolling escalators to our left as if wondering why they couldn't get to the top. These corpses were a mix, just like the last lot—maybe three or four sets of Furnace overalls as well as a number of police and SWAT uniforms. The smell of blood was fresher here, and the taste of gunpowder hung like cigarette smoke in the back of my throat.

"Jesus," whispered Simon. "What happened?"

"Gangs," Zee replied. "Skulls or the Fifty-niners. Or maybe they're all working together now."

Zee's words caused a thought to explode, so powerful and so overwhelming that I almost doubled over. I began to shake my head, trying to deny the revelation, but I couldn't. The truth was there, right in front of me. I couldn't quite believe I had never thought of it before, but I can honestly say it hadn't crossed my mind. I'd been so focused on getting out, on being free, that I'd been blind to the consequences of my actions, blind to the real nightmare.

We were free, but so was each and every inmate in Furnace, the ones who had survived, anyway. And for every kid like me who'd been framed there were ten, twenty, maybe a hundred who were guilty of their crimes—murder, arson, assault, and worse. They were out, on the streets, the same cold-blooded killers who had been responsible for the Summer of Slaughter, the same brutal gangs that had made the streets run red.

They were free, and it was my fault.

"This way," said Zee, leading us off in the direction of the voices.

I did my best to ignore the nausea, to shrug off the guilt, following him with a heavy head and a heavier heart. Signposts showed us the way to the Elizabeth Line, and we followed them around a bend, down another vast escalator, and along a narrow tunnel lined with bare crimson footprints. At the end of it was a staircase that dropped onto the platform. This one was larger, kiosks embedded in the green-tiled walls. Shadows danced and played against the empty stalls like a puppet show. We waited, frozen at the top of the stairs, knowing we needed to get down them but unable to take that first step.

"Jesus, when are we gonna catch a break?" Simon muttered.

"Ignore it," I said. "Whatever's down there, whoever it is, we leave them alone and they'll leave us alone."

"Or maybe we could just wait," Zee said. "They'll be gone soon, surely. We don't want any trouble."

It was a tempting idea, but I knew that no amount of waiting would help. Trouble just had a funny way of finding us.

AMBUSH

WE DESCENDED THE STEPS SLOWLY, every muscle tense, ready to defend ourselves. We didn't know what was down there, but if experience had taught us anything it was to expect the worst.

Zee had taken the lead, but when he reached the bottom he stopped and motioned for me to proceed.

"I don't want to cause them too much damage," he whispered with a nervous grin, flexing his nonexistent biceps. I wasn't in the mood to laugh, stepping past him onto the platform. The noises were even louder down here, but the wide staircase blocked our view. Only the strange shadow puppet show on the wall continued, a parade of phantom limbs and elongated torsos.

"Forget it," a voice pulled itself out of the cacophony, louder than the rest. "You saw those things up there, you wanna die then go ahead, bruv', but I ain't wiv you."

The shouts rose in pitch, a dozen people arguing. I was surprised to hear a female voice in there too, the sound so alien to me after Furnace that at first I didn't recognize it. We moved cautiously around the staircase, the other half of the platform sliding into view. The first thing I saw was three inmates in torn overalls, two leaning against the wall and another—a Skull—pacing back and forth, a rifle gripped in his white-knuckled hands. He pointed it across the platform toward something out of sight, his finger wrapped around the trigger.

"I told you to shut the hell up," he said, his voice desperate and broken. "This ain't none of your concern."

I took a few more steps, lifting my arms into the air and coughing gently. The prisoner with the gun spun around and loosed a shot, the bullet flying up and gouging a chunk of concrete from the ceiling. The sound seemed to startle him as much as everyone else and he almost lost his grip on the weapon. He blinked furiously, seeming to recognize us, but if anything this made him even more wary.

"Hell you doing here?" he yelled. The other inmates had pushed themselves up from the wall and were backing away.

"Looks like one of them," said a small, blond-haired kid. "Shoot it."

"Whoa," I said, raising my arms even higher. "We're with you. We don't want trouble, okay?"

The Skull looked at me down the barrel of the rifle, using his free hand to wipe the sweat from his nose. He squinted, then lowered the gun a fraction.

"You're him," he said. "The one who got us out." I nodded and his face suddenly opened up into a crooked smile. "We sure glad to see you. You guys alone?"

I nodded, letting my arms fall to my sides as I walked around the stairs. There was a small group of people cowering in the corner of the platform—two middle-aged men in suits holding briefcases, a younger guy in builder's fluorescents, and a girl about my age. They were all looking at the floor, glassy-eyed and terrified.

All except for the girl, that was. She glared at me with such intensity that I had to turn away.

"Can't be too careful," said the Skull, pointing the gun at the floor. "You seen what's goin' on up there?"

"Police everywhere," Zee replied, stepping past me and offering a halfhearted wave at the group. "Nearly got us."

The Skull snorted, but it was the blond kid who spoke next.

"Ain't talking about the cops," he said. "You not seen nothing else out there? Not heard nothing weird?"

"Like what?" I asked.

"Like those things back in the prison," said the Skull. "Those monsters. We got jumped by one, it took three of us, started . . . it started to . . ." He let the words fall into silence, swallowing hard.

"Berserkers?" I asked. "The same ones from Furnace?"

All three inmates shook their heads.

"Ain't seen this bastard before," said the Skull.

"Forget it, okay," Simon said, swallowing nervously. "We're just here to catch a train. Heading north, be fewer cops out there."

"Good plan, boss." The Skull shrugged, looking at the tracks. "Won't be catching no train here, though."

"Why's that?" I asked. The Skull didn't answer, just turned to the tunnel at the end of the platform. I started to ask my question again but a soft squeal surrounded by a dull thunder cut me off. The sounds grew in volume, accompanied by a light that bloomed in the shadowed archway. It got brighter and brighter before solidifying into a pair of headlights that tore from the opening and blasted toward us. The train ripped past so fast that it took my breath away, sucked through the other tunnel like it had been hoovered up.

"That why," the Skull said. "You wanna try and climb on board one of them you be my guest. Come every five minutes or so but they don't stop, not for us."

"Must have set up a quarantine," Zee said quietly. "All around this area. Trains won't be stopping here, or any of the nearby stations." He swore, stamping his foot. "And they've kept the trains running up here, which means we can't even walk the lines."

"So what do we do?" Simon asked. "Head up, take the streets? Might be far enough out by now."

"Nope," said the Skull. "No getting out that way, either. All the exits are sealed up tight, we tried 'em. Po-po out there, they'll gun you down the second you poke your noses out."

"Why aren't they coming in?" Zee asked, directing the question to me. "Storming the place."

"They got enough to deal with on the streets," the Skull said. "Something real strange goin' on up there; inmates goin' wild."

"You surprised?" Zee asked. "First time they've been free in a long time, they're bound to go crazy."

"Not what I mean," the boy continued. "They're goin' wild, like animals. Didn't seem human no more."

"You see the bodies?" the blond kid asked. "Cops killed, torn to pieces, but the inmates didn't take the guns. 'S like they're rabid or something. Tearing each other to pieces as well as the po-po."

"Rats?" Zee asked, looking at me. "How'd they get out so fast?"

"Doesn't matter," I replied, confused. The rats had been shut down in the tunnels beneath Furnace, along with the warden. There was no way they could have broken out this quickly. I looked at the Skull. "What's your plan? How are we gonna get out of here?"

"That's what we was just talking about," he replied. "We fresh out of ideas. But now you here, you can tell us what to do, right?"

"You need to hand yourselves in," came a voice from the corner. I glanced up at the girl, her expression twisted by rage. Her fists were clenched by her sides and she looked like she could take down all of us single-handed if she wanted to. "Before it's too late."

"We'll take it under advisement," said Blondie with a shy smile.

She scowled at him, and looked like she was about to say something else when a noise broke free behind us—that same clownish giggle that we'd heard before, scraping over the tiles like fingernails down a blackboard. The Skull aimed his rifle up the stairs, his face a mask of fear.

"They found us," he hissed. "Brought 'em with you. Led 'em right here."

"Who?" Zee asked, stepping behind me. "What's up there?"

The air suddenly grew thin, replaced by a thunder that flooded the platform as another train tore past, seeming to snatch all the oxygen from the air before disappearing with a scream. The laughter came again, mixing with the echoes of the train into a nightmare serenade. It was followed by the thump of bare feet overhead, something big heading our way.

I felt the adrenaline in my veins, felt the nectar start to do its job. I knew what would happen: it would cloud my mind, make me stronger and faster, capable of doing terrible things. But it would also try to make me forget who I was. It would try to turn me into a monster.

"Get ready," I heard myself say, the words coming out as a throbbing growl. "Here it—"

Something blasted from the top of the stairs, a hulking black shape that crashed down them so fast that it was just a blur. The inmates cried out in fear, skittering back across the platform as the immense, knuckled form rolled across the floor toward us.

The Skull fired his rifle, the bullet flying wide and punching a hole in a coffee-shop window, but the figure kept coming, bladed limbs carving the air, threatening to dice us all.

I threw myself at it, but I'd taken only a few steps before it stopped, doing a couple of clumsy somersaults before skidding to a halt on a bed of black blood, its long limbs flopping uselessly beside it. I saw its face and recognized it instantly. The creature was just as I remembered, rigid and scarred as though it had been carved from rosewood, one eye pure molten silver, the other lost in the gaping wound I had punched into its mangled skull.

It was the berserker, the beetle-black one that I had fought inside the prison.

And it was dead.

"I thought you said—" I started.

There was another burst of childish laughter from above us, then something huge leaped over the handrail from the top of the steps and crunched onto the platform, hard enough to create a cobweb of cracks in the concrete. Everybody scattered back like bowling pins, and past them I saw a creature sitting on its haunches, nothing but a ball of tortured muscle.

Then it straightened, its body unfolding to an impossible height—towering three feet over me. From a distance it could have passed for human—pink flesh that was so dark it looked sunburned, its arms and legs bulging but in proportion, its torso covered with a network of scars and dressed only in a pair of faded gray shorts.

But the more I studied the beast the more I realized that although it may once have been human, it was something much worse now. Its hands were huge, far too big for its arms, and swollen into clubs. There was something wrong with its bones, jutting up as if it was wearing a suit of armor beneath its flesh. And between the blades I could see its muscles moving, as though there were snakes in there desperately trying to find a way out.

Its face, though, was the most horrific thing about it. Not because it was disfigured, or because it was unrecognizably alien, but because it was that of a child—swollen, yes, and bruised, but a kid's nonetheless, nine, maybe ten. It swiveled on those giant shoulders, wearing an infant grin so permanent that it could have been painted on. Nectar dripped from that grin as though a tap had been turned on inside its mouth, splashing down the front of its body and leaving a trail on the tiles.

The creature studied us all with eyes that flashed gunmetal gray. Beside me the Skull fired again, the bullet thudding into the berserker's chest hard enough to rock it backward. The creature peered down at the wound more from curiosity than with any sign of pain, and the skin around the ragged hole began to pulse black, revealing a network of veins. In seconds it was sealed by a plug of nectar, the berserker flexing its grotesque muscles and grinning at me with that mannequin's smile.

It laughed, a giggle that danced up my spine. There was no warmth in that laugh, no sympathy, only madness and cruelty.

"Run," I yelled, but before the word had even left my mouth the berserker was on the move, covering a quarter of the platform in one bound. With another cackle of delight it swiped Zee out of the way, sending him flying over the ledge onto the rails below, wrapping its other hand around my head and neck. I felt my tendons stretch to breaking point as it lifted me off the ground, only half noticing that Simon was gripped in its other fist.

The berserker pulled us closer, its jaws distending impossibly wide like a snake preparing to devour its prey. Its whole face seemed to stretch with the movement, its eyes drooping as the skin beneath them was pulled down, its cheeks almost tearing with the effort. Inside its maw were jagged blocks of rotten enamel that had once been teeth, and its breath smelled like the charnel room inside Furnace, like it was engulfing me with death.

Then it leaned forward and sank those teeth into my neck.

My vision sparked, black explosions that slowly erased the creature and the platform from view. The berserker pulled free its barbed teeth, and the last thing I saw was its eyes, pale silver and filled with black tears.

Then the darkness swallowed me.

VISIONS

THE FiRST THiNG I realized was that I was hanging in midair, a hundred meters or more above the earth. And the first thing I saw was a building.

It rose from a burning city, silhouetted against a sky that was so cloudy and so dark it could have been forged from obsidian. Smoke roiled against the encroaching night, and in those coiling tendrils I saw shapes—twisted bodies that swarmed over the streets below, that leaped effortlessly from rooftop to rooftop, and that crouched in dark corners gnawing on hidden feasts. Every time I tried to focus on one of those forms it vanished, becoming smoke once again.

The building was alight as well, smoke pouring up from the windows like inverted waterfalls. I studied it, trying to work out where I had seen it before. It was an office block, similar to all the rest—a tombstone of concrete and glass that rose maybe forty, fifty stories from the inferno at its feet. Crowning the structure was a short four-sided spire, like a pyramid, although against the smoke-stained, blood-reddened sky it looked more like a pyre.

I tried to breathe but hot air, devoid of oxygen, filled my lungs. I struggled, but I couldn't move. Somewhere, behind the illusion of the city, I could still see the creature that held me, fizzing in and out of existence every time I blinked. I twisted my body, trying to find a way to escape the berserker's grasp, but even if I could have done so, the flames beneath me extended in every direction for as far as I could see, as if the whole world was burning.

It is, somebody said, the voice so loud and so close that it was as though the dying city had spoken. *The whole world is an inferno. It will burn until every nation has fallen, until all who oppose us are dead, until people see the true light.*

The building ahead was getting bigger, growing from its bed of fire. No, it wasn't getting bigger, it was getting closer, pulling us toward it with some malevolent gravity. As the voice spoke the tower block grew brighter, the windows near the top coming alive and glowing with a sickly yellow light. I was still too far away to make out what lay inside, but I could see shapes there, as deformed and demented as those I had glimpsed in the smoke below. I fought against the grip but I was powerless, dragged relentlessly up toward the building's spire.

"What do you want?" I screamed, though all that emerged was a whimper strangled by smoke.

You know what I want, the voice replied. It was distorted, comprising the roar of flames and the crack of breaking bones, but I knew who it was. There was no mistaking the tone of Alfred Furnace, filled with power yet tinged with insanity. *We showed you, Warden Cross and I. We showed you what the future would bring. And here it is, a world in flames and a new race ready to emerge from the ashes.*

I thought back to my time in the tunnels beneath the prison, when the warden was turning me into one of his soldiers, into a blacksuit. He had spoken of a war, a judgment day where the strong would destroy the weak once and for all; a new Fatherland that would stand for ten thousand years. I had almost been ready to become a part of it, my mind washed of all sense by the nectar, my body butchered and rebuilt. I had almost staked my place in this new world, given myself to Furnace and his legion.

And you still can, the voice went on, reading my thoughts. *You betrayed me, but you also betrayed yourself. Would you deny yourself a role in a world born from strength, from victory? Look, Alex, and see what awaits you if you answer my call.*

I peered down into the smoke churning like an ocean between the burning buildings. The shapes there were clearer now, row upon row of faceless soldiers marching down the street, goose-stepping toward the tower block. Their bodies were puffed out, packed tight with muscle, their eyes piercing silver blades that cut open the wall of smoke before them. Everything about this force smacked of power, of determination, of strength, of victory, and I felt the emotion vomit up from my stomach.

Is it not better to be a soldier in the new world than to be a corpse in the old? Furnace went on. *You continue to surprise me, Alex. You have fought with courage. You are the kind of soldier who can change this pathetic little world and make it something wonderful. You are the kind of soldier who can fight at my right hand. And I need a new commander, Alex, because my old friend the warden has disappointed me. A man who can't keep his house in order doesn't deserve to have a roof over his head.*

The small nugget of pleasure I got from hearing him insult the warden was lost almost as soon as it appeared. I wanted to scream at him, to tell him that I'd never join his army, but I couldn't find the strength. Or was it something else? My stomach was still churning, my head ringing, and I knew it wasn't from fear. It was excitement I felt, the same terrifying rush as when the warden had shown me what it would be like to crush my enemies beneath my heel, to break their bones and leave their smoldering corpses in my wake. It was power, pure and simple, and it felt good.

There couldn't have been much nectar left inside me, but what little was there began to thump through my veins, turning my blood black and filling my thoughts with violence. I tried to fight it, but as I pictured myself storming through the streets, the entire world on its knees and begging me for mercy, I found myself grinning, a dull rumble of a growl escaping my throat.

See them weep, Alex, Furnace said, his voice emanating from the tower block like a pulse. *See them plead. For I am their new emperor, and you are their new prince.*

It suddenly dawned on me where I'd seen the tower before—in the city, of course, its spire visible on the skyline, replicated in countless postcards and posters. We were closer to it now, and through the windows I caught a glimpse of what lay within. In every room was an operating theater, decorated with blood and crammed to bursting point with wheezers. The creatures breathed through their ancient gas masks, parting flesh with filthy fingers and screeching with delight. I don't know how many windows there were—dozens, maybe hundreds—but they were all portraits of death and decay as Furnace churned out more soldiers for his force of freaks.

Side with me or side against me, he said as we drew inexorably closer. *This vision is the truth of the world. Your antics inside the prison have forced me to play my hand a little earlier than I would have liked, but no matter. Perhaps you have done me a favor, boy, in making me act now.* He laughed, the throb of his lunatic chuckle making the fires rage even more fiercely. *Perhaps, when the last cities fall and the people embrace me, then it is you I will be thanking for giving me the opportunity to lay the foundations of the new world now. Yes, Alex, because of you the war begins this morning. The future starts today. Look at it, Alex, and tell me which side you would rather be on. Look at it, and make your choice.*

My lungs were empty, crying out for air, but even if they hadn't been I couldn't have given Furnace an answer. We were nearly at the spire, and as we approached I saw yet another nightmare emerge through the smoke, through the shimmering haze of heat. A creature was clinging to the sloped roof with hands like blades, bigger than any berserker, its body strangely distorted as though its limbs had been stretched on a rack, its skin shimmering as the nectar pulsed through its veins. And its eyes. Those twin silver moons radiated a power and a strength that cut through everything else, that shone like beacons, like twin beams from a lighthouse, dousing the flames and blasting the smoke away until the city gleamed as if new and the skies blazed blue.

Furnace. Alfred Furnace. It had to be him.

The creature howled, a cry loud enough to rock the world to its knees. Then it began to laugh, a noise which faded into birdsong over the newborn paradise beneath my feet.

Look at it, Alex. Make your choice.

But I couldn't, even as the air flooded back into my lungs, even as my senses returned. I couldn't give an answer because right then I didn't know the truth, I couldn't make a choice.

I honestly didn't know which side I'd pick.

NECTAR

THE VISION OF THE CITY began to clear, dissolving back into reality like sugar in tea, but the reality was no better than the illusion had been. I blinked the tears from my eyes to see the berserker in front of me, its drooping clown's face inches from my own, its fingers wrapped around my neck. It was grinning, the lips forced open so wide I thought they must have been stitched that way, nectar still dribbling out between them. Then, with another infant laugh, the creature released its hold on me.

I dropped like a stone, landing on my back and gasping in a lungful of stale air. I clamped my hands to my throat, feeling the ridge of bite marks there. There was no blood, the nectar had seen to that, but the whole side of my neck and face was itching madly, as though somebody was running a feather duster down the inside of every vein.

Simon was beside me, his back arched in agony. My entire upper body was throbbing, as though I'd been cooked alive in the flames of my hallucination, but somehow I found the strength to sit up and focus on what was happening.

The berserker seemed to have forgotten all about us. It bounded down the platform, running on all fours like an orangutan as it closed in on the fleeing inmates. It was on them in seconds, swinging its hammer fists in a horizontal arc and knocking the blond kid and his quiet friend away. They rolled over the edge of the platform like rag dolls, accompanied by the clack of breaking bones.

The sight of them on the lines made me remember Zee. I scrambled across the concrete on my knees, peering over the edge of the platform to see a motionless shape below. The lower part of his face was a mask of blood, but I could tell by the pale blue eyes it was Zee. They were open, and they weren't blinking.

He must have hit the electrified rail. I knew it. For a second I didn't feel anything, then a blinding flash of white light popped in the center of my head, expanding hot and fast like a supernova. *Not him,* I screamed inside. *Not him, not Zee. NOT ZEE!* With each plea the flare of the supernova darkened, the nectar numbing the emotions the way it was supposed to, killing the sadness the same way it killed the physical pain. I let my guard drop, willing the poison in, urging it on so I wouldn't have to deal with the truth of what lay before me, the body broken and slumped on the tracks.

The body that was moving.

"Gonna kneel there all day," came a whisper of a voice, strained as though he had been badly winded, "or do you think maybe you could give me a hand?"

The words flushed the nectar from my head, leaving me with nothing but a blinding pulse of agony, so deep that it felt as if it had always been there. But, more than that, I felt joy. The sensation was so strong that pearls of tears clustered in my eyes. I looked at Zee openmouthed and wide-eyed, and my expression must have been a sight because he laughed.

"Jesus, Alex, close your mouth before you drool on me," he said, glancing at the rail beside him, the one he had missed by a hair's breadth.

I cast a look over my shoulder just to make sure the berserker hadn't changed its mind. It had pinned the Skull against a wall, its massive hands held out on either side of it to stop the kid from running. Not that he was going anywhere. He was hunkered into a ball, his arms hanging uselessly by his sides, no blood left in his face as he waited for the monster to attack.

I heard a distant squeal, the rattle of the tracks. The air was trembling, as if it was scared of the bullet of metal and glass that was tearing this way. Not wasting another second, I eased myself over the platform and dropped into the pit between the rails, grabbing Zee under the armpits.

"Oh crap," he said as I was hoisting him up. I followed his line of sight to see that the tunnel was growing lighter, two headlights visible and getting bigger with terrifying speed. I threw Zee up toward the platform but his foot caught on the nearest rail and he cried out in pain. I lost my grip and he slipped back into the pit. I took him by the scruff of the neck, using the last of my strength to hurl him upward just as the train exploded out of the tunnel. I crouched, the sheer velocity of the oncoming engine almost enough to make me drop down dead from fear. In the blink of an eye it had reached me, and as I leaped for safety I saw the driver's face, inches away, frozen into a rictus of panic.

I almost made it, ninety percent of me over the threshold of the platform. But the train was too fast, clipping my legs at forty miles per hour. I cartwheeled like a spinning top, the world unraveling as I flipped end over end and came crashing to a halt at the foot of the stairs. Even when I stopped the world was still moving, my brain a gyroscope that threatened never, ever to calm. I screwed my eyes shut, feeling like I was on a white-knuckle ride at an amusement park, my stomach threatening to hurl even though it was empty.

Through the confusion I heard the berserker's spine-chilling laughter and I forced myself to look. The beast was still in the far corner, although the view was spinning so much that I could barely tell which end of the platform was which. It now had the Skull clasped between its bulging palms, and for a bizarre moment I thought it was kissing the kid. Then I realized its embrace was something far worse.

The berserker had its jaws locked around the boy's throat, its blunt teeth in his flesh. There was blood dripping down the kid's prison overalls, but even from where I was lying I could see that it was black, not red. The nectar dripped onto the floor, forming a pool beneath the freak and its prey. It might have just been my imagination, but it looked different from the nectar I'd seen back in Furnace, the poison that had been pumped into me by the warden. The flecks of color in the darkness weren't silver and gold but red, like splinters of rubies.

"You seein' that?" Simon said, and I realized he was kneeling beside me, one hand on my shoulder. Zee was crawling toward us, the strength returning slowly to his limbs but his face as pale as wet paper. "What's it doing?"

"Feeding," I said, although I knew this wasn't true.

"Can you walk?" Simon asked. I nodded, but to be honest I wasn't sure if I could move at all. My legs felt like rubber that had been stretched too far, still no pain as such, just that infuriating itch. "We should get out of here before that thing finishes doing whatever it's doing."

With a sucking sound that reminded me of a foot being

wrenched from mud the berserker pulled its teeth free of the kid's neck. The wound that it had left was as black as pitch, a ring of ragged holes that reached from ear to shoulder, reminding me of a shark bite. The red-flecked nectar was still dripping, but it looked like it was dripping upward as well as to the floor below. I blinked in disbelief, squinting into the shadows to see that it wasn't leaking from the boy's neck at all. It was spreading beneath his skin, radiating outward like channels of dirty water beneath ice.

Was that what it had done to me? No, it had bitten me but it hadn't pumped me full of nectar, not like this. I'd have felt it.

The Skull, still held by the berserker, began to tremble, his entire body rocked by spasms so violent that I thought he was going to shake himself to pieces. His veins were pulsing with the nectar inside them, resembling a cobweb of black lines that slowly spread over his face and beneath the collar of his overalls. He thrashed for a moment longer, then he arched backward, unleashing a desperate, deafening howl at the ceiling. His eyes snapped open and I could see that they were black wells, so deep and so dark that they could have been hollow pits inside his face.

The Skull's cry went on for what felt like forever, filling the platform with white noise. Then his head lolled on his shoulders, his eyes looking right at me. I stared into those sockets as tears of ink drew down his cheeks, black blood leaking from his nose and joining the fluid that gushed from his mouth. It looked as if he had been pumped full of nectar, so much so that it had split open his skin, gushing out of every pore.

The berserker laughed again, then it hoisted the Skull over its shoulder as though the boy was nothing but a sack of meat. With a single leap it threw itself over the platform and back toward the stairs, not even sparing us a look as it crouched and propelled itself upward, landing on the top step.

It paused there for a second, as if to get its bearings, and as it did so the Skull lifted his head and gazed down the stairs through those blood-blackened eyes. I could see the fabric of his overalls stretch and split as the limbs inside grew, his fingers bulging out joint by joint like sausages fattened and flyblown. His face too was almost unrecognizable, swollen like a month-old corpse.

But even though the kid had been disfigured beyond repair, even as his face began to warp and split like old wood, there was no denying the expression there. His eyes, as dark as they were, were hungry. And his mouth was twisted upward manically, the lips drawn, teeth glinting against the nectar.

He was smiling.

FEEDING

WE SAT AT THE FOOT of the stairs long after the slap of the berserker's footsteps had faded, long after we heard the last echo of its sinister toddler's giggle ebb from the passageways above us. We sat there in silence, trying to make sense of what we'd seen, trying to get our heads around this bizarre new twist.

The platform was deathly silent, no sign of life from the two other inmates who'd been knocked onto the tracks. Zee had been lucky, and I offered a silent prayer. It was about time we'd had a little luck. The angry girl was peeking out from the doorway of the coffee shop, but there was no sign of the other civilians.

"We should probably go," Zee said. He was sitting on the bottom step rubbing his right leg. His new jeans had been torn open but I couldn't see any blood there, just a bruise that was blossoming on his calf.

"Go where?" I asked, struggling to find the strength to move my mouth. My neck was stinging furiously where I had been bitten, as if I'd been rolling in nettles. The sensation was migrating down my right arm, the skin there tender to the touch.

Nobody answered. What could they say? I mean, if Furnace had sent in his berserkers, freaks like the one that had just been down here, then we wouldn't be safe anywhere. Hell, nobody would be safe with those things running amok. I thought about my vision, the image of the city in flames, tried to work out what Furnace had been talking about. What had he said?

"The war begins this morning," Simon whispered, as if reading my mind. I looked at him and he glanced back at me almost shamefully.

"You saw it too?" I asked.

"Saw what?" Zee said as Simon nodded. "What did I miss?"

"Trust me," said Simon. "You don't wanna be part of this club." He looked up the stairs, then at me. "You think what he said was true? About the city, about the war?"

"Guys!" Zee snapped.

"We had a vision," I explained. "It was Alfred Furnace, talking to us, I don't know how, exactly, but—"

"The nectar," Simon interrupted. "He talks to us through the nectar, I guess."

"It's like he's right there, inside my head," I said. "Like he's in there screaming. It's not possible, but that's what it's like. It feels like he could just dig his fingers into my brain and make me do anything he wanted."

"Only he can't do that, right?" Zee said. "Otherwise he'd have just killed you. Made you commit suicide or something. He may be talking to you, but he can't control you."

"Right," I muttered back, unconvinced.

"Anyway, what did you see?" Zee asked.

"The city in flames," Simon said. "Full of monsters. Did you see that freak on the tower, right at the end?"

"Yeah," I replied, picturing the beast as it howled at the streets below, looking like it was ready to tear the world apart brick by brick, bone by bone. "Furnace, right? That was one evil-looking hombre."

"You're not wrong there," Simon went on. "If I never have to come face-to-face with him in the flesh, then it will be too soon." He turned back to Zee. "He said it was our fault that his creatures were loose, our fault that he had to start his war today."

"War?" Zee said. "That doesn't make any sense. Unless he's declaring war on us, on the prisoners."

I tried to think back over my hallucination but it was fragmenting like a dream, erased by consciousness. Maybe Zee was right, maybe that was all he meant—a war against the kids who had escaped from his institution. That had to be it, didn't it? My head was still reeling and I felt my body give in to gravity, lying back against the stairs. I tried to sit up straight but I just didn't have the strength. It felt like all my bones had been stolen.

"He was giving us the same old crap," I went on, struggling to find the energy to breathe in. "Telling us he'd forgive us if we just gave ourselves in, that we could help him fight, that we could be his new right-hand men, blah blah blah. At least he was slagging off the warden, it was worth it just to hear that. I think that bastard Cross might have had his day."

I looked at Simon and realized he'd lost even more color. He flicked me a glance, too quick for me to make out the look in his eyes.

"He didn't—" he began, then stopped and turned away, staring at the wall. I ignored him, feeling my neck turn to jelly, my head dropping against the chipped tiles of the steps. If I could just rest here for a bit, then maybe I'd be okay. Or maybe this was it, maybe my body had finally run out of fuel. Perhaps it wouldn't be so bad if it all ended here, I thought. At least it was quiet, at least I was with friends. I closed my eyes.

"Did Furnace say anything else?" asked Zee, making me jump.

"I don't think so," I slurred, too tired to remember.

"The tower," Simon said. "The tower the beast was standing on."

"What sort of tower?" Zee said.

I heard Simon shrug before he said: "An office block, in the city. I think it must be his. All kinds of sick stuff going on inside."

There was more, but I zoned out, my thoughts covered by a pleasant blanket of darkness and quiet. The stinging in my neck and my arm had settled into a deep buzzing pulse that beat in time with my heart. I don't know how much later it was that I felt hands on me, shaking me hard. I tried to open my eyes but couldn't, the sudden terror of paralysis turning my blood to ice water. I struggled against the grip of sleep, eventually managing to peel my eyelids open. But that was pretty much all I was capable of.

"You look like crap," Zee said.

"It's the nectar," Simon replied. "It's running out."

"What happens if it does?"

"Bad things," Simon said. "Seen it happen to the rats, back down in Furnace. If the nectar dries up, then all the crap that's happened, all the wounds and broken bones, fast catches up with you. And Alex here, he's been beaten to death and back I don't know how many times. He runs out of nectar, he runs out of time."

I tried to comment but my words were still locked tight by tiredness. Somewhere in the conversation my eyes had closed again and I hadn't even noticed. This time the darkness was far from comforting. It felt a bit like I was being buried alive.

"So what do we do?" asked Zee, his voice laced with desperation. I realized he had his hand on my head and the touch felt good. "I'm pretty sure Mickey-D's hasn't started offering nectar shakes yet. What do we do?"

"Something gross," Simon said. I heard the scuff of feet as he left the steps, followed shortly by a sound that could have been a lobster claw being pulled from the socket—a disgusting symphony of cracks and slurps and grunts.

"No way," said Zee. "That's just wrong. Wrong, wrong, wrong."

"Yeah, but we don't have a choice," Simon said. I heard him swallow something, then gag, then swallow again. "If he doesn't get some more nectar into his system then he's going to die, if not now, then pretty soon. I mean, look at him."

I sensed Simon standing before me and I felt something drip onto my neck, tickling my skin as it ran beneath my hoodie.

"Open wide," said Simon. I did as I was told, feeling another drip on my chin as he held something over my head. The next drop of liquid struck my tongue, bringing with it the foulest taste I'd ever experienced—as if all the food in a fridge had been left for years until it was covered in mold and putrefied to a mush; a liquefied mess of sour, lumpy milk and maggot-infested beef. I felt my throat close up, my stomach heaving, but Simon held my mouth open with one hand and kept pouring in whatever it was he had in the other.

I swallowed, only to stop myself from choking. The instant I did the disgusting taste was forgotten as my brain recognized what the substance was. My pulse shifted up a gear, hammering in my ears. Even though my eyes were still closed my vision went blacker, tiny pinpoints of golden light sparking like exploding stars against the night.

It was nectar. Somehow, Simon was feeding me nectar.

It hit my stomach like a living thing, like it had a mind of its own and knew exactly where to go. It felt like it channeled itself instantly through my gut and into my arteries, lining them with lightning and bringing my exhausted muscles back to life. The wound in my neck was on fire, although burning with power, not pain. The sensation seemed to spread down my right arm, all the way to my fingers, as if the veins there had been stretched and widened to hold as much of the poison as possible.

I gulped harder, craving the liquid that filled my mouth, like this was my first glass of water after a month in the desert. I didn't care about the taste, I just wanted more of it—it filled me up like fuel, my body an engine suddenly gunning and ready to go.

I sat upright with a choked growl, opening my eyes and looking through the pulsing black veins of my retinas to see a severed limb over my head. I recognized the boy who held it, but all memories were obliterated by the need for nectar. I lashed out at him, grabbing the arm and pressing my face to the leaking veins, sucking the nectar out with relish. In seconds it was dry, and with another guttural roar I leaped to my feet, pouncing on the corpse of the beetle-black berserker and tearing into its cold carapace.

Somewhere in the frenzy I heard a voice telling me to slow down, telling me not to drink too much. I didn't know if it was somebody else or if it was me, that same internal thought that had kept me sane back in the prison. I ignored it, sucking poison from the torn cavity of the creature beneath me, filling my belly with nectar. That infuriating hunger that I'd felt for what seemed like forever was gradually being sated, every cell of my being turning from a dry, useless husk into a swollen vessel of power.

I raised my head from the corpse and let my dripping mouth

hang open. A noise escaped me, a roar that came of its own accord. I lifted the dead berserker, now as light as cotton wool, using both hands to tear the cadaver in two. I threw the bloody pieces away, turning to the platform to find something else to test my strength on, something else to destroy. The nectar was screaming at me, sluicing through my brain and shrieking a single word with each pulse—*kill, kill, kill*—and on top of that the sound of laughter resonating in my head, a low, deep cackle that I knew belonged to Alfred Furnace.

You have made your choice, he said, the nectar carrying his voice into the deepest reaches of my soul, the words borne on another wave of mirth. They seemed to sprout into visions, images that blossomed into full bloom—me at the head of an army, raining hell down onto the world, me locked in combat with somebody who looked like the warden but who couldn't be. *Whatever you do from this moment on, whatever path you decide to take, you have made your choice.*

I clamped my hands to my ears but it did no good. Furnace was howling as though he had torn open my skull and stepped inside. The nectar carried on flowing, healing my wounds, turning my muscles to rock, smashing my thoughts like china plates. I searched the pieces, trying to keep my mind, but all I could hear was that endless laughter, like thunder, and that same relentless order telling me to kill.

If I obeyed, maybe it would make the madness stop.

I scoured the platform, saw two faces I knew but at the same time didn't. They weren't worth my time. Turning, I saw the girl, watching from the doorway.

She'd do.

I no longer knew what I was doing, crossing the platform in

three giant strides until the pathetic creature was beneath me. She heard me coming, scrambling to her feet and holding her hands up to protect her face. Her eyes glared at me, still full of fight, never wavering.

You wanted to help her, remember? You wanted to save her.

More voices in my head, all fighting each other, contradicting each other. And the only way to banish them was to make that choice, to take a life. I raised my hands, ready to twist her neck like a chicken's, to end it once and for all. But still she fought me with that gaze, two piercing points of white light that held me back as firmly as a hand on my chest.

She's looking at you like you're one of them, but you're not one of them, Alex, you're not one of them, you're not—

I threw my head into my hands, the voices jumbling together into an insane chorus. I screamed against my palms, only half noticing that there were words in there.

"Who am I? Who am I? *Who am I?*"

I lifted my fist again, knowing that all it would take was one simple movement and the girl would be dead. Then Furnace would be right, my choice would have been made. I wouldn't have to fight anymore. To my side came the sound of an explosion as a train flew from the tunnel, the deafening noise the final straw. I moved fast, faster than I'd ever moved, turning, screaming as my fist descended like a guillotine blade, driven earthward by the nectar, by its nightmare desire to destroy.

The train was almost gone but I caught the end of it, my fist punching through the last window in the last carriage, the force of the blow so great that it reduced the Plexiglass to splinters, tearing a chunk from the metal frame. The impact felt as though it had ripped my arm right out of its socket, dragging me along the platform on my heels. But it was the train that lurched, the carriages rocking against one another almost hard enough to pull it from the tracks.

With an ear-shattering squeal it accelerated through the other tunnel, plunging the platform into silence. I dropped to my knees, cradling my fist, the nectar's pounding song beginning to quiet, quenched for now, leaving me alone with my sobs and with the endless echo of *his* whispered delight.

You have made your choice.

.

LUCY

IT TOOK ME A WHILE to realize that somebody was talking.

I swam out of a trance, breaking free from the ocean of dark thoughts that I'd been drowning in. I don't know how long it had been since I'd fed, the last few minutes—or maybe hours—nothing but a blur. My hand was itching furiously, and I focused on it to see blades of glass protruding from between the knuckles, surrounded by smudges of greasy black blood. The wounds had already healed, the nectar plugging the holes in my skin, knitting the flesh back together.

But there was something more. My hand seemed to have grown, swelling so much that the skin was tight, and an ugly shade of bruised black. It wasn't just my hand, either, it was my whole arm. I felt beneath the sleeve of my hoodie, running all the way up the bulging flesh until I reached the bite mark in my neck. It was pulsing with every heartbeat, and when I lifted my hand away my fingertips were stained with nectar.

Gradually the rest of the world settled, growing still and clear as if I'd been looking at a reflection in a disturbed puddle. I was on my knees on the lip of the platform, rats scurrying about below, sniffing curiously at the pools of dark liquid I had left between the rails. My head was ringing, almost loud enough to drown out the words from behind me.

I eased my head around to peer over my shoulder, aware that my whole body felt tender. There was no pain, the nectar had made sure of that, but there was something else, a deep-rooted tickling sensation that stretched from my neck down my spine and finished in my hips. I tried to remember what had happened, had a fleeting image of me bringing my fist down on something.

On a girl?

As my eyes gradually made sense of the shapes behind me I saw to my relief that the girl was there, sitting on a bench against the wall of the staircase, her head resting against her chest, her hands playing with a small silver medallion that hung around her neck. Zee was next to her, although he was perched uncomfortably on the other side of the bench, leaving as much space as possible between him and her. Simon was pacing up and down urgently in front of them, all trace of pain from the gunshot wound in his shoulder now apparently gone. I realized that he must have consumed some nectar too; not much, just enough to patch him up.

It was Simon who noticed me first. He flinched when he made eye contact, his entire body stiffening. Then, when he saw that my senses had returned, he relaxed.

"Welcome back," he said.

Hearing his words, both Zee and the girl looked over, her face twisting into an expression of terror. She tucked the necklace out of sight, then pushed herself back into the bench, pulling her knees up to her chest. Her eyes were still haunted, still defiant, still fierce.

"Don't let him near me," she hissed. "Don't you dare let him anywhere near me."

"We told you—" Zee started, but the girl cut him off.

"I don't care if he's your friend or not; he's a psycho. You hear me? You're a psycho!"

I turned away as a fit of dizziness rocked me. Then I swiveled around, shuffling away from the tracks. The girl started to protest and I held my hands up in surrender.

"It's okay," I said, my voice throbbing. "I won't come near you. I'm sorry, sorry I scared you."

"Scared me?" she said. "You almost killed me!"

"Then you decided to punch a moving train instead," Zee said, raising an eyebrow. "I'm not really sure what to say about that. How's your arm?"

"It's fine," I said, his words bringing back the memory. I tugged one of the shards of glass from the soft flesh between my knuckles. It fell to the floor with a tuneful tinkle, followed by a single drop of black blood. "I really *did* punch a moving train."

"Nectar'll do that to you," Simon said. "Makes you do craaaaazy things. Better than being dead, though. I think. And you fought it, you came back."

"I almost didn't," I replied. Every time I got a fresh dose of nectar I toppled a little closer to oblivion. It had happened in the prison, when I'd fought those first two berserkers. And it had been worse just now. Christ, I'd nearly beaten an innocent girl's brains in. How many more times would I have to take the nectar to stay alive? And what would happen when I couldn't find my way back? I'd belong to the warden, and to Alfred Furnace, for good.

Simon was wrong, that wasn't better than being dead.

"Anyway, let's forget about it," Zee said. "You're awake, and you've got your strength back. You're gonna need it. We're *all* gonna need it."

I nodded at Zee, then nodded an acknowledgment at Simon. Despite everything, he'd probably saved my life by feeding me nectar. I'd been on my last legs. Hell, I'd been on my last everything. And I really did have my strength back. I got to my feet, my whole body singing, feeling as though it was capable of anything.

The girl seemed to press herself even farther into the bench, so I backed off another few steps, keeping my hands by my sides. I wasn't quite sure what to say, and I doubted there was anything I could do to win her over after what had happened, so I settled for an awkward attempt at a smile.

"Well, this is Alex," Zee said. "Alex, this is Lucy."

"I thought you'd be running for the hills about now," I said.

Lucy wiped her eyes, smearing mascara over her cheek, and with her dark hair hanging in untidy strands over her cheeks it made her look like a Goth. She was wearing jeans and a neat blue suit jacket over a Led Zeppelin T-shirt, a pair of scuffed sneakers on her feet. Up close, and free of the nectar's malevolent grip, I noticed she was older than I'd first thought, maybe sixteen or seventeen.

"You kidding me?" she said. "With those . . . those *things* up there? Not to mention a prison-load of your ex-cellmates."

"We're not like them," Zee said. "I told you."

"Yeah, you're all innocent, you said." Lucy snorted a humorless laugh. "You just happened to be walking by and they threw you in Furnace. You're all as bad as each other, thugs and killers, don't try and pretend you're not. My dad was a copper, you know. He'd have sent you all back down there before you'd taken three breaths of fresh air."

I wondered how much they had told her, asking the question out loud.

"Enough," Simon answered. "You were zonked out over there for a good twenty minutes."

"You told her about the berserkers?" I asked. "About the experiments?"

The girl spluttered, scoffing at the story she'd been told. But it was a little difficult to deny, given the evidence, and the way she turned her tired eyes to the floor, her mouth drooping, I could tell she was finding it harder and harder to maintain her disbelief.

"Told her everything," Zee said. "Don't think she believed me. But I don't think it matters. She trusts her own eyes."

"It's impossible," she said. "You can't . . . you can't just make something like that, you can't just turn a . . . a . . ."

She sneaked a look at me and gave up, chewing her lip instead.

"Told her all about you too," Zee went on. "That it's not your fault you're . . . y'know . . . all messed up and everything. Not your fault you look like Shrek's uglier brother."

"Thanks," I muttered.

Lucy's head lifted, and she must have seen something human in my eyes—or maybe it was the smiley face plastered over my hoodie—because she let her legs unfold, dropping her feet to the platform below. She sat forward, her elbows on her knees, her fingers smearing more mascara over her delicate features.

"That all true?" she asked, staring at the scars on my neck, on my face, around my silver eyes. "What he said. That they took you apart and put you back together again?"

"You think I was born like this?" I said, uncomfortable under her scrutiny. I angled away, raising a hand and pretending to scratch my forehead, leaving it there for longer than it needed to be. "None of it matters, though. It's all history. All we need to think about is finding a way out of here, out of the city."

"It's bad up there," Zee said, hauling himself off the bench and smoothing down his ripped jeans. "Lucy says all the main roads out have been closed off, the mainline train stations too."

"We were told to stay home," she said. "It was all over the news. But hardly anyone believed it was as bad as they were saying. I couldn't take a day off work; needed the money. I reckon most people felt the same. Thought the cops would get it under control; thought it was safe enough." She snorted again, this time in disgust. "Thought wrong, didn't I?"

"Whole city's in lockdown," Simon mumbled, kicking out at an imaginary stone. "It's hopeless. May as well stay here till we're rounded up."

Till the city burns, I thought with a shudder.

"Haven't been no trains since the one you tried to kill," Zee said. "Guess they figured it was too dangerous, people on the tracks and stuff."

"So the tunnels are clear?" I asked. There was a round of shrugs.

"Maybe, maybe not," Simon said. "I don't fancy getting halfway down one and finding out they're just running a bit late."

"What, then?" I asked. "You didn't think of any amazing plans while I was out? Jeez, guys, what am I paying you for?"

At this the girl actually smiled—the smallest twitch of one corner of her mouth, gone a heartbeat later, but a smile nonetheless.

"Well, feel free to dock my salary," Zee said. "Because I've got zip. Far as I see it, we can either risk the tunnels, keep heading north for a quieter station, or—"

"Don't get much quieter than this," Simon interrupted, looking around at the deserted platform.

"You know what I mean," Zee went on. "We either try that,

and risk a train, and find ourselves in exactly the same position half a mile closer to the center of the city. Or . . ."

"Or . . . ?" Simon and I said together.

"Or we breach the surface now, see what the situation is up top." He peered longingly up the stairs, snatching a ragged breath. "If there are cops up there then we'll have to fight, I guess. But they might be busy with those other things. We might be able to sneak out onto the streets."

"And then what?" I asked. "Hot-wire a car again, get the crap shot out of us by another helicopter?"

Zee's shoulders lurched up and down in resignation.

"Guess it's a risk," he said. "But the alternative is to stay here and wait for trouble to come to us, whether it's the cops or another of Furnace's sick freaks."

"Great," I said. "So it's get hit by a train, get shot at by the cops, or get eaten by a mutant kid-faced gorilla. Jesus, what a choice."

"You lot are better off heading up top," Lucy said. "If everything you say is true—and I don't for a second believe it is—but if even some of it is true, then you should hand yourselves in, let the courts sort it out."

Simon pointed a finger at the girl, his face growing overcast.

"How do you think we got here in the first place?" he said. "I'll never give myself back to Furnace. I'd rather die than do that."

I felt the same, but Lucy had a point. If the berserkers were up there, if the public had seen them, then there was a chance that people would believe us. At the very least they'd keep us in a normal jail with windows and televisions and luxuries like that, and they'd have to investigate what had been going on. It wasn't as if they could shove us back into a burning prison. No, things had changed since last night. The world might listen.

I started to voice my thoughts when a jolt of pain gripped my neck, cramp twisting the muscles all the way down my arm. I grabbed it, massaging it with my good hand, feeling the scarred tissue beneath my skin writhe and pulse as if there was something living under there. Something living and *growing*.

"Wassup?" Simon asked, seeing my discomfort. I shook my head, the pain already ebbing.

"It bit you, didn't it?" Zee asked. "That thing. Took a chunk right out of your neck."

"Doesn't matter," I replied. "I've been through worse. Come on, what's the plan?"

Zee and Simon shared a look, then Zee spoke.

"Let's just poke our heads out. Not for long, just to see what's what. If the streets are crawling then we'll try the tunnels, yeah? Either way, we keep heading up into the city and out the other side."

I nodded, looking at Simon. He glared at me, wiped his nose with the back of his hand, then shook his head in a way that said he didn't like it but he'd give it a go.

"But you're poking your head out first," he said to Zee, clipping him around the back of the neck. "That way, if I see your noggin pop, then I can get mine out of the way."

"Deal," Zee said, setting off up the steps with a weary sigh. Simon followed, and I looked at Lucy.

"What about you?" I asked. "Are you going to wait here for the cops?"

The girl took an uneasy look around her then jumped to her feet, smoothing down her shirt and making for the stairs.

"Are you mental?" she muttered. "That *thing* might be back at any time. No way, Psycho Boy, I'm coming with you."

THE STREETS

IT SHOULD HAVE BEEN a five-minute walk to the surface, but it took us three times that long.

We went slowly, stopping at every corner to make sure the coast was clear, pausing with our breath held each time we heard the ghost of a noise spirit down the passageways. The last thing we wanted was to walk in on a berserker midway through a meal, or to swing around a bend into a barrage of bullets from an over-zealous SWAT team.

At the top of the platform steps we followed a winding trail of black blood all the way down the passage to the escalators. The dark line continued up one of the three moving staircases, a macabre signpost showing us the way out of Twofields station. I stepped onto the other upward escalator, not wanting to go anywhere near the mess even though I knew it was nectar, the same filth that was fueling my muscles, powering my heart.

"Anyone know where we'll come out?" Simon asked as we traveled slowly toward the level above.

"Twofields," Zee said unhelpfully. He noticed we were all looking at him and added: "Um, it's in the financial district, I think. By the banks and all that. I've never been around here, sorry."

"It's the cathedral, not the bank," Lucy said. I hopped off the escalator, scanning the hall ahead to see no sign of life apart from the same bloody trail. Simon followed, then Zee, and Lucy was still talking as she stepped gingerly onto the tiled floor. "St. Martin's, you know? Banks are over the river, Morgan Heath and Central. Why, you thinking of robbing one?"

"I told you—" Zee started, but he didn't get a chance to finish.

"I know, I know," Lucy said, holding up her hands. "You're all innocents, you'd never dream of robbing a bank."

"Well, apart from Simon," Zee added, almost apologetically. "He used to rob stuff."

"Gee, thanks for sharing that," Simon muttered as we set off across the hall. It was deserted here too, although there was more evidence of violence—crimson streaks splashed up against a pillar, decorating a map of the underground. As we passed it I couldn't help but think that it looked like the whole city was drenched in blood. It bled freely onto the floor, dripping like an open wound, which meant it was fresh. I held my finger to my lips to keep everybody quiet as we walked up a small flight of steps onto the main concourse.

"Jeez Louise," Zee said when the station foyer came into view. "What the hell happened here?"

Twofields station looked like it had been hit with a cruise missile. The various pillars scattered between us and the main doors had crumbled into dust, the ceiling drooping like a canvas tent. Every single bench had been overturned, and one was embedded in the glass door of a Marks and Spencer's. The striplights in the ceiling had been daubed red, casting the entire scene in a weird, muddy glow that reminded me of the infirmary back in Furnace.

"Oh God," Lucy moaned, wiping her mouth. "Oh God, what's going on? What's wrong with you people?"

Zee started to defend us again, attempting to rest his hand re-assuringly on Lucy's shoulder only to have it shrugged away. I left them to it, treading carefully across the sticky tiles, through the open ticket gates, and around a corner. There was a noise here, the faintest whisper, and flickering too, like somebody was fidgeting manically in the shadows. I raised my hands, praying I wouldn't come across the berserker that had caused so much destruction.

To my relief, the source of the noise and light was a television. It hung precariously off its wall mounting, a string of something red and wet drooping over the screen and looking like the only thing keeping it from toppling to the floor. The volume was almost muted, but I didn't need it. The images told their story effortlessly as they flashed on and off behind a pale-faced broadcaster.

"That looks bad," said Simon from behind me. "Is it real?"

I thought it was a stupid question, but I could see why Simon had asked it. I'd seen this city attacked a hundred times—blown up in films, invaded in computer games, blazing on the cinema screen—that it was easy to believe what was taking place in front of me was make-believe, nothing but special effects and acting. Except that wasn't how the news worked.

No, those images were real. They were happening right now, and right outside the doors of this station. The shot of a building on fire—a residential block, by the looks of things, smoke-blackened faces screaming from windows twenty stories above the ground; the footage of street blockades on every major route out of the city, bridges sealed off with police vans and . . . had that been a *tank*? Fleeting, blurry video of a huge, muscular creature scaling a wall like King Kong, vanishing through a window with a flash of silver eyes and a lunatic grin; aerial shots of the city that looked too close to my hallucination—pillars of smoke rising from three or four major fires, smudging the blue sky; CCTV feed of gangs of inmates running wild; and the vision I knew would become iconic, the one that we'd be seeing everywhere—a girl, maybe five or six, sobbing into a wide-eyed corpse that had probably been her mother while an inferno raged behind her, camouflage-clad soldiers trying to drag her to safety.

JAILBREAK THREATENS CITY, ran the headline beneath the anchorwoman, an understatement if ever I'd seen one. Below that the rolling text bar ran its relentless course, telling people outside the city limits to get the hell away from town, and everybody inside the perimeter to lock their doors and start praying. **_POLICE WARN OF A NEW "SEASON OF SLAUGHTER."_** And the thing that was more ominous than anything else, a flashing warning stating **_ALL EMERGENCY LINES HAVE BEEN SUSPENDED. DO NOT CALL._**

When the emergency services stop working, you know you're in serious trouble.

"No way," Lucy sobbed. She had a hand to her mouth, looking both ten years older and ten years younger than when I'd first seen her. She buried her head into Zee's shoulder and this time she didn't protest when he rested his arm around her. He had tears in his eyes too. They rolled down his cheeks leaving meandering trails in the layers of dirt that had accumulated there. "This can't be happening." Lucy's muffled protests were the perfect accompaniment to the images on-screen, a sound track of misery and disbelief that bled into our ears as we watched the reports file in, the body count rising by the second as the unknown threat surged through the city. And then the picture changed.

"There's the bastard," Simon said, his voice low and menacing. On-screen was a motorway, army trucks rumbling down it and

flooding into the city. There was a police barricade at the junction
and the barrier was open, the trucks passing through it under the
scrutiny of several more camouflaged soldiers and . . .

My heart almost stopped.

It was *him*. The warden.

He stood surrounded by hulking blacksuits, his gray suit as
smart as ever, his hair parted neatly. There was no sign of the injuries that he'd suffered during our escape. He could have been anyone, a middle-aged man who had turned up to watch the show.
Only even from here, halfway across the city, even as a tiny figure
on a TV screen, it was clear that he radiated power. His posture
made the soldiers around him hunch their backs, lower their eyes,
and his leathery face—so much like a rotting mask pulled tight
over a skull—seemed to dominate the entire picture.

"Arrest him, you idiots," Simon yelled. "Go on, you want to
know who's behind this, he's *right in front of your stupid eyes!*"

But the police and the soldiers showed no sign of doing so. Instead they were talking to him, and from the looks of it they were
hanging on his every word. He waved a long, thin arm and three
uniformed men vanished out of the shot, running.

The camera began to zoom in as more vehicles crossed the
bridge, this time something that looked like a cross between a
truck and a tank, its caterpillar tracks tearing up the tarmac. The
warden slid closer to the edge of the screen, looking like he was
about to climb right through the glass and into the station. Before
I even knew what I was doing I had taken a couple of steps back.
We may have beaten him, we may have escaped his prison, but
that man still scared the crap out of me.

I braced myself, studying his expression. He looked deadly serious as he addressed the men and women around him; furious,

even. But just before he fell out of shot, in the instant before he vanished, he turned his crooked face to the camera and smiled, a wicked glint that was gone before I could even be positive it had been there. But it *had* been there, it was scored into my retinas, his face like a Punch doll carved in bone, flashing up in negative every time I blinked.

"Come on," I said, desperate to get away. "The longer we leave it, the less likely we are to get out alive."

We all turned our backs on the television and shuffled toward the exit. One last flight of steps took us up to the main doors, thrown into shadow by the smoke that billowed and blustered beyond. It was so dark out there that for one terrifying moment I imagined the entire city had been plunged beneath the ground, a chamber of solid rock growing overhead and sealing us in this tomb forever. I had to close my eyes and literally shake the image from my head, stepping from the door to see slivers of blue sky through the relentless smog.

"Looks clear," said Zee between coughs. I don't know how he could tell, as visibility was reduced to maybe thirty meters. The street outside was lined with cars that all looked empty. Some still had their doors open and their engines running. The buildings here were all shops and offices, and the fire was coming from one farther up the road. It was engulfed, flames licking from the doors and windows as if jeering at the fact that there was nobody there to put them out. Walls exploded, raining lethal shards of glass and masonry down into the street. Several alarms were going off in shops and cars alike, rising like some demented morning chorus.

I pulled my hoodie up over my mouth to keep the smoke out, but still I felt dirty fingers stretch down into my lungs. It was like being back in the incinerator in Furnace Penitentiary, and I coughed so hard I thought I was going to puke.

"Which way?" I wheezed.

"Away from that," Zee replied, pointing at the burning building.

We'd taken three steps from the station doors when a cop sprinted out from behind an abandoned truck. He saw us straight-away, raising his pistol and pointing it at us with shaky hands. It was impossible to gauge his reaction because a gas mask covered his face, only a pair of wide eyes visible beneath. I raised my hands above my head instinctively, hoping he wouldn't notice the writh-ing muscles and tendons in my right arm. Zee and Simon lifted theirs too, but Lucy started running toward him.

"Thank god," I heard her say as she bounded across the street. The cop saw her coming and angled the weapon toward her.

"Stop," he shouted. Lucy slowed to a walk, holding her hands in front of her.

"Officer, I'm not one of them; I'm innocent, a civilian; I need help."

The cop flicked his eyes at us but kept the gun pointing at Lucy. Beside me I could feel Simon tense up, knew that as soon as he saw a chance he'd be across the street, fists at the ready.

"I said don't move," the policeman barked at Lucy. "I'm warn-ing you, take another step and . . ."

He trailed off. Beneath the mask his eyes were blinking furi-ously and I thought I recognized the expression. He was in shock.

"Lucy," I said. "Back off, he can't help you."

Lucy ignored me, taking another couple of steps toward the policeman. I could hear her pleading, asking him to take her with him, to arrest us, just to get her off the streets. But he was paying no attention, looking at us like a rabbit about to get hit by a truck. I could hear muffled sounds and I realized he was talking, a stream of words blurred by his gas mask. From here, it sounded like a prayer.

"Come on," Zee whispered. "Let's go."

We started to move down the street, keeping our steps small and slow so we wouldn't alarm the cop. He swung his weapon toward us, his mumbles ending abruptly.

"I can't let you go," was all he said, his gun shaking.

Lucy was crying now, holding her hands out to him, fingers clasped together. Somewhere nearby a siren welled up, barely audible over the sobs and the constant roar of the fire. And there was something else too, the patter of feet running this way, getting louder, faster, accompanied by hoarse breathing. I risked a look up the street but I couldn't see anything past the smoke.

Somebody cried out, a noise that might have been a yelp of pain or a whoop of excitement. The cop turned toward it, his eyes blinking even more furiously behind the sheen of his visor, as if by opening and closing, opening and closing they might erase the madness from sight. He lifted the gun, pointed it in the direction of the sounds, but there was nothing there but a wall of smoke backlit by shades of orange and red. That call came again, echoed by another, and this time there was no doubting that they were shouts of delight, like monkey screams.

The cop looked at Lucy, his eyes lifting into a sad smile, a look so full of warmth and sympathy that it almost broke my heart.

"I'm sorry," he said. "May God help you."

Then he swung the gun up to his own head and pulled the trigger. The shot echoed between the buildings, then was engulfed by the smoke, and before the cop could hit the ground two shapes bounded from the shroud of darkness, black eyes bloodshot, swollen, and full of rage as they tore toward us.

OLD FRIENDS

AT FIRST I thought they were berserkers, their bodies muscle-bound and misshapen, as if they had been sculpted from clay by a child. Nectar dripped from their eyes and lips—just like the kid back in the station—making them look like those weird mimes you get on street corners, face-painted to look like they're crying. Only these things weren't crying. Their mouths were twisted up into grins, teeth bared, and fat, black-veined tongues slopping away at the mess that dribbled down their chins. And in the soul-less depths of those inkwell eyes I saw nothing but glee.

But they weren't berserkers. How could they be? They were wearing prison overalls, torn around their bulging chests and limbs and stained with fresh and drying blood, but unmistakable. Their faces, although swollen, had no mark of the scalpel, no stitches or scars. No, they couldn't be berserkers, because they were prisoners like us who had just escaped.

They couldn't be berserkers because I *knew* one of them. He was called Bodie. I'd talked to him no more than a few hours ago, just before we'd made our bid for freedom up the elevator shaft. He'd been a boy then, not a wild, slavering beast hammering across the hot tarmac too fast for a human, hands like claws held out to our throats, eyes promising not just violence but a painful and bloody death.

I didn't have time to call out his name before he leaped onto a car hood and soared through the smoky air. He thumped into me, sending us both rolling over the pavement into the wall, him on top, his claws raking my skin, slashing, scratching. His head lunged forward, his teeth snapping shut, and I realized he was trying to bite me. Nectar swept through my system, making me act without thinking. I lashed out, my fist catching Bodie on the head. It snapped away but he didn't seem to feel the pain, lurching forward for another attack.

Of course he didn't feel the pain. Judging by the amount of nectar that was flowing from his ears, his nostrils, squeezed from his pores, he was pumped full of the stuff. I managed to get an arm between him and me, pushing him back just before his teeth could get purchase.

"Bodie!" I called out, shoving him away. He toppled but gained traction, leaping back onto me. There was no white left in his eyes, those black pits like a demon's, feral and full of something that wasn't quite rage, wasn't quite delight, but some sick hybrid of the two. Nectar dripped from his open mouth, and as it splashed onto my skin I noticed that it was flecked with red, the specks glinting like molten lava. He was almost vomiting the stuff, so much of it that my clothes were drenched, a sparkling black pool spreading out beneath us.

He leaned back in and this time I snapped my head forward, butting him right on the nose. It broke with a crack but he didn't even register it. I did it again, bright lights bursting in my vision, then again, harder this time, knocking him backward. I sat forward, grabbing his head in both my hands and holding it as steady as I could. He jerked and trembled in my grip, his body epileptic.

"Bodie," I said. "Bodie, stop it. It's me, Alex."

I caught movement behind Bodie's head, noticed that Simon and Zee were both wrestling with the other inmate. There was no sign of Lucy. Bodie raked his nails across my throat, his jaws snapping like a piranha's, that fat slug of a tongue darting out and licking his lips between each attempted bite. I could feel the adrenaline kicking in, bringing the nectar with it, clouding my thoughts and my senses. If I didn't end this quickly then I'd be pulled under again, and there was no guarantee I'd be able to find my way back to the surface.

"Last chance," I said, my heart in my throat, pumping hard enough to explode. "Bodie, if you're in there then you better let me know."

He rocked hard enough to dislodge one of my hands, throwing himself at me. I grabbed him again, then, as the emotion boiled up from my stomach, bursting from my mouth in a wail of grief and anger, I twisted as hard as I could. His head almost turned through a hundred and eighty degrees, but he didn't stop fighting. His hands thrashed, his hooked fingers like the blades of a combine harvester, reaching for my throat even though he couldn't see me.

I backed away and watched for what must have been half a minute as he scrabbled on the street, his body a broken machine driven by the nectar inside him, the poison refusing to give up control even as the vessel cooled and stiffened. Eventually it ground to a halt, the eyes clearing as though a storm cloud was passing. Bodie stared sightlessly at the smoke that whirled above him, those slivers of daylight lodged in the glassy sheen of his gaze.

I remembered Zee and Simon, looked across to the opposite sidewalk to see them both sitting on the other inmate, kicking and punching at his body even though he showed no sign of moving. Zee slid off onto the concrete, rolling away onto his feet. His knuckles were black. He looked at me, an expression of utter desperation.

From farther down the street came a muffled scream, followed by the honk of a horn. I wiped the tears from my eyes—tears that weren't caused just by the smoke—and got to my feet, pulling Simon up as I passed him and jogging away from the burning building.

As we ran the view ahead grew clearer, emerging from the burning air like the picture on a television that's just been turned on. There was another rabid inmate standing on the hood of a small red car, using a shotgun like a bat to try to smash the windshield. It was working, a web of cracks spreading out across the glass, and beyond them I could make out Lucy's face. She pressed the horn again as if the sound might knock her attacker away, but he just hunched over her, the gun descending again and again in a terrifying frenzy.

Simon moved first, running past another car and ripping the bumper clean off, swinging it like a club and catching the inmate's legs. The strike was hard enough to spin him head over heels in a clean circle, and he almost landed perfectly on the hood like an acrobat. But his balance failed him and he stumbled backward, arms flailing. Simon swung again but the inmate fell beneath the curve of the weapon, pushing himself off the hood and throwing himself on Simon, arms and legs wrapped around him and his teeth going right for the jugular.

I slid over the hood, grabbing the boy by the collar. Beneath his skin I could see veins of black, pumping visibly, and there were beads of ruby-flecked nectar there, like dew, that had been squeezed from his pores. I wrenched him away from Simon, throwing him against a wall. There was a pop, like a balloon filled with water, and something beneath the kid's overalls burst. Nectar began to drain out of him like a tap had been turned on, the weird swellings that covered his body and face shrinking, making him look like a paper bag that had been left out in the rain. It looked as if he was dissolving. He was growing weaker too, his desperate lunges slowing.

I heard an engine roar to life beside me. The red car's headlights blazed, and with a crunch of gears it jolted forward, accelerating fast, bouncing up onto the curb and pinning the inmate to the wall. He flopped onto the steaming hood, twitched violently, then was still.

For what seemed like a long time we stood in silence, trying to catch our breath. Then Lucy opened the car door, letting it swing out on its hinges, broken glass tinkling from the windshield and the side windows. The air bag had deployed, and she was covered in white powder, making her look like a ghost.

"Is it dead?" she asked.

"I'd say so," Zee replied.

He stepped toward the car and offered Lucy a hand. She stared at it for a moment as if she wasn't sure what it was, then grabbed it and let him help her out. Simon was leaning over the hood, prodding the dead inmate with his foot.

"What the hell are they?" he asked. "They look like, well, us— us as in me and you, Alex. Only, they haven't been under the knife. That's impossible."

"Full of nectar," I added. "But it's not the same nectar we had back in Furnace."

"It's got red in it," Simon said, dipping his finger into a puddle of the filth and studying it in the smoky sunlight. "It's as if it's, I don't know, supercharged or something. It's turning them straight-away."

"Yeah," I said. "The one who attacked me, that was Bodie."

"Bodie?" said Zee, the corners of his mouth dropping. "Seriously?"

I nodded, and we were silent for a minute more. Bodie had been a Skull, but he'd been a good kid. He'd helped us get out. To see him reduced to a mindless animal, full of poison and hell-bent on destruction, was devastating. Zee took another look at the corpse on the hood, then glanced at me. He seemed about to say something, but instead he frowned, walking over.

"You okay?" he asked. "That bite on your neck looks nasty."

I raised a hand to where the creature in the station had gripped me in its jaws. It didn't hurt—of course it didn't—but my heart sank anyway. It was another scar that would forever remind me of what I'd been through, what I'd become. Zee put his face close to mine, peering up at the wound.

"I can see it," he said. "I can see the nectar in your skin."

I wasn't surprised. That's what it did—prowled through your veins, plugging wounds and healing wrought flesh. But Zee had obviously noticed something else. He walked to the red car, reached inside and pulled the rearview mirror free from its mount.

"Look," he said, handing it to me. I took it, peering into the glass reluctantly. The wound was worse than I'd thought, and there was something more. Clumps of nectar grouped around it, caked in drying saliva. I moved to clean it off, but as I did so I thought

I saw those thin trails move, edging closer to the ragged bite mark. I blinked, tried to focus, saw it again—tiny beads of red-beaded nectar defying gravity and rolling up my neck. With a grunt I drew my sleeve across it, wiping until every last trace of nectar had gone, then throwing the mirror to the ground.

"What the hell is going on?" I asked, my skin itching at the thought of what I'd seen. "Nectar doesn't do that."

Zee looked down at the broken mirror, then back at the dead inmate, whose skin hung in loose folds, empty of the fluid that had swollen it.

"I'm not sure," he said quietly. "But it looks like these kids, these inmates, were *infected* by the nectar."

"Infected?" said Simon, walking to Zee's side. Lucy was there too, listening to the conversation with the expression of somebody who has just woken from their worst nightmare to find out it's real.

"Yeah, infected," Zee said. "That's why the berserker in the subway carried that kid off rather than killing him."

"So it could set him loose up here, you mean? Let him infect others?"

Zee nodded. "The berserkers fill the kids with nectar, turn them into psychos, and those infected inmates do the same with new victims. That rat was sure as hell trying to bite me just now."

I remembered the way Bodie had been trying to sink his teeth into me, nectar spilling from his throat.

"I don't think this is an invasion," Zee went on.

"So what is it?" Lucy asked him.

Zee looked once more at my wounds, wiping his tired eyes with the back of his hand.

"I think it's a plague."

ST. MARTIN'S

WE STARED AT ZEE as if he'd gone mad, as if he'd suddenly snapped under the pressure. Simon even snorted a laugh in his direction, shaking his head in denial.

"You're off your head, Zee-boy," he said as he ran his hands over his body, checking for injuries, for bite marks. "Nectar don't work that way. It's not *contagious*."

"Isn't it?" Zee asked. He walked over to the car Lucy had been in, looking down at the shotgun the inmate had been using to smash through the windshield. He seemed as if he was about to pick it up but then obviously thought better of it, turning back to us. "How do you know?"

"Duh," Simon replied, gesturing at his enormous, misshapen arm.

"But look at Alex," Zee said. "He's changing."

I lifted my right arm, the muscles so big now that the sleeve of my hoodie had ripped. It still looked as if something was moving under my skin, black worms that appeared then vanished before I could make any sense of them. It wasn't sore, though. In fact if anything I felt stronger than I ever had. I felt as though I could take on every single one of Furnace's freaks with that single bulging limb.

"It doesn't matter what's going on," I started, cradling my arm against my chest. Zee cut me off.

"Doesn't matter?" he said, one eyebrow raised. "Look around you, Alex, and tell me it doesn't matter if the city is overrun by . . . by whatever Bodie was."

I did as I was told, not that I could see much with the ocean of smoke churning around us. It had grown thicker, blocking out all but a halo of dull orange that sat just above the horizon. It hung in the back of my throat, burning like acid, and I hawked up a ball of dirty spit.

"He was a rat," Simon said, and Zee nodded. I didn't believe them—I mean, how could Bodie have been turned into a rat without the surgery, without days spent in the infirmary, in the screening room, slowly losing his mind as the warden's poison went to work?—but now wasn't the time to argue. The fire behind us was spreading fast, there was no sign of the emergency services. If we didn't get moving soon then we'd be barbecued.

And I could hear more screams from close by, chirruped cries of menacing delight carried on the filthy air. If Zee was right, and this was a plague, then the streets would be crawling with those things.

But he *couldn't* be right, could he?

I thought about the new nectar, the crimson insect eyes that swam inside it, the way it had seemed to crawl inside my wound, like it was alive, and I shuddered so hard I almost lost my balance.

"So what now?" asked Lucy. She was leaning up against the car, her arms folded over her chest and her chin almost resting on them. She spoke in a robotic monotone, one that I recognized from Furnace—the voice you used when your brain went into survival mode, switching off everything but the bare essentials.

"We keep moving," I offered. "North, I guess. We stick to what we agreed, get the hell away from here. If we just keep moving, then we'll think of something."

It wasn't the best plan in the world, but nobody had a better one. With a collection of weary shrugs and sighs we set off up the road, sweatshirts pulled up to our mouths to keep the smoke out. We could have taken a car, there were enough of them around—too many, in fact: the road was littered with vehicles, like an assault course. It was quicker on foot, and we made good time considering we had to stop again and again as those relentless shrieks faded in and out between the buildings.

With each step the smoke grew thinner, its acrid touch weaker. I studied the shops and offices that emerged from the smog—a travel agent, two betting shops, a computer service company, a pawnbroker, a drugstore—wondering if we'd be better off taking shelter. But it felt good to be moving, even though we didn't know where we were going, or what was waiting for us. Every step carried us farther from Furnace Penitentiary.

SOMETIME LATER WE REACHED a crossroads, the signals blinking from red to green and back again controlling nonexistent traffic. There were vehicles here too, one sickly yellow sports car buried deep into the side of a white van, the windshield broken, the driver nowhere to be seen.

Ahead was what looked like another fire, this one blazing on both sides of the road, spreading into a small park between offices, the trees like burning hands held up to the heavens. It looked like there were shapes in the flames, figures dancing between the trunks, reminding me of some weird pagan ceremony. It had to be an illusion, but it creeped the hell out of me and I turned away only to see something that scared me a million times more.

To my left was another street, a wider avenue with flowers planted down the divide between the two lanes, abandoned cars spilling along its length. It stretched downhill, all the way into the center of the city, to the distant skyscrapers that stood there like sentinels. And among them was the spire-topped monolith of black glass that I knew from my nightmare.

My ears began to ring, and for an absurd moment I swore I could feel that building searching for me, like a giant eyeball scouring the city. The ringing grew more intense, unbearable, like a high-powered drill working into the flesh of my brain.

And suddenly the view before me changed, the other buildings crumbling slowly into a cloud of debris, like they had been demolished, the city glowing red as the steel foundations of every building began to melt, ashes incandescent as they rained upward toward the roiling black sky. All that remained was the tower, and perched on the throne of its sloping roof a monstrous, merciless creature that howled into the flames, claiming victory over the world.

Then I blinked, and the street was back, looking positively heavenly compared with the vision. I swallowed and my ears popped, the ringing ebbing away into silence. I peered up to see Zee's eyes on me, but he didn't say anything. If he wasn't used to my sporadic moments of madness by now, then he never would be. I pointed down the street, toward the city, but it was Simon who explained.

"Furnace," he said.

"The prison?" asked Lucy.

"No," Simon replied. "The man. That's where he is, that tower," and he explained what the two of us had seen.

"In that case, my friends, I suggest we go this way," said Zee, setting off along the street opposite, one that led away from the city, away from the tower.

"That's the wrong way," Simon called out after him. "You're going east."

"Doesn't matter," Zee said over his shoulder. "Running into the police is the least of our worries now. Whole city is a death trap. We're better off heading out of it while we still can."

He was right, and I was happy to turn my back on the distant skyscraper, even though I imagined I could feel its depthless windows boring into my head, making note of where I was, keeping track of every step. I did my best to ignore it, focusing on the road ahead.

After a hundred meters or so it divided into two. The bigger branch was blocked by a barricade of concrete blocks, a police van stationed behind them. The door of the van was open and from inside I could make out the sharp static bursts of a radio. We stepped closer, warily, until the jumbled words began to make sense.

". . . need backup, immediately. Ten-double-zero, ten-twenty-four, repeat we are under attack—"

The cop swore and I heard gunfire, the noise too loud for the empty street we were on. There were more curses, then a deafening bleep as the radio cut out. Almost instantly there was another broadcast, a woman this time.

". . . everywhere, don't know . . . Can't . . ." Screams, then a growl loud enough to make the van's speakers vibrate. "What the hell? Ten . . . Ten . . . Screw it, just get to the CC fast, they're everywhere!"

More followed, but by that time we were walking again, taking the smaller road, which angled gently to the left. There was more smoke here, starting as a fine, gossamer-like mist that hung a few feet off the ground, thickening quickly as we approached a burning car. We gave it a wide berth, worried that it would suddenly blow up, pressing through the worst of the smoke to see a shape looming up before us. It was huge, emerging from the gloom like a tanker coming to dock in a fog-drenched harbor. I smeared the tears from my eyes and the silhouette took on a shape, a round dome that I recognized.

"St. Martin's," I coughed. I'd been here once before, years ago on a school trip—memories of cold stone, uncomfortable pews, and beating up a kid called Andrew Spragg in the shadows behind the pillars until he'd handed over the money he'd brought to buy a souvenir. I felt my cheeks redden, wondering—not for the first time or the last—whether I even deserved to be saved from this nightmare, whether I should have just stayed in Furnace, accepted my punishment for who I used to be.

The enormous baroque building sat in the middle of a tiled plaza, deserted apart from the army of pigeons that huddled in the center and cooed curiously at us. We started across it, making for the other side, and had taken a dozen steps when we heard somebody calling. We froze, expecting the worst, but there was no malice in that voice, no menace, just concern.

"Over here!" it hissed, the whisper carrying across the open ground. "Quickly!"

The front of the cathedral was a sculpture of pillars, reminding me of a matchstick house. It was difficult to see into the darkness behind them, but as I looked I could make out a black-robed figure standing there and waving at us.

"What does he want?" Simon asked. An answer leaped into my head from nowhere—*trouble*—but I left it unvoiced. The figure stepped past a column, glancing nervously to the left and right before gesturing at us even more enthusiastically. I saw the white collar, realized he was a priest.

"You kids need to get off the streets," he shouted. "Haven't you heard? Come, you're welcome here, it's safe in the House of the Lord. Come, pray with us."

"This guy has no idea," Simon said, but Lucy was already hurrying across the plaza without so much as a backward glance.

"We should take a look," Zee said as he watched her go. "It's safer than out here, right?"

"But we need to get out of the city," I said, although I couldn't deny that a chance to rest my weary body would be welcome. Besides, those relentless calls were still rising up over the rooftops, shrill whoops and barks that set my teeth on edge. It wouldn't hurt to take shelter for an hour, get a better idea of what was going on.

"Come on," said Zee. "It looks safe enough."

"Yeah, like that's all you're concerned about," Simon replied with a smug smile as he followed. He put on a falsetto, clasping his hands to his heart. "Oh, Lucy, wait for me, I'll look after you."

Zee turned and scowled, the blood rushing to his face. And, incredibly, we were all laughing as we entered the vaulted doors of St. Martin's.

GOD'S HOUSE

THE CATHEDRAL was just as cold and as dark as I remembered.

The priest—a short, wiry man with a neat beard and clipped gray hair—led us through a small lobby into the main body of St. Martin's, muttering as he walked. Lucy was tucked beneath his arm, crying soundlessly, her shoulders twitching.

Inside, it was more like a cave than anything, the stained-glass windows vast but leaden, the smoke outside like old curtains that cut out all but a trickle of dirty light. Two rows of pillars lined up on either side of us, between which were the rows and rows of wooden benches, which made my ass feel numb just looking at them. Resting on these, draped in dusty shadows, were a number of people, all with their backs to us. Some were hunched forward in the pews, obviously praying, while others talked in hushed voices.

I noticed that the biggest group was clustered around something on the floor in the main aisle, close to the altar, a small shape that I couldn't quite identify. A couple of them turned around when they heard our footsteps, their faces full of fear.

"I found some more," the priest called out, his voice swallowed instantly by the immense space, as though the cathedral was demanding us to be silent. The thought brought gooseflesh out on my arms.

He turned to us, squinting into the darkness, and his smile suddenly grew nervous. I knew why. Our clothes covered up most of the scars and the surgery—except for my bulging arm—but mine and Simon's eyes must have been glowing a fierce shade of silver in the half-light beneath the dome. He swallowed, cocking his head and clutching Lucy tighter to his chest.

"Are you children of God?" he asked. I almost burst out laughing, managing to bite my tongue before it erupted. The air was thick with incense, the smell making me sleepy, sitting on my eyelids and pressing them down. "You may rest here, if you are. Each of His flock is welcome."

I looked at Simon, unsure what to say. Luckily, Zee stepped in.

"And I saw the beast," he said, the cathedral turning his shout to a whisper. "And, um, the kings of the earth and their armies gathered together to make war."

The priest's face opened up and he lifted one hand from Lucy, holding it out to us like the Pope addressing the faithful. I threw Zee a look and he returned it with a bashful smile. He didn't have to speak for me to know he'd heard it on one of the documentaries he used to watch with his parents.

"Revelation 19:19," the priest beamed. "You are welcome, child; you are all welcome. Come, pray with us."

He led us forward toward the group of people. I counted seven of them, and as we drew closer I realized the shape on the floor was an eighth. It was a kid, and he groaned feebly, writhing on a bed of hassocks and tucked beneath a blanket of coats. His face was a sickly shade of yellow, and it was filthy, dark lines like warpaint stretching from his neck to his forehead.

"Take a seat, anywhere you like," the priest said, helping Lucy onto a pew. She put her head in her hands, staring at the Bible on the shelf in front of her and rocking gently back and forth. "The more voices we have, the better He will hear us."

"He okay?" Zee asked, nodding at the kid.

"I don't know," replied a young man in a suit. He was kneeling by the child's side, holding the boy's hand in both of his own, and he looked up at us through a thick pair of glasses. I noticed that the kid was wearing a green sweater. He didn't look like an inmate. "We've called an ambulance."

"Fat chance," said somebody else. A woman three rows farther down peered over her shoulder, glaring at us. I noticed she was wearing a hat and a uniform, and I thought for a second she was a cop before realizing she must have been a security guard. "All over the radio, emergency numbers are down. We're on our own."

"We have God," the priest interrupted, but the woman waved his comment away with an impatient hand, turning her attention back to the altar. The other adults—a mix of men and women, mostly older, in their forties and fifties—shuffled uncomfortably while the kid strained and whimpered beneath them. I did a quick head count. There were eighteen of us in total.

"What's it like out there?" the man in the glasses asked. "You see anything?"

"Saw plenty," Simon replied. "She's right, there's no cops." I tried not to think about the policeman we'd seen, putting a gun to his head and blowing out his own brains. "Sure as hell didn't see any ambulances."

"What happened to him?" Zee persisted, pushing through the small crowd and kneeling beside the kid.

"I'm not sure," the Glasses Man replied. "I was on my way to work when everything kicked off. He was outside, on Slate Street, around the back there. There was blood everywhere; I thought he was dead." His voice lowered to a whisper. "The blood belonged to his parents, they were . . . They were . . ." His voice caught in his throat and I thought he was about to vomit. "I couldn't get through to EMS so I brought him in here. He's alive, but he's been hurt, pretty badly."

He reached out, pulling back the brown cord jacket that was covering the boy's neck, and I felt my heart drop right to my feet. There was a bite mark there, unmistakable even in the cathedral's sulking light. I could make out the teeth marks, blunt stab wounds that stretched from his collarbone to his windpipe, embellished with bruises. And what I thought had been dirt was something worse. Those dark trails were nectar, pulsing beneath his skin, spreading out through his body. The kid seemed to grow more anxious under our scrutiny, attempting to burrow deeper into his makeshift bed.

"Oh Jesus," said Zee, earning a stern stare from the priest. "He was bitten."

"Bitten?" asked several of the adults together. The man with the glasses finished. "By what?"

Zee ignored them, standing up and walking toward Simon and me.

"I'm telling you," Zee went on, quieter than before, leaning in so that even with every eye in the cathedral fixed on us he wouldn't be heard. "It's a plague, it's spreading. If you get bitten, you turn."

"Come on, Zee," Simon replied. "These aren't zombies we're talking about. That's crazy."

"Excuse me?" said the priest, taking a step closer. "Do you know something? Any information would be helpful at this point."

We kept our mouths shut, unsure what to say. But Lucy seemed to wake from her daze, peering out at us through eyes that reflected the dappled mosaic of light from the windows.

"They're from the prison," she said softly. "They escaped. They know what's going on."

The priest stumbled back, clutching a pew to stop himself from falling over. Several of the adults retreated too, some even uttering absurd cries of distress. The rest looked as if they were preparing for a fight, their eyes steely and their knuckles white.

"Is this true?" asked the priest, making the sign of the cross over his robes. "You're from Furnace?"

I nodded, getting ready to run. I didn't honestly think this bunch of geriatrics would turn on us, but I knew what people were like. You take away the things they take for granted and they soon go mad. It's like ripping out the foundations of a house and watching it crumble. When you think about it, we're all insane, we just don't know it till we're given a little push in the wrong direction.

"But they're okay," Lucy went on, aware of the growing tension. She looked at Zee and offered him the ghost of a smile, which almost knocked him off his feet. "They seem okay. They saved me, really. I'd be dead now if they hadn't showed up. And they do seem to know what's happening, as insane as it sounds. You're better off listening to them."

The crowd seemed to relax, although their bodies remained

stiff, mouths screwed into little more than slits. The priest recovered himself, smoothing down his robes and looking at Zee.

"Is this true?" he asked. "Do you know what's going on?"

Zee shook his head.

"Not everything, not even close," he said. "I'll tell you what we know, but first things first." He pointed at the kid on the floor. "You need to tie him up, and tie him up good."

TOILET BREAK

I THOUGHT we were in for a force-ten riot. The second Zee gave his order the man with glasses stood bolt upright, hands knotted into small fists.

"Don't you dare touch him," he said, his voice so low and so hoarse it sounded demonic. His eyes too were flaring in a way that made me think of the devil—except I'd already been to hell, I knew the truth about demons. "I swear . . ."

He didn't finish. He didn't need to. His body language did all the talking. Zee held up a hand, silently begging them to listen.

"I'm not saying we should hurt him," he said, his voice calm. "But trust me, if he was bitten then something's going to happen to him. He's going to . . ."

He looked at Simon and me, his eyes imploring us to help.

"He's going to become a monster," Lucy said, pulling herself up from her seat and leaning on the carved wooden finial of the pew. "There's something in him—what do you call it?"

"Nectar," said Zee.

"Nectar," Lucy repeated, dropping down onto her haunches near the boy. People in the crowd were protesting, those who had been seated making their way toward the aisle to hear our story.

Lucy spoke over their muttered remarks. "I'm a nurse. Well, I'm training. I wouldn't have believed it if I hadn't seen it, if someone just like him hadn't tried to kill me. But it's true. If that nectar stuff is in his veins then he's turning. He'll become feral, aggressive. He'll lose his mind."

"Look," said the man, "I don't know who you are, but you're talking nonsense. He's in shock, he's got a serious wound in his neck, and he needs rest, warmth, and water. You can't tie him up, I forbid it."

"Forbid all you want," Lucy said. "If you don't get some restraints on him then I'm getting the hell out of here. You want the truth, you poke that head of yours out the door and take a look at what's going on. There are kids out there . . ." She paused for long enough to reach out a hand and press it against the boy's cheek. "There are kids out there and something is happening to them. They're tearing the city apart."

"Start from the beginning," the priest said. "Please."

"You sure?" Zee asked. "It's a long story."

"From the sound of things, we've got a long wait before anybody comes to rescue us," replied the priest.

Zee opened his mouth, but before he could begin I burst in.

"Is there a bathroom here I can use?" I asked. The priest nodded, pointing behind him.

"Over there, by the transept, down the stairs in the crypt." I thanked him and set off, only to hear him shout: "Please don't steal anything from the gift shop or the cafeteria."

"I need to go as well," Simon shouted, trotting to catch up. Zee was mumbling something at us, but the crowd had surrounded him now and were urging him on. We left him to it, squeezing past the last few stragglers and following the nave to the huge open space beneath the dome. I looked up as we walked, but the vaulted ceiling was lost in shadow. It was easy to believe there were creatures up there, clinging onto the rafters, faces like gargoyles, ready to drop down and feed, so I let my head fall, concentrating on the floor. It took us a while to find the entrance to the crypt, and when we did I felt my throat choke up.

"Underground again," I said as Simon ducked through the low stone archway and traipsed down a narrow spiral staircase. He laughed without humor, keeping one hand on the newel post as he led the way. We walked deeper and deeper, the twisting stairs seeming to go on forever, but just as claustrophobia began to grip me we emerged into a light, airy corridor. To the left were two doors marked MEN and WOMEN, respectively.

Simon pushed through into the gents, holding the door open for me. There were two urinals and I took one, surprised when he squeezed himself in next to me.

"Um . . ." I said, suddenly self-conscious.

"You want me to use the cubicle?" he asked as he went, grinning that lopsided grin of his. "Too late. Come on, don't be shy. Unless . . ." he leaned in even closer. "The warden didn't experiment on your you-know-what, did he?"

"No!" I retorted, the mere idea killing off any last hope of relieving myself. I waited until Simon had finished before trying to relax, the sound of the taps running doing a bit to help.

"Wow," Simon said. "Warm water. You remember that?"

I rinsed my hands under the tap, the sensation of hot water on my skin bringing back too many memories—showers at home after soccer training, washing up the dishes after dinner—and the sense of loss was so overpowering that my face screwed up, hard enough to make it ache. Simon must have noticed because he turned away with an uncomfortable expression, then thought better of it and clapped me twice on the shoulder.

"Come on," he said. "Poor old Zee probably needs some help. You know how he gets when he's stressed."

We walked back to the spiral staircase and started climbing, but after a dozen or so steps Simon stopped, turning to face me.

"Alex," he said quietly. "How the hell did it get so bad so quickly?"

The stone walls pressed in, trapping us in a bubble of darkness that felt protective rather than threatening.

"I don't know," I replied.

"It's just . . ." Simon seemed to choke on his words. "How did Furnace manage to get his army into the city so quickly? I mean, his creeps were here almost as soon as we got out."

"He knew we were escaping," I finished when Simon faltered again. "The warden told him, remember that phone? That's why Furnace sent those two berserkers to the prison, that's how he had time to get everything else in place."

Simon looked unsure, and it took a nudge from me to make him spill the rest of his thoughts.

"It's more than that. In the vision, back in the subway, he said that we forced his hand, made him start his war today, right?"

I nodded, trying not to think about what I'd seen after the berserker had bitten me, what Alfred Furnace had told me. Simon shuffled uncomfortably, then looked me right in the eye.

"This break, us getting out. It wasn't a blow for Furnace. It was exactly what he wanted. And I don't think we escaped . . ." He left the sentence hanging, and all of a sudden the silence in the stairwell was replaced by the roar of my pulse in my ears as I realized what he was saying. "I think he let us out."

"That's impossible," I said, shaking my head as I remembered everything we'd gone through to force our way out of the prison. There was simply no way that Furnace could have engineered all of that. "Why would he let us all go just to try and catch us again?"

"He's not trying to catch us," Simon said. "The police are, sure, but Furnace—he's trying to *turn* us. He wants us out here, tearing the world apart."

I was still shaking my head, but I only had to look out onto the streets of the city to know the truth.

"No," I barked, pushing past Simon and almost tripping up the stairs. "There's no way. We're wrong. Furnace is crazy. He's off his head. They both are, him and the warden. The army is here now, anyway. They'll handle it. We just need to stay alive."

"But they don't know what they're dealing with," Simon said. "If Furnace is filling this city with berserkers, if his rats are pouring into the streets, infecting everyone they bite, then the army's just walking into a trap. They'll get eaten alive out there."

I don't think he was talking literally, but I know we both had the same image in our heads. Simon was right. The rats—these new ones—were fast and they were angry, and by the looks of things their numbers were spreading. They'd attack without mercy, without hesitation, and those of their victims who didn't die stood a good chance of turning into bloodthirsty freaks themselves. I thought about the faces of those soldiers we'd seen on television, how young some of them looked. I didn't know how the nectar worked, only that the warden had told me adults couldn't handle it. But where was the cutoff point? Sixteen? Eighteen? Twenty?

"Coming in here was a mistake," Simon said as we walked through the arch into the main body of the cathedral. "City's gonna be swarming; there will be nowhere left to hide. We should grab Zee and Lucy and keep moving, get out of here before—"

"There will be no getting out of here." The words were spat from the shadows and we both flinched. The priest was standing there, bathed in darkness. "Our only plan is prayer, our only escape is God. This is Armageddon, the last battle of good and evil before the Day of Judgment. We must believe, my children. And we must sacrifice. Oh yes, we must sacrifice."

I shared a look with Simon as we walked toward the door, a look that was echoed in his furrowed brow. Out there was hell, but inside this cathedral a storm was brewing, I could feel it.

And I didn't like it.

Not one bit.

TROUBLE

IT WAS DARKER in the cathedral now and it took me a minute to work out why: the huge doors at the front of the building, the ones we had entered through, were now closed and bolted, chains looped between the handles and sealed with padlocks better suited to a medieval dungeon.

"Looks like we're here to stay," I whispered to Simon as he stepped out after me. The priest was close behind, his eyes like burning suns as he stepped around the last bend. I noticed that the white band in his collar had come loose, folded up like a broken bow tie.

"Join the flock," he commanded, and it was a command, there was no doubt about that. Any hint of the friendliness and warmth he had displayed when we arrived was now long gone. He ushered us across the open floor beneath the dome, back toward his congregation. They were huddled together even more tightly now, watching us approach with a mix of expressions, all unreadable in the growing darkness.

The kid hadn't been moved, but I was relieved to see that one of his arms had been secured with a plastic cuff to the leg of a pew. The security guard was standing over him, one chubby hand resting on her holstered pistol. The man with the glasses was back on his knees, cradling the child's head and glowering at Zee, who sat on a pew a few rows back, Lucy beside him. I made straight for Zee, excusing myself as I pushed through the crowd.

"Thanks," he snapped, sitting forward. "You left me to tell the whole story on my own!"

"We'd have just messed it up," I replied. "You're good with words. Besides," I nudged him, "you had Lucy to help you."

His elbow nudged back hard into my ribs, but he couldn't completely hide the smile on his face as he crashed back against the pew. The priest was standing by the altar, genuflecting so energetically that it looked as if he was conducting an aerobics class. His strangled prayers drifted back to us, garbled words that meant nothing to me.

"Did they believe you?" Simon asked. Zee studied the crowd, then looked at Lucy.

"No idea," she replied for him. "I'm having a hard time believing everything you've said, and I've seen it for myself."

"Well there's a pretty good chance they're about to see it first-hand too," I said, nodding at the kid on the floor. His face was growing darker, like a dead flower decomposing in the sun. "How is he?"

"Getting worse by the second," Zee replied.

I felt hot breath on the back of my neck and turned to see the security guard there. She was short and stocky, and her face was fierce, but she had a sliver of warmth in her eyes.

"Feeling better?" she asked. It took me a moment to realize she was talking about our toilet break, and I nodded. "Good, 'cause I got a funny feeling things are gonna get weird." She leaned in, whispering conspiratorially. "That man, he's not a priest."

"Seriously?" I asked, a little too loudly.

"He's the caretaker," the security guard went on. "I work here sometimes, do the night shift; I've seen him before but wearing overalls and carrying a mop. He's a real dyed-in-the-wool, right-wing, Bible-spouting head case, if his talks down in the staff room are anything to go by. The bishop would normally get here about now, but something tells me he ain't coming to church today. He lives over in the palace; he'd never get across town, not now."

"So what's *he* doing?" Zee asked, staring at the man in black robes. The guard shrugged her hefty shoulders, standing straight, massaging her lower back with both hands.

"I don't know, and that's what worries me. He's started spouting on about the Armageddon or the Apocalypse or some such. Trouble is, these people," she gestured across the church with her hand, "are divine nut jobs too and he's stirring them up something wicked. Most were here for an early Sunday prayer or two; the cathedral's doors are never locked."

"They're locked now," I said.

She nodded, her chins doubling in size and number. "We heard noises out there when you were downstairs doing your business. I don't know what they were, sounded like feedin' time at the zoo." She was fiddling with her holster, popping the stud and clicking it back in. "Saw something too, out on the plaza. Looked like . . . Well, I don't know what it looked like."

"A berserker," Zee finished. "Might have been the one from Twofields."

"We all agreed it would be better if we locked up," the guard said. "If what you told us is true, then there's nothing out there but trouble."

She peeked at the priest, still prostrating himself at the altar.

"Trouble out there, trouble in here too, if you ask me. Now I know you kids have been in prison, but you seem all right. I never approved of that bloody penitentiary anyway. Just watch out for yourselves, okay. In my opinion, there's nowhere more dangerous than a church on the eve of the End of Days. 'Specially if people think you're on the wrong side."

A shadow swept across the pews, a fleeting shape forged of light and color that fluttered from the altar to the doors in the blink of an eye. Every head in the cathedral shot up in time to see a silhouette scamper over the window ledge outside, vanishing just as fast to leave nothing but the clack of feet on stone and a high-pitched howl, ebbing into silence.

"Think they know we're in here?" Simon asked. Nobody answered, but I didn't think those freaks did. If they had any idea there were human hearts beating warm blood in the cathedral they'd be in here like a shot. They were probably just using the building as a lookout point. If we were quiet, they might leave us alone.

But from the looks of things, quiet wasn't going to be an option.

"This is not a time for talking," bellowed the priest-caretaker from his altar, his hands held high, beseeching the cathedral's invisible ceiling. "This is a time for praying. Call upon the Lord to carry us in His arms, to keep us safe from the Great Annihilation. Together we shall offer Him a sign of our faith; together we shall rise into His kingdom."

"I ain't rising into *anyone's* kingdom," muttered Simon.

But most of the crowd had taken to their pews, or were on their knees in the center aisle, their mouths moving in time with the priest's as he recited something from the Bible. His voice grew more shrill with each verse, specks of spittle flying from his mouth, his eyes even wider now, not blinking. I heard scraping from above us, like there was something running on the roof, running fast.

And the kid on the floor was in bad shape. He began to cough, the man with the glasses lifting the boy's head just as a fountain of black liquid exploded from his mouth. It spattered over the uneven tiles, seeming to squirm and wriggle like a puddle of beetles, red flecks sparkling. The kid's throat had swollen to the same size as his head, his breathing wheezy and ragged. His hands were bigger than they had been, poking out from the pile of coats like rubber gloves filled with tar. He lurched, hard enough to pull the pew toward him. The plastic cuff gouged into his mottled arm, letting loose another trail of nectar.

"Think you can loosen this?" Glasses Man asked, but the security guard just shook her head. I didn't blame her, those pews weighed a ton and it had to have taken some strength to move one.

Another shape landed on the window ledge, slipping for a moment as it tried to gain purchase. Somebody in the cathedral screamed, but there was a hand over his mouth before the noise could really get going. We all stood there, as still as the statues around us, until with a guttural roar the shape launched itself from the ledge back down to the street below.

Almost instantly the imposter priest's shrill prayers continued, deafening after the silence.

"The two of them were thrown alive into the fiery lake of burning sulfur!"

"Hey," the security guard hissed, firing the word at the priest. He showed no sign of hearing her, calling out with even more force as he talked about a white knight and a golden sword. She tried again, louder this time. "Hey! You! Shut up for a minute or they're gonna hear us."

The priest kept talking, each sentence capped with a chorus of "Amens" from his flock. The hum of voices was swelling like a tide, filling the cathedral with white noise, threatening to spill from the windows into the streets beyond.

"Stop it!" the security guard went on, her own voice now too loud. "Just stop it. You're only the bloody cleaner, for God's sake."

At this the man's eyes—so wide, so motionless they could have belonged to a corpse—rotated in their dry sockets toward her. There was no expression on his face, but beneath that, in the way his jaw muscles danced, the way the tendons in his neck bulged, I could see a fury of insanity and delusion fit to burst.

"No," he said, "I am more than that. I am God's servant, called here today to lead His flock into the new world. He has appointed me his earthly messenger, and through me you shall all be saved."

"Christ, who does this whacko remind you of?" Simon asked. And it was true. What he was saying now could have come right from the mouth of Alfred Furnace himself, without all the religious stuff, of course. The priest turned his lunatic gaze our way.

"Not everyone can be saved," he said, his voice high and wavering, like a child's. "Judgment Day is approaching, the Lord is testing us, for only the most faithful shall pass through the Valley of Death."

"He doesn't even know what he's talking about," Zee said. "Can you take him, d'you think?"

"I can," Simon said, edging forward. The priest pointed at us with one bony finger.

"He is testing us with these demons," he screamed. "The devil's spawn who have only today broken free from the bowels of hell. They are not part of His flock; they are not destined for the Kingdom of the Light. Seize them, my children. For only by slaying the legions of the Beast will we be judged worthy."

"Oh boy," said Zee, using the pew in front to pull himself up. "Here we go again."

"You're insane!" I shouted at the crowd. "We're not demons, we're kids, like your own!"

But my silver eyes must have looked pretty unholy in the dim light of the cathedral, because people were already easing themselves out of their seats and advancing up the aisle. I bunched my fists. I didn't want to hurt a bunch of pensioners, but now that the doors were locked there was nowhere to run.

The promise of violence was charging the nectar up inside me, my body an engine about to be shunted into gear. I fought it, taking deep breaths, trying to stay calm, but black veins were already throbbing in the corners of my vision, common sense and self-control fading into the background as the poison turned my thoughts to murder.

I clamped my eyes shut, the outline of the massive cross of the altar splashed across my retinas. It didn't fade, it expanded against the backdrop of my eyelids, morphing from a crucifix into what looked like a tower. Yes, it was a tower. It took shape like a photographic negative being developed, windows and doors and a spire slowly emerging. And all around the tower the night seemed to flicker, sparks dancing as if the world was on fire.

Demons? said a voice, that same age-old, ground-shaking whisper. Alfred Furnace, once more in my head. *Show him the truth.*

Show him that you are not a creature of his god, nor of his devil. Show him
that you are a work of man, a genius creation, one of the soldiers of the
Fatherland who has claimed this time as his own.

I realized I was groaning, each word splitting my skull open
a little wider. I opened my eyes, saw the flesh of my arm begin
to swell even more, the nectar that raged through my mind also
wreaking havoc with my body.

"No," I mumbled, poison rushing up my throat, into my mouth,
almost gagging me. I spat a mouthful, not caring where it went.
The image was still there, the tower layered over reality like a
transparency. And I saw it again, that creature perched on the
spire, a beast that could have been a devil, or maybe a god, baying
at the flames, preparing to unleash a nightmare upon the world.

Go on, Alex, show this pathetic man his future. Were those words
coming from the creature I saw, that giant of twisted flesh? Was
that *thing* really Alfred Furnace? It was impossible to tell. *Take him*
by the throat and show him the true religion—not a benevolent deity but
a new race.

Another noise spilled from my mouth, more a growl now than
a groan. I felt my new arm itch and I ripped the tattered sleeve of
the hoodie away so that I could dig my fingers into the pus-bloated
skin. It was roasting, so hot that it felt as if I'd put my good hand
against a grill. I pulled it away, my face crushed into a grimace of
confusion.

"See their true form!" the priest spat, pointing at my arm, almost jumping on the spot. "They are demons. 'Take your son,
Abraham, sacrifice him as a burnt offering.' It is so written, so
shall it be. Burn them, and earn your place by His side."

The priest and his flock were still coming, faster now, urged on
by the panic in the man's voice.

"Take one more step and I'll shoot your heads right off," the security guard screamed. Her pistol was out, shaking so much she could have been standing on a fun-house walkway at the fair. The crowd must have sensed her fear because most were still advancing—men and women who yesterday had probably been loving parents, who had cuddled their grandchildren, who now had that same psychotic gleam in their eyes. "Stay back, I'm warning you."

I saw a man behind her—tweed jacket, white hair—but I didn't realize what he was doing until it was too late. Even as he lifted the candlestick I was running, leaping over a pew and stretching out a hand to block the strike. I was too slow, the huge silver club thumping down on the guard's head, her hat crumpling. She dropped like a bowling pin, wearing a look of surprise that was almost comical. The man snatched the gun from her hand before she hit the floor. He saw me coming and pulled the trigger, the shot zinging over my head. I slid to my knees, hands held up in surrender. At this range, if he fired again, he couldn't miss.

For the few seconds it took the pistol shot to fade nobody moved. Then the priest strode forth, hissing his orders through an idiot grin.

"Yes, the time has come to act. We shall honor you, Lord. We shall sacrifice in your name."

He held up his hands to the heavens, foam spilling from the corners of his mouth.

"We shall burn them."

BURNT OFFERINGS

I NEVER THOUGHT there would be a time when I wished myself back in Furnace.

But as I knelt on the floor and watched that crowd approach, fear and desperation turning their faces into cruel masks, as I stared at the man who held me at gunpoint, knowing he would shoot me dead if I so much as moved, I found myself wishing just that.

It wasn't that I would be safer in the prison. Of course not— these men and women were just that: men and women. They were weaker than me, slower than me. They were nowhere near as dangerous as the rats and the berserkers that had stalked the tunnels beneath general population. They were nowhere near as wicked as the wheezers and their filthy blades. And they'd have all run screaming, or dropped dead from heart failure, if they'd so much as glimpsed the warden.

No, it was something else that made me pray for Furnace, pray to be back in my cell. Because down there, so deep that no amount of screaming would ever reach the surface, I had a memory of the world as a place where good things could happen. Even though we were buried alive I could still imagine life up here, people going about their business, smiling, laughing. Even though there was a small corner of the earth that was rotting away in madness and bloodshed, life still went on above us, it would always go on.

Now, however, nowhere was safe. There were no more smiles up here, no more laughter. That dead core was spreading outward, infecting everything. It had been only a few hours and already these people were broken beyond repair. They'd had a glimpse of hell outside their window and their sanity had been snapped in two as easily as a dry twig. And they hadn't seen the half of it, not yet. What would they do when they finally set forth from this cathedral and saw the streets running red, the monsters that were treading this city into bone dust?

It suddenly struck me how easy this would be for Alfred Furnace, if what he had said was true. All he had to do was rock this one city to its knees and the cancer of fear would spread. The world would crumble all by itself.

"Secure them," the priest was saying as he strode forward. He stepped over the kid on the floor, the boy's face resembling a rough carving in mahogany, lumps like woody knots bleeding black sap. The man with glasses hunched over him, glancing at us with an apologetic expression. I knew that look, the one that said he was on our side but too afraid to do anything about it. I'd worn it enough times. "Fetch the lamps."

Simon grunted, started walking toward the priest, but the old man with the gun lifted it toward the ceiling and fired again. I heard the bullet ricochet off the stone, scraps raining down over the pews.

The kid on the floor reacted to the shot, his eyes snapping

open, bottomless pits devoid of color. He stared at the ceiling, his lips peeling back to reveal stained teeth, his back arching as if he was in agony.

The smoking barrel dropped right at Simon, freezing him in his tracks. We were all standing in the center aisle, the armed man closest to the doors, the rest of the crowd clustered around the priest, and the four of us in between them.

"Time is short," the priest said. "We must exorcise the spirits from this child by slaying those who have engineered his possession."

"This isn't necessary," Zee quavered. "We're not demons."

"You and the girl can stand back," the priest said. "Your eyes don't shine with the light of the devil. Your souls can be saved."

Zee started to argue but Lucy grabbed his arm, pulling him away. He looked at me, arms held up, mouthing, *What can I do?* I shook my head, warning him to stay away. Then I met Simon's eyes, saw exactly what he was thinking. *Let them get close enough, then give them hell.* We closed ranks, standing shoulder to shoulder as we had so many times before.

An elderly woman had run to the altar, lifting a ceremonial lamp from the cloth. She hurried back with it, handing it to the priest. He walked closer, ten steps away, then five, before coming to a halt. He made the sign of the cross over his chest, kissing the base of his thumb. All the time he circled the lamp in his hand, the oil sloshing inside.

"I really wouldn't do this if I were you," I said. "I'm sure God doesn't take too kindly to killing kids."

"You've never read the Old Testament," Zee muttered.

"You are not children," the priest went on, eyes bulging so much they looked as if they'd pop right out of his head.

"They're not children!" somebody behind him yelled. The way they were acting reminded me more than anything of inmates inside the prison, the pack mentality which spread like wildfire, devouring common sense and reason. Right now these people were animals. They had their leader and they'd follow him into the heart of madness because it was safer there than standing alone.

"Easy," came a voice from behind the crowd. I recognized Glasses Man, his words lost behind a deep growl of pain, like an injured animal. "Hey, guys, I think he's waking up. Can I get some help here?"

But all eyes were on us. I backed up, feeling the hot barrel of the gun sting my neck. This was crazy, there was no way they could just burn us alive. But even as I watched, somebody else had fetched a candle, a small man, younger than the rest, clutching it to his chest with both hands like a cross to ward off vampires.

"Give me strength, Lord," the priest wailed. "Place your hand on me and give me the courage to do what must be done. Accept this sacrifice, trust us to kill these devils in your name."

He unscrewed the top of the lamp and held it up high, drops of oil spilling down his arm and onto the stone. Some of the crowd were stepping away now, their sense of reality returning.

"Wait," said one woman near the back. "You're not actually going to do this, are you?"

And behind it all that same pitiful moan of the kid on the floor, growing louder, deeper.

"He's coming out of it, I think. Will somebody help down here?"

Simon leaned into me, a whisper dropping from his lips.

"You get the gun, I'll take the priest."

I'd barely registered what he'd said before he darted forward. I felt the pressure of the gun leave my neck and swung my right arm back as hard as I could. It was a lucky strike, my elbow clipping the pistol just as the man pulled the trigger. The bullet went wide, thudding into somebody in the crowd and catapulting them over a pew. A mist of blood blossomed upward, painting the faces around it, but I wasn't paying any attention. I twisted my whole body, bringing my fist around hard into the gunman's face. He'd probably never been hit in his life, especially by someone with a blacksuit's punch, and the impact knocked him out cold.

By the time I'd turned back the cathedral had descended into anarchy. Simon and the priest were wrestling with the lamp. Simon may have been taller and broader than the priest but the man had a psychopathic strength. Oil was spilling everywhere, glistening green and blue against their clothes. Most of the crowd was retreating now, reality forcing its way back through their wide, timid eyes. But two or three were doing their best to help the priest, punching Simon in the head and neck and trying to push him over. Zee was running along one of the pews, making for the skirmish, and I headed that way too.

The man with the candle got there first.

He held it out for a moment, his saggy face crumpled with panic. Then with a soft cry he let it tumble from his hands. It missed Simon, the flame almost guttering out as it tumbled earthward. Then it landed in a puddle of oil and roared to life, the fire like a hand rising from the stone and grabbing both Simon and the priest in its embrace. Even with the flames around them they carried on wrestling, the priest refusing to let go of the lamp despite the fact it had become the center of the inferno.

"Simon!" I cried, ignoring the clawing heat as I ran to his side. I threw a punch into the raging fire, feeling it connect with the priest. He staggered backward, the lamp now welded to his hands.

The flames had engulfed him and he reeled toward the altar, collapsing on the steps. He writhed for a moment, then was still. The fire, still hungry, began to chew up the carpet, catching hold of the altar cloth and the tapestries that surrounded it.

"Alex, help me," said Zee, and I forced my eyes from the smoldering corpse to see him tearing coats from the kid on the floor. Simon was on his knees, beating at the flames on his clothes. But the oil was burning thickly, smearing his fingers, stretching tongues of flame up toward his neck and face.

Zee gave Simon a shove, sending him sprawling onto his back. Then he pounced on top of the blazing body, slamming coats down everywhere he could.

"Hold these!" he yelled, and I did as I was told, crouching beside him and pressing the jackets over the flames. Zee's hands were a blur as he slapped until the fire had been reduced to pockets of charred cloth that smoked weakly. He collapsed on top of Simon, all three of us coughing up a lung and panting for breath.

I scanned the crowd, waiting for the next attack, but with their messiah gone and one end of their haven blazing nobody would even meet my eye. Most were collapsed against the pews, puking and crying and all the other things you do when you realize you've become a monster. I should know. I've been there too.

The man with the glasses was doing his best to hold the kid still but the boy's tremors had grown much worse. The boy was thumping up and down, each motion causing a squeal of wood as the pew was dragged over the stone. He was mewling, a horrible sound that reminded me of a newborn animal. And looking at the kid, that's what he was like. He wriggled against the man's grip like an oversize baby, gnashing the air, clawing helplessly at the plastic cuff, dribbling mouthfuls of black liquid.

"What do we do?" the man asked. "What's wrong with him?"

I knew exactly. He'd woken up, roused by the nectar that surged inside him, by the smell of burning flesh, of spilled blood, the cries of pain. I knew because the nectar inside me was firing up too, boiling in my veins. I felt the wound in my neck pulse as though there was something living in there. My arm twitched, the skin swelling, and I held it to my body as if that would keep it from expanding any more.

"Get back," I told the man in glasses. He didn't argue, easing the boy's head off his knees and shuffling away. A spasm rocked the kid's body, the pustules on his broken face bursting, his insect eyes never blinking. Then he opened his mouth wider than should ever have been possible and unleashed a cry of anguish.

Too late I realized what that cry was. It was a call for help, the same way a cub calls for its mother. And moments later, as the windows grew dark, silhouettes thrashing against the leaded glass, I realized that its call had been answered.

They'd found us.

INVASION

THEY CAME THROUGH the window hard and fast, led by the same berserker we'd seen at Twofields station. It pushed its fat, grinning baby face through the leaded glass, emitting that same spine-chilling giggle. Then it dropped the ten meters or so to the floor, snapping a pew and scattering Bibles like leaves.

A window smashed on the other side of the cathedral, two shapes pushing through a vision of angels, not seeming to notice that the glass was cutting their skin to shreds. Judging by the amount of nectar that was spilling from them, streaming down the walls, those wounds would be closed before they hit the floor. They were both inmates who had become rats, their overalls scuffed and torn almost beyond recognition, their faces darkened by the fluid pumping beneath their skin. One had already grown enormous forearms, reminding me of Popeye. It bared its teeth at us, growling like a dog, then dropped, landing awkwardly and sprawling on its side. The second followed, scampering on four limbs toward the fire as though it was the first time it had ever seen one.

The only sound I could hear was, incredibly, laughter. One of the men in the crowd was chuckling to himself as he watched events unfold. Everybody else just stood there, breath held, as if by sheer collective will they could stop this from being real. I realized I was doing exactly the same, praying that if I was still and silent enough that berserker and its spawn would leave us alone.

No such luck.

The berserker advanced first, scrambling over a pew, moving on all fours. It sniffed the air, evidently catching the scent of the kid, loping toward him. Glasses Man was sitting on the floor, between the kid and the berserker. He shuffled backward, his specs hanging off one ear, his hands held up.

"I was just trying to help him," he said. "Please, I didn't—"

The berserker lifted the man in its massive arms, throwing him across the cathedral. He hit a pillar with a chilling thwack, bouncing off into the shadows beneath a pew. It was the sound more than the sight, I think, that suddenly propelled everybody into action. Where there had been stillness there was now chaos as people ran, nobody choosing the same direction.

A woman thumped into me as she bolted. She made exactly five steps before one of the rats got her, bounding up the southern aisle and cutting down between the pews. It leaped onto her back, teeth lodged in her throat, sending them both crashing to the floor.

I felt a hand on my arm, flinching at the touch before realizing it was Zee.

"Let's move," he ordered, taking his own advice and running along the length of the pew toward the northern aisle, Lucy close behind. Simon was after them like a shot, not looking back.

I watched the second rat take down another member of the crowd, the man who had been holding the candle. It didn't pause to feast but propelled itself up, felling another victim with a gargled cry of delight. Somebody threw a punch at the rabid inmate.

It connected with a crack, but the creature didn't show any sign of feeling it, using one hand to knock the fist away and the other to claw out the man's throat. Behind it all was a backdrop of smoky flames as the altar continued to burn, the fire somehow making its way up the stone walls in search of fuel, finding the ancient wooden rafters.

"Alex," Zee yelled from the other side of the cathedral. "Come on!"

I remained motionless, watching the berserker lean over the kid on the floor. Not that he was a kid anymore. There was nothing of the child left in that swollen mass of blackened tumors that struggled to free itself from its plastic binds. With surprising tenderness the berserker grabbed the kid's hand and pulled, the plastic snapping. Then it pushed the boy to his feet, nudging him with its snout the same way an animal might do to its offspring before it takes its first steps.

I can honestly say that it was the most terrifying thing I had ever seen.

The kid—the rat—took a hesitant step forward, then caught sight of somebody cowering behind a column. It moved clumsily but fast, so fast, covering a dozen meters in a second. And it knew exactly what to do with its prey, tearing into it with expert precision.

"Jesus, would you get a move on?" said a voice to my side. I realized Simon had come back for me, tugging furiously on my sweatshirt. One side of his face was charred black but he didn't seem to be in too much pain. "You've seen it all before, come on."

Still I didn't move. The berserker lifted its head, studying me from the other end of the aisle, then started moving, stepping over the still-warm bodies in its path.

"Screw you," Simon said, retreating for the second time. "You wanna die, then go ahead and die."

And that's precisely why I wasn't moving, I realized.

Because I wasn't going to die.

The berserker reached me, towering up to its full height—a meter or more above my head. It grabbed me by the throat, the same way it had done before, turning its ugly head this way and that as if trying to get a good look at me. But it didn't need to.

It knew exactly who I was. *What* I was.

With another infant chuckle it released its grip. Then it turned its back on me, scouring the cathedral for new victims. In a rush of anger the nectar detonated inside my head, firing off so many synapses that time seemed to unravel—the fire burning, the rats moving, the people screaming all in slow motion like a movie whose projector was running out of power.

"Don't you dare," I heard myself say as I watched the berserker slope off. "Don't you dare!"

I ran forward, shoving the berserker in the back with everything I had. It lurched, using its forelimbs to stay up. But all it did was angle its head over its shoulder and hiss at me. I heard a shot from somewhere in the cathedral but I ignored it, my anger swelling up inside my head, making my vision flicker on and off. This was by far the worst thing that could have happened, worse even than me being torn to pieces, being eaten alive.

The berserker didn't kill me because I was a part of its family, because it could sense the same life force in me that flowed through it, because we had the same father, and that man wanted to keep us both alive.

It didn't kill me because it knew that I was one of them.

"I'm not," I screamed, picking up the candlestick that had been used to brain the security guard. "I'm not one of you. I'm not the same as you!"

And in my head, out of nowhere, came his voice—that same impossible half whisper, half shout of Alfred Furnace.

But you will be.

I lifted the heavy candlestick, a solid silver bar that must have weighed as much as a lead pipe, and as the nectar forced a battle cry from me I brought it down on the berserker's back. It hit with the same sound a car makes when it drives into a wall, a weird metallic clang that reverberated around the cathedral. The berserker toppled forward, falling flat on its face. But it didn't stay down for long, scuttling away and unfolding once again to its full height. This time the look it gave me was more threatening, but still it didn't attack.

Another shot, and I glanced over to see Zee firing the pistol. There was one dead rat by his feet, the body twitching. Another had the sense to duck down behind a pew, the wood splintering as Zee fired. The berserker uttered a wet screech as it retreated, and the two remaining rats burst from their hiding places, following it toward the broken window. It ushered them up the wall and through the glass, leaping after them and pushing its way out into the open air. It looked back only once, and as its eyes met mine I once again heard that voice, reverberating around my head as if the very bells of the cathedral were ringing.

You will be.

CLEAR SIGHT

AS SOON AS THE BERSERKER had gone, Zee, Simon, and Lucy made their way back to the nave. Lucy was staring at me with a mix of fear and suspicion, and I noticed that the boys were doing exactly the same. I lowered myself down onto a pew, looking at my right arm to see the bulging tendons pulsing with nectar. It had swollen so much that it could have belonged to a skinned gorilla. The itch from the bite was spreading down through my chest and my stomach, even as far as my right leg, but I didn't dare peek beneath my clothes to see what was happening.

Zee came and sat next to me, his head in his hands. It took me a moment to notice he was crying.

"It's never going to end, is it?" he said, wiping his face with his sleeve. I slung my good arm over his shoulders, feeling them heave. Before I knew it I had tears of my own, Zee's frustration and fury contagious. He lashed out at the pew in front, his bony fists not budging it. "It's never going to end. Not now."

I wanted to reassure him, calm him, but what could I say?

"It's gonna end pretty damn quick if we don't get out of here," Simon said, nodding at the fire. The whole eastern end of the cathedral was blazing, fueled by the draft that cut between the broken windows. A thick blanket of smoke hovered just above head height, filling the inverted bowl of the dome and dropping steadily closer. I was grateful to it as I wiped my eyes, blaming my tears on the burning air.

"Why didn't it kill you?" Zee asked, looking up at me through red-rimmed eyes. "It didn't even try. What's that all about?"

"Maybe it had a crisis of conscience," I replied, attempting a smile. "Decided it wanted to be a pacifist."

"Yeah, because it was real gentle with everyone else," Zee retorted. He looked at Lucy, who had made her way from body to body. The ones that hadn't been savaged beyond recognition, that was. "Any survivors?"

"They're all dead," Lucy said, her hand resting on the throat of a woman for a second before she shook her head. "Jesus, they killed everybody." She stood, throwing an expression my way almost fierce enough to knock me dead. "See what they did? Your friends? They killed everybody!"

"They didn't kill her," Simon replied, nodding at the security guard who stared unblinking at the ceiling. "That was *your* friends."

Lucy turned her glare on him and Zee stood up, his tears apparently forgotten as he walked between them like a referee. She looked back to me malevolently.

"That thing treated you like you were its brother."

"Look at me," I hissed back. "I look more like those things every second. Soon I'm gonna look more like them than I do you. In its eyes I *am* its brother."

"But the rats by the Metro, they attacked you," said Simon.

"They're just animals, though," I replied. "They're feral. They attack everything, even each other." I'd thought the berserkers were mindless killers as well, but they were something far worse.

They possessed intelligence—not human intelligence, but they were clever enough to recognize friends from enemies. Clever enough to follow orders. "I think Furnace wants me alive for some reason," I went on. "Maybe he wants us all alive. I don't know why, though."

"So he can kill us himself, probably," Simon said. And even though I knew that was far too simple an explanation, I still nodded.

"Let's forget it," Zee said, swallowing hard. "It's pointless trying to work out what's going on when none of us have a clue." He turned to the cathedral doors, still chained, then looked at the window, the fire now licking at its sill. The flames had also reached the first row of pews, devouring them with relish. He set off toward the northern aisle, taking Lucy's arm as he went. "Come on, I think it's time for some fresh air."

I didn't get up straightaway. Part of me just wanted to sit there until the flames consumed me. Surely there was some rule that if you died inside a cathedral then you had to go somewhere good afterward. It's not like I believed in heaven or anything, but I'd seen hell—hell was right outside this building, spreading fast—and anywhere had to be better than that. My arm throbbed, the sensation passing to my fingers, the nectar singing inside me. I was changing, again. And if my suspicions were right, if my worst fears were coming true, then it would be far better to be cremated right here than to find out what I was turning into.

But if I was really part of Furnace's plan, maybe I could find a way to stop it. Maybe I could find a cure. Reluctantly, as I felt the heat getting closer, I pushed myself up from the pew and followed the others.

Zee walked through an archway into a small anteroom, passing through it to another spiral staircase, this one stretching upward. He set off at a pace.

"Er, Zee?" I asked. "I know I shouldn't question your wisdom, but isn't it a bad idea to go *up* when you're inside a burning building?"

"You're right, Alex," he said, and he must have been feeling better because his exhausted laugh echoed up the stairs, emboldened by the stone. "You shouldn't question my wisdom."

We seemed to go around and around forever, my head growing dizzy with both the rotation and the effort. At one point we passed another arch which led off into smoke-filled shadows but Zee ignored it, clomping relentlessly upward. I don't know how much later it was before sunlight began to filter into the staircase, and after three more upward loops we stepped out onto a sweeping balcony.

"Whoa," I said, my head still spinning, my eyes screwed almost shut against the blinding light. I made out the cathedral's dome to my right, rising endlessly, and to my left was a stone balustrade that ran the length of the balcony. It was as tall as I was, but windows had been punched into it at regular intervals, and through them, bathed in gold, was the city. I blinked until I was used to the glare, then walked to the nearest one.

"Come on," Zee said, bracing his hands on top of the stonework and struggling up. "There will be emergency access ladders on the roof. View's better from up here as well."

"How do you know?" Lucy asked, looking reluctant but eventually accepting Zee's hand.

"You telling me you never came here with school?" he asked as he hauled her onto the ledge. "We got in so much trouble for climbing up here, detention for a week. But it was worth it."

I looked at Simon and we shrugged at each other, then I effortlessly vaulted up to join him. It was solid stone, and wide at the top, which was a relief. But still the sheer drop onto the cathedral roof far below made my stomach clench and my ears ring. I gripped the stone hard, trying not to grimace. Simon had turned a strange color and I noticed that his eyes were closed.

"You okay?" I asked.

"Not used to heights," he grunted.

I wasn't either. It had been so long since I'd been above ground at all that being all the way up here didn't seem real. To see the city opened out before me, a tapestry of streets and buildings whose every shade was given life by the sun, made me smile so hard my face hurt. I could see for miles, all the way over to the distant hills that bordered the suburbs. The sensation of being so high—almost as far above the ground as we had once been below it—made my heart sing. It was so powerful that it took me a while to make sense of what I saw.

At first I thought I was hallucinating again, Alfred Furnace filling my head with terrifying visions. But this was no nectar-inspired nightmare.

The golden glow came not from the sun but from a thousand fires. The entire city was burning.

"No way," said Zee. "This is insane."

Pillars of smoke rose from every direction, making the city seem like another cathedral whose vast roof was supported by blackened columns. The worst fire was over by the river, where an entire block of office buildings was being consumed. There was no sign of fire engines there, the flames blazing unchecked, spreading fast as they caught the wind. Another inferno was closer, near what I thought was the city library. Luckily the smoke from this one fanned out like a charred canopy, blocking the view into the center, concealing the skyscrapers there.

"Why is this happening?" asked Lucy, her face a mask of calm but her words trembling. "Why isn't the government doing something?"

It looked like the authorities were trying their hardest to contain the situation. At least five or six helicopters could be seen hovering over the streets, military birds bristling with guns and radio equipment. And from up here I could make out the rattle of trucks and orders bellowed from below. There was gunfire too, plenty of it, each burst shattering the unreal sense of stillness and distance that we felt up here, perched on the roof of the world.

But there was only so much they could do. Guns were useless against a beast of hardened skin and rippling muscle whose veins flowed with nectar. You could shoot a berserker a hundred times and the chances were it would get back up and keep on coming.

And the rats, these new ones, there could have been hundreds of them. I don't know how many inmates had been caught, turned, but from what we'd seen already the streets were crawling with freaks that had once been kids.

"We should just be thankful it's a Sunday," Zee said. "And that it's so early. Imagine if this was a shopping day, at lunchtime, the city would be jammed."

"Imagine if it was a school day," Lucy added, making us all shiver.

A burst of gunfire rose up from close by, and we craned out over the main body of the cathedral below to see a pack of soldiers advancing across the plaza, taking cover behind an armored truck. They were all firing across the street that ran parallel to us, at a shape in white overalls that threw itself through a shop window and vanished. The face of the shop exploded into dust as the bullets impacted, and we watched as the soldiers surrounded the building, lobbing in a flash-bang before clambering through the window in pursuit.

"We should get down there," Lucy said. "They'll be able to take us to safety, right?"

Wrong. Seconds later one of the soldiers flew back through the window, rolling across the street spouting a vivid helix of blood. Another followed, tripping onto the pavement and firing wildly into the shop. He ripped a grenade from his belt and lobbed it inside, seeming to forget about the rest of his unit. There was a muffled pop that blew out the remaining windows. We watched, half in amazement, half in horror, as the rat launched itself through the dust with a cat-like pounce, landing on the soldier and going to work with untamed ferocity.

"Jesus," said Zee.

The armored truck accelerated, the rat too busy with its meal to even notice. Its bumper connected with the creature at what must have been forty miles an hour, carrying it over the plaza and disappearing out of sight behind the cathedral roof below. We all heard the crash, though, and after that nothing but the roar of flames.

"We have to get out of the city," Zee went on. He squinted into the horizon and I followed his line of sight. It took me a while to get my bearings, but when I did I grew so faint and dizzy I almost tumbled right off that ledge.

In the distance, over the river, past a cluster of high-rise flats—one of which was also smoking—past the park whose serpentine lake sparkled in the morning light, out toward the hills, was home. I couldn't see much from here, of course, the houses a gray smudge, like the froth of a wave next to the immense ocean of the city. But it was there, somewhere, the house I'd grown up in, the house where my parents lived. If I'd had a telescope and a little more time then I'd have been able to find it.

I wondered if they were there, sitting on the worn-out green velvet sofa in the living room, watching the news on the tiny television Mom had won at work in a Christmas raffle. I wondered if they thought I would be trying to get home, trying to find them. And in that instant I wanted nothing more than to do just that, to get home, to sit between their feet on the dusty carpet like I'd done as a kid, my dad ruffling my hair and kicking me playfully with his slippers. They'd accused me and abandoned me like everyone else, but I could forgive them. Right now I *would* forgive them.

"Alex?" Zee's voice broke through the emotion and reality flowed back in. "What do you think?"

"Huh?" I asked, not knowing what I'd missed.

"We get down to that truck," Lucy repeated. "Make a break for Meriton, there's a police station, a big one. My dad used to work there. It's a mile away, maybe two, but it's on the way out of town."

"And the truck will have a radio," Zee added. "We can let somebody know what's going on. It can't hurt to try."

I nodded, but my mind was still elsewhere. I pictured my house, my parents, only now I watched as the plague spread, as the berserkers tore down my street, trailing rats like the Pied Piper, ripping the doors open, pulling apart the people inside, feasting on the warm corpses, spreading the nectar to the children, all the while their ranks swelling, more of the world decaying beneath their bloodied claws.

The wind gusted, dividing the pillar of smoke that rose from the library, and for a fleeting second I saw the skyscraper beyond, the black monolith whose pyramid spire seemed to beckon in the flickering heat haze. I thought of Furnace's message, his invitation to be part of his grotesque army. The itch in my arm flared at the thought and I clutched it to my chest again, feeling the skin burn and bulge, slowly changing, becoming something else.

"Alex?" prompted Zee.

"Yeah, it sounds like a plan," I said when I realized they were all waiting for me. "You three head for Meriton."

"You're not coming with us?" Simon asked.

"No," I said. "I've got something else to do."

I watched the curtain of smoke heal itself, blocking the view once again. But beyond it that tower was still there. It was still waiting. And when I spoke again I was speaking to it.

"One way or the other, I'm going to end this."

RESCUE PARTY

THEY STARTED TO ARGUE with me, as I'd known they would. But their words were drowned out by the sudden thump of helicopter rotors, the thunder growing to an unnerving crescendo as two choppers broke past us, one on either side of the cathedral dome. We clutched our heads, the whirlwind threatening to spill us over the edge into oblivion. Lucy screamed, jumping back down onto the balcony and crouching against the curved wall, her face buried in her hands.

The helicopter to our right dived earthward, its side door open and a machine gun mounted there, manned by a soldier in camouflage. He swung it toward the cathedral, flames spouting from the barrel as he fired at something we couldn't see. The very stone of the building seemed to groan, heat shimmering from the tiles, as if the fire that raged inside had brought this ancient Goliath of wood and stone to life.

The other bird stayed high, another machine gun swiveling over the roofs of the surrounding buildings, a helmeted face visible in the dark interior. Zee stood, waving his arms and calling for help. It was a bad idea, but I didn't have time to tell him that before the door gunner caught sight of us, sweeping the .50 caliber cannon our way and unleashing a torrent of lead. The balustrade to the right of us exploded into shrapnel, bullets puncturing the dome, bombarding us with chunks of stone. I toppled backward, dragging Simon with me, the pair of us landing awkwardly on our backs.

"Stop shooting!" Zee yelled, holding his ground. After what felt like forever—but had probably been no more than a second—the gunner must have realized his mistake. The weapon fell silent, the chopper suddenly angling down toward the street. Zee swore at it, hurling abuse at the soldier who had tried to kill us. "We're on your side!" he called out. "Take us with you!"

There was no way they could have heard him. I ran to the gap the shells had made, holding on to a fractured stone post and watching the two helicopters hover twenty meters or so over the plaza. They were both now shooting at the base of the cathedral, at the place where the truck had crashed, although we couldn't see what was going on.

"Look out!" Zee yelled.

Something was moving along the roof of the cathedral beneath us, its feet scrabbling for purchase, sending tiles flying in every direction. I recognized the baby face of the berserker as it blasted forward on all fours, heading right for the choppers.

It launched itself from the roof, hitting the first bird's tail and causing it to veer wildly to one side. The berserker's grip slipped but it held on. It lashed out with one leg, catching the tail rotor and causing it to spin off, tearing a chunk from a shop. The chopper started to spin, the berserker clawing its way down the fuselage and swinging through the open door. The gunner fell, already in pieces, and the bird screamed up toward us, its blades clipping the cathedral dome meters from where we were standing.

With a deafening crunch the rotor came loose, the helicopter dropping fast. The berserker threw itself from the door, grabbing hold of a metal drainpipe on the cathedral wall, not even pausing for breath before bounding out of sight. Then the chopper landed on its side, its rotating blades catapulting it over the plaza and into the shops beyond where it disappeared in a fireball.

The second helicopter was rising, but it was too close to the cathedral. The berserker did exactly the same thing as before, launching itself through thin air as the bird drew level with it.

This time, however, the pilot knew what to expect. The machine tilted at the last second, slicing up toward the airborne berserker. The creature flailed, desperately trying to change direction. But there was nothing it could do, hurtling into the rotors and exploding in a black mist. What was left of it sailed over the rooftops, impossibly far and impossibly graceful, falling out of sight streets away. A shower of black blood splattered the plaza below.

"Result!" yelled Simon who had run to my side, his arm looped around my waist so that he could lean over the balcony. He punched the air with his other hand.

But the chopper had suffered too. I heard the whine of the engine, smoke pouring from the exhaust. It struggled, banking hard one way then tilting back toward the cathedral. Even from up here I could hear the constant beep of the alarm as it began to spiral toward the street. The pilot managed to keep it steady, landing with a bump next to the corpses of the soldiers. The engine cut out, the growl growing quieter as the rotors slowed.

"Come on!" yelled Zee. He was clambering down onto a rusted iron ladder bolted into one of the huge columns that surrounded the dome. "This is our chance."

"Our chance for what?" I asked, waiting for Lucy to follow

before doing the same myself, telling myself I shouldn't look down but unable not to. The sloped roof wasn't too far beneath us, though, and we reached it in under a minute. Zee teetered to the edge, scanning the wall before jogging over to another ladder, wedged in the right angle of the building's cross. He vanished, Lucy next, Simon pushing in front of me with a mumbled "Excuse me."

I peered over, noting that we were about two stories from the ground, and decided to give the ladder a miss. I climbed over the vaulted wall, dropping effortlessly onto a ledge halfway between the roof and the plaza. Then I skipped off that and landed in time to greet Zee at the bottom. He gave me a puzzled double take when he stepped off the ladder and turned around to see me waiting.

"Take your time," I said, glancing at a watch I didn't have.

"Show-off," he replied, helping Lucy find the ground in a way that was a little more touchy-feely than it needed to be. I gave him a knowing smile before she could turn around and he scowled at me, his cheeks glowing.

The northern arm of the cross-shaped cathedral was between us and the helicopter, but there was evidence of the battle everywhere. Across the street was the row of shops that had been decimated—the wreckage of the first chopper long lost beneath a blanket of flames. Heat hovered over the entire plaza, fierce enough to have made some of the trees here spontaneously combust. And everywhere there were splashes of black where the blood of the berserker had rained down, glistening in the firelight like spilled oil.

I realized Zee was off again, jogging around the stone wall of the cathedral. I caught up with him just as he was rounding the bend, seeing the helicopter resting on the sidewalk between the plaza and the street. It had crushed a bench and a bin, rocking unsteadily as its rotors slowed. The pilot was standing in the doorway peering up at the engine, the rattle of which drowned out our approach until we were halfway across the plaza. As soon as he noticed us the door gunner swiveled his machine gun our way, his finger on the trigger.

"Hold it!" he yelled, startling the pilot. She clambered inside the chopper door, ripping her pistol from a holster. The four of us froze, but Zee took one step closer, his hands raised.

"We're human," he said, his choice of words making the situation feel even more surreal than it had before. "We're human, like you. Don't shoot."

"On the ground," the pilot shouted, a young woman with cropped chestnut hair. "Spread your arms and legs. Do it now; I won't tell you twice."

We did as she ordered, resting on the cold, damp stone as the pilot walked cautiously over and patted us down. She left me till last, prodding my swollen arm with her pistol. The barrel came away wet, a strand of clear fluid like saliva trailing between her weapon and my skin. I waited until she had moved back before pulling my shredded sleeve down as far as it would go, suddenly ashamed.

"You can all get up," she said. "Except you."

I didn't have to look at her to know she was talking about me. I watched as Zee, Lucy, and Simon all got to their feet, brushing themselves down. The pilot holstered her pistol, resting her hands on her hips, but the chopper gunner never took his sights off us.

"Identify yourselves," the pilot demanded.

"Zee Hatcher," Zee replied. "This is Simon Rojo-Flores and Alex Sawyer and Lucy . . . Sorry, Lucy, I don't know your last name."

"Wells," she said. "You have to help us. There are things out here; we've been attacked."

"Yeah, you and everybody else in the city, sweetheart," the pilot said. She looked at me.

"What's going on with that arm of yours? Looks infected. Looks a hell of a lot like one of those *things* to me."

"I'm not infected," I replied, not knowing if I was lying or not. "I'm a good guy, honestly. I'm one of you."

I didn't know if that was a lie either, but the pilot seemed to soften.

"Okay, okay. I'm Captain Annabel Atilio. D Company, First Battalion Home Defense. Why don't you kids tell me what you're doing out here."

No sooner had she spoken than a rally of screeches broke free from the constant roar of the fire, trailing down the street and echoing off the cathedral walls. The pilot stiffened, peering into the smoke that blocked off the route back into town.

"Hold that thought," she said. "The chopper's nuked. Let's get some wheels and you can tell me when we're moving."

GROUNDBOUND

CAPTAIN ATILIO LED THE WAY to the truck we'd seen earlier. It was resting against the cathedral wall, surrounded by chipped stone and the remains of the rat it had squashed there. It looked like a Hummer, painted beige, with metal plates bolted over the windows. There was a gray cloud rising from the hood but it looked more like steam than smoke.

"M-ATV," said Atilio. "Designed to survive roadside bombs so it should be okay." She pulled out her pistol again, holding it in one hand while she tried the door. It took a little work, but eventually it opened and the body of a soldier slid out. Atilio felt for a pulse in his neck, shaking her head. "Dammit. Roke, get over here, and bring that fiddy. You lot, get in the back."

We did as we were told, pulling open the rear door and climbing into the darkened interior. It was a bit of a squeeze with four of us on the seat but we managed, peering through the porthole-like windows to see the gunner lugging his weapon over the plaza, a bronze tail of ammo sweeping the ground behind him. He clambered onto the roof turret and mounted the machine gun.

"Hey, guys," he shouted down, offering a smile to Lucy. "Don't mind me."

"Right," said Atilio as she climbed into the driver's seat, firing up the engine. "Let's get this show on the road." She pulled the radio handset from its socket. "Checkmate 5 this is Airborne 32, do you copy?"

A voice buried deep within static whistled from the speakers. I couldn't make out what it said but the captain obviously could.

"Status is groundbound, sir," she reported. "Something pulled us right out of the air. Airborne 14 too, now KIA. What do you need us to do?"

The voice again, barking out orders made up of numbers and code words and not much else.

"Roger that, XO," Atilio said. "Got some civvies, I'll drop them off with the PMCs over by Pear Street."

She waited for confirmation then replaced the receiver, slamming the gearstick into reverse and revving hard. The powerful engine pulled the truck from the wall, the vehicle bumping as it rolled over the rat. The gears groaned as she fought to find first, then started forward across the plaza.

"Where are we going?" I asked.

"We need to head to Meriton," Lucy interrupted. "The police station, it will be safe there."

"You kidding me?" Atilio replied. "Meriton's gone, everything up there is gone."

"Gone?" Lucy asked. "What do you mean?"

"I mean gone, not there anymore. You haven't seen the fires?" Atilio eased the truck over the sidewalk and onto the street, accelerating toward the smoke. She saw us all nodding in the rearview mirror. "They took out the police stations first, hours ago. Meriton, Raymondtown, even as far north as Colette."

"They?" I blurted, not quite believing what I was hearing, and even though I knew the answer I added, "Who?"

"We don't know," she said as the world turned to night, smoke nuzzling against the tiny windows, flowing in through the open roof. Above us the gunner coughed into his sleeve. Atilio flicked a switch and the headlights came on, doing little to cut through the confusion. "It all started with the prison break, but this is more than that. There are creatures out there, like animals, only not like any animal I've ever seen before. They're big, they're fast, they're savage, and they don't go down when you shoot them."

I opened my mouth to try to explain but for some reason Zee rested a hand on my arm, offering a tiny shake of his head. Atilio angled the truck around a burning car. It was the one we had passed earlier. She was driving us into the city.

"We got the call at around 0600," she went on. "Standby orders. By that time the hospitals were already filling up with cops and the emergency services had gone into meltdown. First Battalion is stationed just outside the city. We're an anti-terrorist squad, really, ready to roll if something bad ever goes down."

"Don't get much badder than this," the gunner added, swinging his machine gun around to cover the road ahead.

"You can say that again," Atilio said. "Half an hour after that we got the green light: move in. Our orders were to shoot on sight, clear the streets. And that was fine, when we thought there were only prisoners to shoot."

Zee opened his mouth to protest, then obviously thought better of it.

The smoke peeled away from the windshield to reveal that the road ahead had been completely blocked by what looked like a

collapsed building, bricks and tiles and furniture spilled everywhere and smoldering. Atilio swore, doing a clumsy three-point
turn and heading back the way we'd come.

"Keep it sharp up there, Roke," she ordered. "This feels wrong."

"Yessir, ma'am," came his reply, muffled by the wind as the
truck accelerated. Atilio hung a left at the first junction we came
to, accelerating down the street before turning left again. The
road here was narrower but clearer and I could see right down it
into the heart of the city. Above us there was a roar as another
chopper soared over the streets, disappearing toward the distant
skyscrapers.

"Lucky bastards," muttered the captain. "I hate being groundbound."

"Excuse me," Lucy asked, leaning forward. "But where are we
going? Shouldn't you be heading the other way, taking us to safety?"

"Sorry, kid," Atilio said, her face in the mirror bearing a genuine expression of concern. "We've got our orders and rescuing
civvies ain't part of them. We're grateful that this is Sunday, not
too many people in the city. But it's spreading, and fast. We had
reports of disturbances as far out as the estuary, and if it gets any
farther then we won't be able to stem it. Like a bleeder, y'know?
Got to nip the artery or you're bang out of luck."

"Then where are you taking us?" Lucy persisted, wiping the
tears from her eyes.

"Closest place I can think of as safe," Atilio replied. "Most of
the Batt is broken up and sweeping the city, and the police have
been moved to the outskirts to prevent panic setting in—the ones
that are still alive, that is. But we're not alone out here. Bunch of
PMCs have been called in and I know for a fact they're stationed
down this way. Got a camp there, and I reckon that's your best bet."

"PMCs?" I asked.

"Private military companies," Atilio explained, the truck speeding up as it thundered down the hill. "Back in my training days we'd have called 'em mercs—mercenaries—but we don't use that word anymore. They're soldiers, only they don't work for the government. They— Oh boy, hold on."

I glanced out of the window to see that we were approaching a junction. There was less smoke here, and I could make out a café on the corner, and next to that a grocery shop. It would have looked like a perfectly normal city scene if not for the two tanks that wheeled noisily from the street to our left, the tarmac crumbling beneath their squeaking caterpillar tracks. Atilio honked her horn and maneuvered the truck between them, offering a salute out of the window. If anybody inside saw her they didn't show any sign of it, the enormous machines rolling out of sight behind a kebab shop.

"This city is gonna be dust before the day is out," she said once the thunder had passed. "So anyway, what exactly were you kids doing on the roof of St. Martin's in the first place?"

"Hiding," Zee said. "We were out on the streets, saw what was going on. Looked like the best place to take shelter."

"And you just happened to be in the middle of the financial district at half-past dark on a Sunday morning?" she asked, although I could tell by the way she looked at us in the mirror that she already knew the truth.

"Would you believe we were sightseeing?" Zee tried, not very convincingly.

Captain Atilio nodded. "Yeah, right, and this here is the Queen's carriage and Roke up there is her footman. You a footman, Roke?"

"If I am, I'm wearing the wrong uniform," he shouted down.

"And you lot aren't tourists, either," she said. "I've seen enough prison eyes in my time. Don't look so worried; a few escaped juvies are the least of my concerns at the moment. Right now the more of you lot we see who aren't punching through solid steel and biting off heads the better." She turned in her seat, glancing at my arm. "Though the brains'll want to take a good look at you with that tree trunk you've got there."

"The brains?" I asked, and for some reason found myself thinking of the wheezers and their wicked blades.

"Don't worry about it," Atilio said. "Military intelligence has set up shop a dozen clicks away. I can't take you there. We'll drop you with the mercs for now, then it's back into the fight."

"So you have no idea what's going on?" Zee asked, leaning between the seats. Atilio shook her head and let out a rueful laugh.

"Kid, I haven't got a clue. All I know is that there are things out there that make al-Qaeda look like fluffy bunnies, and we've got orders to shoot 'em dead. Until someone tells me different, I pull the trigger first and ask questions never. Welcome to life on the front line."

I don't know if she said any more because it suddenly felt as if the sky above me had opened up, a noise like the world ending. I didn't know what it was until a shell casing landed on my lap, bigger than my thumb and red hot. I brushed it off, feeling more drop down, a rain of burning brass as Roke fired the cannon. I clamped my hands to my ears, feeling the truck veer wildly to the right, something bouncing off the bumper with a dull thud. Above me Roke swung the weapon around, shooting it back the way we'd come.

"You see that?" he yelled as Atilio steadied the vehicle. "Man, it was bigger than a horse!"

"You get it?" the captain yelled.

"Hit it with about a dozen rounds," Roke replied. "Just threw itself over a roof. I think it's still up there."

He grunted in frustration, pulling the trigger again. I looked out the back, saw the enormous shells punching through random walls, tearing chunks from the brickwork, smashing windows into dust. Then he stopped, spitting out a couple of choice swearwords.

"It's getting worse," Atilio said. "It's like there's a nest of these things somewhere."

"I think we may know where," I said. Atilio glanced at me in the mirror. I started to explain but she stopped me.

"Save it for the XO," she said. "The mercs have set up a command center in the Pear Street multistory. We're nearly there. I'll have a couple of them swing you over to HQ, get you out of town. They'll want to talk to you, especially if you have the slightest clue as to what's going on."

"Take the next right," Roke shouted down. "Road ahead's jammed, use Freeman Street, then cut around the back."

Atilio followed his directions, the car turning right and speeding down a narrow street before skidding left through a barrier and into a parking lot. It didn't quite fit through the gap, sparks flying up from the sides and sounding like a finger scraping down a blackboard.

"Whoops," Atilio said. "Glad this ain't my car. Where the hell are these guys, anyway?"

"Sitting up top crying to each other like little babies, most likely," Roke suggested with a snigger.

"Not this lot," Atilio said, steering the truck carefully up the first ramp. "From what I hear this crew is a bunch of coldhearted killers, built like outhouses and with surgical enhancements to boot."

The car bombed through the empty parking lot, swinging up to the next level. She glanced in the mirror for long enough to see our nervous expressions.

"Don't worry, these guys can be a foulmouthed and filthy bunch but they're usually harmless. We call this lot the Blues Brothers, you'll get that when you see what they all wear."

We swung up again, pressed against each other as we swerved around another bend.

"Don't let them give you any lip, right? They may be freelance but right now they answer to my XO, and don't be afraid to remind them of that. Besides . . ."

She stopped for long enough to ease the truck up another ramp.

". . . Something tells me you'll feel right at home with them, judging by the state of those eyes of yours."

We bombed up the last ramp back into the blinding sunlight, and by the time her words had sunk in it was too late. The truck squealed to a halt and several hulking shapes approached, one of them pulling open my door with a dull throb of laughter. A pair of silver cat's eyes peered into the gloom, a razor-sharp smile slicing open his face.

"Well, well. Just look at what we've got here."

Then he grabbed my arm in an iron grip I'd hoped I'd never feel again, ripping me from the truck into the cold, cruel glare of a dozen grinning blacksuits.

PMCs

THEY'D CUFFED ME before I even knew what was going on, cold steel against my wrists, my right arm swollen so much that the clasp almost didn't click shut. I felt a boot connect with my leg, sending me crashing down onto my knees, then the unmistakable metal ring of a gun barrel against my neck, pushing my forehead against the huge front wheel of the truck. That's all it took, a second or two, and they had me again, their smoky laughter rumbling across the roof of the parking lot as if this building too was gripped by an inferno.

"Hey, what do you think you're doing?" Captain Atilio appeared from behind the hood, one finger pointing at the blacksuit above me. "Let him go, you've got no authority to—"

"It's them!" I heard Zee yelling from inside, banging on the tiny window. "Captain, these are the men responsible."

"You shut it too, kid," Atilio snapped. "I want quiet. You, I need your name and rank, and I need to see your commanding officer right now."

The truck had seen better days, but I could still make out some of the scene behind me reflected in the hubcap. There were at least half a dozen figures there. I wanted to believe that it was the battered metal that distorted the men, that they weren't really Goliaths of muscle, their silver eyes glowing in the sun. But I knew Furnace's soldiers when I saw them, when I heard them.

The only difference between this lot and the guards back in the prison was that some of these wore red armbands over their suit jackets, a white circle and a black motif emblazoned there. I studied the blurred reflection, realizing after a moment that it was the Furnace logo, three circles joined by a triangle of lines.

"We've got all the authority we need," growled the one who had me pinned to the wheel. He wasn't wearing an armband. "These are escaped convicts, property of Furnace Penitentiary. You want to see paperwork then we've got buckets of it over in the tower." I heard the focus of his voice change. "You, get them all in cuffs, and call Warden Cross, let him know who's back."

Just the sound of the warden's name made my stomach churn, and with it came the nectar, called into action by my pounding heart. A dark flower began to bloom over my vision, reality peeling away like dead skin, exposing nothing but raw nerves beneath. The blacksuit must have sensed something because the pressure on the back of my head grew stronger.

Somewhere behind me I heard the bleep of a radio, a blacksuit speaking into it too quietly for me to make out his words.

"Captain Atilio, please," Zee's voice again. "Don't listen to them. They're responsible for all this. They're the ones who're trying to take over the city. Please, don't leave us here."

Another couple of blacksuits approached and I heard scuffling from inside the truck, shouts and screams and swearwords all blasted out in one indecipherable chorus. Gradually each voice became clearer as Simon, Zee, and Lucy were pulled into the daylight, squirming powerlessly against the mammoth fists that held them.

The car door slammed shut and I felt somebody grab my legs. I was pulled flat onto my face, more cuffs fastened around my feet, then yanked back and chained to those around my wrists. I fought against it but even with the rage building inside me, the nectar flowing to my muscles, I couldn't budge my restraints. All I could do was wriggle onto my back, my hands and feet pinned painfully beneath me as I rested my head against the wheel. At least I could see what was going on now.

"Listen, I don't care if these kids are prisoners or civilians," Atilio shouted, marching up to the first blacksuit and staring him right in the eye, even though her head only came up to his chest. Then she actually prodded him, which made me respect her just about more than anyone else I'd ever met. "You've got no right to throw them about like this. I was going to leave them with you, because I thought we had bigger fish to fry. But I'm taking them with me."

She turned to the semicircle of blacksuits that had formed around us—the ones on the outside were all wearing armbands, but those closest to me weren't—pointing in turn at the ones who held my friends.

"I'm ordering you to let these kids go."

Nobody moved, just another purr of laughter spilled from a dozen pairs of grinning lips. The sound made me want to puke, flooding my head with memories—the night I was caught, when the blacksuits shot Toby, the countless times they had threatened us in Furnace, and my own soulless laughter when I had nearly, so very nearly, become one of them.

"Captain," I started, wanting to warn her, wanting to tell her to get out of here before it turned nasty. But my words were choked off by a hammer of a fist that slammed into my jaw. Black stars burst into supernovas, plunging the parking lot into a flash of night. That darkness pulsed out of my eyes into my head, the nectar pleading to be given control. *Let me loose and we can kill them,* it seemed to say, each word knocking a little more of my sanity away. *We can kill them all.* I shook my head, silently screaming the words away. I couldn't lose myself to it, not again.

"That's enough!" I heard Atilio shout, and by the time my vision had cleared I noticed she had her pistol out, swinging it back and forth between the blacksuits. There was a rattle from the truck and I hoped that Roke was up there. Berserkers might be bulletproof, but blacksuits wouldn't last long against a cannon loaded with armor-piercing rounds. "Kids, just get back inside the truck. Roke, if any one of these creepy PMC mothers so much as puts a finger in the way then you know what to do."

The first blacksuit, the one who had cuffed me, turned to the guard who was on the radio, waiting for something. It came seconds later in the form of a nod.

"Captain," said the blacksuit, turning back to Atilio, still grinning insanely. "I'm afraid we can't let you do that."

There was movement at the back of the parking lot, where a couple of black vans had been parked. The glare of the sun off their chrome trim was too bright to make out exactly what was going on, but I thought I heard a throbbing snarl rise up from inside as two blacksuits broke free from the pack and walked that way.

"Hey, stop right there," Atilio yelled at them. "Don't think I won't shoot you in the back, merc." When they ignored her she turned back to the first. "You're gonna be neck deep in crap when my XO finds out about this. Now I'm gonna give you one last chance. Let the kids go. I don't care who they belong to, chump, right now they're coming with me."

"Oh, it's not about who they belong to," said the blacksuit, his teeth and eyes glinting. "It's about what they know."

"What they know?" Atilio said, and for the first time I saw her gun waver. "What's that supposed to mean?"

"Don't you dare," said another guard, this one wearing an armband. He took a step closer, raising a finger toward the blacksuit who'd been talking. "You shut your mouth."

The first blacksuit ignored him. At the far end of the parking lot the two men were wrestling with the van doors, but I knew they weren't responsible for the way the vehicles rocked on their wheels.

"It means they are right, Captain," the blacksuit hissed through his smile. "We are responsible for what's going on, we are taking—"

Atilio didn't so much as pause. She squeezed the trigger and the blacksuit stumbled back, his expression one of surprise, his hand held to his chest and the round hole that had been punched through his shirt. She loosed another two rounds, one hitting less than a centimeter away from the first, the second catching the suit in the forehead. His head snapped back and he flopped to the ground, twitching.

I couldn't keep track of what happened next, it was too quick. Another of the blacksuits lifted a shotgun and fired, Atilio either rolling out of the way or sent flying by the shot. Simon butted the back of his head into the face of the blacksuit behind him, bringing his hands around like a club to try to finish him off but missing and tipping earthward like a felled tree. Roke opened fire with the cannon, his aim wild, tearing over everybody's head, and all the time I heard him shouting:

"Jesus, what are they? *What the hell are they?*"

Four shapes were bounding across the parking lot, teeth like broken glass, their skinless bodies almost glowing red and blue in the fierce sunlight. And those eyes, like two silver pennies, promising nothing but pain.

"Dogs!" I found myself screaming as the warden's pets charged, so much saliva floating from their jaws that they could have been running through surf. My fear suddenly turned to downright panic and I squirmed against my chains, feeling them cut through my skin as I tugged at the metal.

Roke must have recovered his composure because the trail of fire cut down past two blacksuits and caused the lead dog to flip over in an explosion of blood. But the other three were on him in a heartbeat, pouncing over the blacksuits and me before landing on the truck so fast and so hard that it was shunted over the concrete. He had time for one scream, so utterly desperate that it didn't sound human, then there was nothing but the horrifying sound of tearing flesh.

They'd come after me next, and it was that thought that spurred me on. I gritted my teeth, pulling on my restraints with everything I had. The cuffs were strong, designed for people with my strength. But the chain that linked my arms to my feet obviously wasn't. I could feel it stretch behind my back, then with a ping one of the links snapped. I eased my cuffed hands under my feet then pushed myself up, black veins still pulsing behind my eyes.

"Get him," boomed one of the suits, pointing at me.

Two blacksuits threw themselves at me, but one flew back before he could make contact, a perfect circle punched into his forehead. I snapped around to see Captain Atilio lying in a puddle of blood beside the truck's hood, her face contorted with pain as she squeezed off the last few rounds from her pistol. She missed the second suit but she got his attention long enough for me to attack.

I squatted down then launched myself, wrapping my cuffed hands around his neck and pulling him toward me, using my momentum to bring my forehead down on his nose. He dropped to the floor, squirming. I couldn't keep my balance, making use of my fall to angle my knee down on his neck. There was an almighty crack, then he lay still.

Atilio was up, even as the rest of the blacksuits opened fire. She ducked behind the hood and ran to the passenger door, diving inside. I saw her hand pull the radio from its rack. One of the blacksuits moved to stop her, sliding around the truck so fast he was nothing but a smudge of black against the sun. But he wasn't quick enough.

"Mayday, Mayday, Mayday. Under attack by PMCs on Pear Street Parking Lot. Repeat, PMCs are hostile. Mayday, May—"

Atilio's voice fell silent, replaced by radio static. I felt arms on me, a blacksuit hoisting me up to my feet and adding a punch to the gut for good measure. When my eyes had stopped watering I saw that Simon had been rounded up too, Zee and Lucy held tight by their throats. Two of the dogs were still feasting on the remains of Roke, their bloodied muzzles rising up every now and again to sniff the air. The third had found its way inside the truck, howling through a wet throat. One last heartbreaking shot echoed from inside the cab, followed by Atilio's final, indecipherable words, then quiet.

The guards that Atilio had shot weren't going anywhere, and neither was the one whose neck I'd snapped. Only one of the downed blacksuits was struggling up, and he and the rest were glaring at me, the smiles wiped from their faces. I flashed them a grin, charged by nectar. They should have learned not to under-estimate me back in the prison.

"What now?" I said to them. "You can't kill me. Your boss needs me alive."

Those blacksuits who weren't wearing armbands broke into that same pulsing laughter. The others looked uneasy, although I had no idea why. I realized that the suit was back on the radio, listening intently to somebody on the other end. I remembered Furnace's words, his invitation to the tower. They wouldn't kill me, there was no way, not when their master, their creator, was waiting for me to make my choice, waiting for me to choose which side I was fighting on. At least, that's what I was banking on.

"Hey, Sawyer," said the suit with the radio. "It's for you."

He approached, holding the handset out so I could hear the voice on the other end. It scraped through the receiver like gravel, terrifyingly familiar.

"I warned you," the warden said, the words like needles in my ears. "I warned you that your betrayal would cost you everything. Look at what you have done. Look at the destruction you have wrought upon your own city. And this is just the start. This is your punishment, forever knowing that you were the one responsible for the end of the world."

"Yeah yeah," I said, my heartbeat so loud I could hear it in my words. "And when I'm lying on the operating table being cut to pieces by your freaks I'll come to regret the error of my ways. Come on, Cross, I've heard it all before."

A burst of static blasted out of the handset, one that might have been a laugh.

"Oh no, Sawyer, no no no," the warden said, and even though I couldn't see him I knew he was wearing that corpse's smile. "Dr. Furnace may want you alive, but I don't. I've wasted enough time on you. Take one more look at the city, Alex, take one more look at the world you have created. Because it will be your last."

The blacksuit pulled the walkie-talkie away, but not before I heard the warden's final words fizz from the handset.

"Kill them," he said. "Kill them all."

CHANGING

I THOUGHT THEY'D TAUNT ME for a while, dangle the inevitability of my death in front of me the way they always did, driven by the sick sense of humor that all blacksuits possessed.

I was wrong.

The closest blacksuit lifted his shotgun, pointed it at my chest, and without so much as a word or a laugh he pulled the trigger.

The world came apart, becoming a blur of sky and concrete and black suits that dissolved into a sickening spiral. I realized I was airborne, and for a crazy moment wondered if I'd managed to shed this grotesque body, if that fistful of lead shot had somehow released me from the warden's curse, let my spirit soar free into the sunlight.

Then I hit the floor, my flesh wrapping itself around me again, even tighter than before. And this time there was pain, not the itch of the nectar but real agony that scrubbed the inside of my chest like a cheese grater. I tried to lift my cuffed hands, to feel the wound the shotgun had opened up, but nothing seemed to work. I had no control. I was the pilot of a sinking ship, my body slowly descending into the depths and there was absolutely nothing I could do about it.

I heard another shot, the growl of the dogs, a scream. Was it Zee I heard yelling "no" over and over again at the top of his voice? Or was it a blacksuit?

I dropped beneath the waves of unconsciousness, the world vanishing for what might have been a second or an hour. I fought it, trying to stay afloat, trying to keep my head above the darkness. The pain in my chest was pounding harder, and by sheer force of will I managed to open my eyes. Sunlight screwed its way in, but past its glare I could see what they'd done to me.

My arm—the one that was mutating—had taken the worst of the shot. It had almost been torn clean off, just a knot of elbow bone and a few threads of twisted ligament still connecting it. The limb lay on my chest, concealing another ragged hole there that was oozing dirty blood. The impact must have stripped my shackles clean away as well because they were nowhere to be seen. I cried out silently, my lungs refusing to lend precious air to my fear, my disbelief. Nectar was pouring out of the severed artery in my arm, pooling beneath me, trickling away on the sunbaked concrete.

Or was it? I squinted into the light, tried to make sense of what I was seeing. The nectar was being pumped out, but it wasn't draining away. It looked as if it was forming a black web between the two halves of my arm, as if a spider was hard at work there. The skin of my ruined limb was bulging, swelling out then shrinking, almost like it was breathing.

And inside that nectar I saw fragments of fire, red flecks that burned alongside golden ones under the morning sun.

"Let the dogs have them," I heard a blacksuit shout, followed by more screams. And then another voice, surely a blacksuit, ordering somebody to stop. An argument was breaking out between the guards, but I couldn't understand the words. I couldn't make sense of what was going on up there, my eyes refusing to focus on anything but my wound. I could barely even remember why I was lying on the floor. It was as if every single resource in my body was being diverted to my arm, the nectar doing its best to patch up a wound that should have been fatal.

The web was twisting itself into thicker strands, knotting together as though an invisible pair of hands was manipulating it. The black liquid had covered my entire arm now, from my fingers all the way up past the exposed bone to my shoulder. It looked like it had been burned to a crisp, only the sensation was cooling, like a breeze blowing against my skin. Gradually, incredibly, the pain was lessening, settling back into that infuriating, unscratchable itch I knew so well.

I heard a blacksuit swear, a dark silhouette rising above me, casting the world into shadow.

"Go on, finish him off. Don't mess it up this time."

"No, Dr. Furnace forbids it. Get away from there. That's an order!"

"Screw your orders."

I heard the pump of a shotgun, the acrid smell of gunpowder stinging my nostrils. I blinked twice, the world gradually swimming back into shape and revealing the smoking pit of a shotgun barrel like a black hole in my vision.

I was moving before I even knew it, my broken, blackened arm sweeping up from my chest and smacking into the weapon just as the guard pulled the trigger. He obviously hadn't been expecting me to move, as the gun clattered out of his hands, the shot carving a hole in the concrete inches from my head and making my ear pop into silence.

The suit bent down to reclaim the shotgun, but the same arm—the limb that had almost been severed in two, which should have been nothing but a hunk of meat on the parking-lot floor—shot out and grabbed him around the neck. I watched, half in horror and half in fascination, as strands of nectar rose from my fist like scorpion tails, darting forward and puncturing the blacksuit's throat. He tried to pull away but the nectar wouldn't let him, the claw fastened in his flesh, lodged there until the color drained from his eyes, turning them from silver to lead.

I didn't know what was going on. I didn't want to. All I knew was that the strength was filtering back into my body, the nectar's insatiable bloodlust taking over. My arm seemed to have a mind of its own, tossing the corpse of the blacksuit to one side, raining nectar down onto the floor.

I pushed myself to my feet, and this time when I stretched out a leg the ankle cuffs snapped as if they were made of silk thread. One side of my head was ringing, the other drenched in silence, making me feel even more unbalanced. The world seemed to have slowed down again, the blacksuits lurching toward me like clumsy puppets, firing off shots that were too far away to do any damage. Somewhere in the confusion I noticed that Zee, Simon, and Lucy were on the move, heading for the ramp that led down into the parking lot.

And next to them . . . Were two blacksuits locked in battle?

Another guard was pulling a dog from the army truck, yelling. Even though I couldn't hear him I could lip read his words: *Kill him, boy.* But the dog wasn't having any of it, its gaze refusing to meet my eyes, its body hunkered, tail between its legs. I watched as it turned on the suit, clamping its jaws down on his arm, then retreated back across the roof, ears flattened to its head. The other two followed with nervous backward glances and I didn't blame them.

I was changing, and fast.

My arm seemed to have doubled in size in the seconds since I'd found my feet, hanging from my shoulder like a broken branch. My fingers now reached past my knees, still coated with nectar, marbled with those glowing red galaxies, but somehow being fused together into an obsidian blade. I tried to move them, to separate them, to wiggle them, *anything*. But they were stuck fast.

"No!" I heard myself shout, tearing at my arm with my other hand, the good hand. It would have been better if the mutant limb had been lying on the roof, better to spend the rest of my life with only one arm than to see myself turning into one of *them*.

A blacksuit was suddenly in front of me, moving fast. I flinched, but once again my arm knew what to do, the nectar in my system operating it automatically. It twisted back then thrust forward like a spear, my fingers slicing into the blacksuit's stomach. His mouth became an "O" of surprise and he looked down to see my arm inside his guts, up to the elbow. He grabbed it, shaking his head in denial.

With a grunt of effort I swung my body around, flicking him away. He slid off my arm, tumbling end over end across the roof and sliding to a halt on his side, sunlight pouring through the ragged hole in his torso. The sight of him there, the knowledge of what I'd done, sat over my thoughts like a weight, a pressure that pushed everything else to one side. I growled, the noise throbbing up my throat, making me smile.

No, I called out again, but this time it was just in my head, lost beneath the rolling swell of a sea of nectar. I scanned the parking lot, seeing the blacksuits close in, their eyes full of fear. Right now they were all just meat, already dead even though they didn't know it.

None of them could fight me. I was unstoppable.

I had set off toward the nearest blacksuit when I heard the sound of thunder above me. A shadow threw itself over everything and I teetered around to see a chopper hovering next to the edge of the roof. There was a hiss, like a snake, and four missiles slithered out of the launchers, two from each side, heading right this way. Three sailed over my head, and I lashed out at the fourth, managing to swat it away like a fly. It darted off on a tangent, hitting the vans on the other side of the roof and detonating in a fireball the size of a house. The floor shook as the three other missiles found a target, a fistful of heat and noise catapulting me over the concrete.

Something was cutting through the nectar, and I realized it was fear. The air was on fire, bringing a scalding pain with each breath. In every direction was heat and smoke, and above it all the relentless buzz of the chopper. There was another hiss, two more white trails blasting overhead and causing another wave of destruction. The flames around me danced in the shock wave, curling up and splashing down like I was swimming in a burning ocean. If I didn't move now, then I'd be cooked alive.

But there was nowhere to go.

I panicked, throwing my huge arm over my face. I'd have to run for it, into the flames. I couldn't even keep my eyes open, the force of the heat drying them out, hot enough to make my eyelashes wither.

I started running, keeping my eyes closed, my hand up. I bumped into something soft, sending it flying. Then everything went white, a light so fierce it seemed to ring in my ears. My sneakers stuck, melting on the concrete, but I kept running, not breathing, not looking, not feeling, only throwing one foot in front of the other.

I struck a wall, momentum flipping me over. Then I was falling. I hit something solid, too soon to be the street below. I risked opening my eyes, seeing that I'd landed on the ramp. Flames had taken hold of my clothes, burning off the smiley face on what was left of my hoodie, and I patted them out as I got to my feet.

Above me, through the gap, it looked as if the heavens were burning, and I retreated down the ramp into the glorious darkness of the level below. I hurdled the barrier down onto the next floor, and again, dropping level by level until the carnage was just a whisper overhead. Eight floors later and I was back on solid ground, the parking lot's lights now off and a constant rain of dust drifting from the steel rafters.

I slumped against the wall, my body drained, my arm so heavy that it felt as if it had been stuffed full of rocks. It looked like it too, the skin stretched over the expanding muscles, rubbing against sharp ridges that could only be bone. Those weird strands of nectar stood up from my wrist, undulating like sea plants. The limb was a mess, and I wanted nothing more than to find a saw and get rid of it, cut it off before whatever was inside could spread. What had Captain Atilio said about the plague in the city? That it was like a severed artery, you had to stem the flow before it bled out. It was the same inside me. If I didn't stop it now then it would be too late. I would become one of them.

I would become a berserker.

Since the moment my arm had begun to grow I'd suspected as much, but it was the first time I'd admitted it to myself. There was no denying it. The bite wound, the infection, the red-flecked nectar that was somehow spreading inside me. I'd been turned. The knotted limb that hung from my shoulder could have been that of the berserker I'd fought back in the prison, a beetle-black weapon that should have belonged to some nightmare, not to me.

I was distracted by the sound of a door opening farther down the parking lot. Three familiar shapes barged from it, checking the shadows before scampering toward the sun-dappled entrance. I lowered myself into a pool of darkness. It was better that they didn't see me. They'd stand a better chance of surviving this if I wasn't with them.

But I guess when you've been through so much with somebody, when you've traveled to hell and back, when you've experienced the very worst of the world, and laughed together even though death is just around the corner, then you share a bond with them, some link that can't possibly be there and yet somehow still is. Because just as they were running up the slope, vanishing into the golden blur of day, one of the figures stopped and slowly turned.

"Alex?" said Zee, his eyes scouring the parking lot, eventually finding me. I pressed myself farther back against the damp concrete, but in a flash he was there, bathing me in a smile. Simon appeared next to him, his own grin a lot less even but welcome all the same.

"Come on," Zee said, offering me his hand. I didn't accept and he grabbed me by my new arm, yelping at the heat but hanging on, Simon helping him.

"Glad I'm not the only one who's lopsided now," the bigger boy said. "You're starting to make me look almost normal."

Together they helped me up, Simon lumping my arm over his shoulders to help me support the weight.

"We need to get out of here," Zee said as we shuffled forward, looking like contestants in some weird three-legged race. Lucy was waiting for us by a pillar, looking at me even more uneasily than she had before. "The army'll blow you to pieces the moment they see you, looking like that."

We were halfway to the entrance ramp when the stairwell door opened again. This time it was a blacksuit who stumbled out of it, his clothes charred and ripped, the red armband crumpled around his elbow. He was coughing into his sleeve as he made his way toward the light, so fiercely that he didn't notice us.

"Yeah, we'll get out of here," I said, lifting my arm off of Simon, glaring at the suit as he struggled up the ramp. "But there's someone I want to have a word with first."

INFORMATION

TEN MINUTES LATER I was sitting inside a small burger joint three streets away, peering through the grease-smeared windows as yet another convoy of trucks rattled past. That had been the second one we'd seen since leaving the parking lot. They were all heading into town, more and more meat for the berserkers and the rats to feast on.

Zee was busy barricading the back door, where we'd broken in, and Lucy was fiddling with her mobile phone, repeatedly slamming it against the counter in frustration. Simon was crouched on the floor over the blacksuit, who was still out cold. We'd tied him up with electrical cords cut from the kitchen appliances.

Getting out of the parking lot hadn't thrown up any difficulties. The blacksuit hadn't even heard me coming, which was no surprise given the number of burns that coated his bare scalp like old jam. A single blow with my new arm had done the trick, then I'd thrown him over my shoulder and followed Zee as he led the way out onto the street.

The helicopters—three of them—had been busy bombarding the upper levels of the parking lot with more incendiaries, the smoke too thick for them to notice us. There had been troops on the ground too, a long line of trucks, tanks, and infantry approaching from the west. We'd gone the other way, unseen among the wreckage of the city, eventually stopping here when the weight of the blacksuit became too much.

"Well, it won't keep out anything that really wants to get in," came Zee's voice. "But I doubt anyone will notice that we broke the lock. He awake yet?" I turned away from the window to see Zee walk past one of the half-dozen tables that occupied the living-room-sized space, looking down at the blacksuit who was snoring gently. "Guess not. You must have hit him pretty hard."

"Dammit!" shouted Lucy, throwing the phone against the wall. "It's just *bleep, bleep, bleep* every number I try."

She reached into the neck of her T-shirt, pulling free the small silver medallion she wore. It flashed between her fingers, the brightest thing in the room.

"Where the hell do we go from here?" she went on, no anger in her voice now, just exhaustion and despair. She rested her elbows on the counter, dropping her head into her arms. "I want to go home. I don't want to be here anymore. I can't even call my mom to let her know I'm okay." She sobbed into her hands, never letting go of the necklace.

"Did she give you that?" I asked. She glanced at the necklace for a second as if she'd never seen it before, then stared back at me.

"What do you care?" she snapped.

"Sorry," I said, holding up my hands. "Just showing an interest."

"Well, don't," she said, tucking the medallion away, slumping against the counter again.

Zee put an arm around her shoulder. "It will be okay, Lucy," he said. "I know it will. Things may look bad, but . . ."

He seemed to run out of things to say.

"Wow, thanks for the pep talk, Zee," said Simon. "I feel so much better now."

I laughed, and it felt good. Even Lucy cracked a smile. But Zee was right; things could have been worse. I'd suffered a few burns running through the fire, but other than that my body seemed to have healed itself completely. The haze of the nectar had cleared in the time it had taken us to walk here, leaving me with only the unpleasant buzz of a headache.

Zee picked up a salt shaker, studying it as if it might give some clue to getting out of the city.

"So where *do* we go from here?" he said, prodding the blacksuit with his foot. He'd pulled off the armband to get a better look at it, the unmistakable logo mounted on red looking more like a swastika than ever. "And why did we lug this numbnuts along with us?"

"For information," I answered.

"You think he knows a safe route out of town?" Lucy asked. I shook my head. That wasn't what I had in mind. Zee replaced the salt shaker, nodding at my arm.

"Does it hurt?" he asked. I lifted my hand, the fingers still fused by nectar, fashioned into a lethal point that looked as sharp and as hard as chipped flint. My hand seemed too far away, the arm now half as long again as it had been, knotted and scarred like old wood. I shook my head. It didn't hurt, not physically, anyway.

There was a grunt from the floor, the blacksuit's snores becoming a moan.

"Here he comes," Simon said, moving onto his knees ready to hold the guard down if he needed to. The suit's eyes fluttered open, and in the gloom of the shop they didn't look silver at all, they looked pale blue, the eyes of a child. Then I saw the memories flood back into the blacksuit's face and all of a sudden his gaze grew fierce, the cold fire returning to his pupils. He struggled to get up but only succeeded in kicking a table across the room, his bonds holding as he flapped on the floor like a fish out of water. Simon pushed two hands down on the blacksuit's chest until the man stopped wriggling.

"You're gonna pay for this," the suit growled, staring at us all in turn. "You'll pay in pain when they find me."

"They won't find you," I replied. "Not in one piece, anyway."

I lifted my arm, flashing the blade of my hand, and his face seemed to melt into itself.

"You know what's happening to me," I said, a statement not a question. He glanced at my arm and nodded. His hair had been burned off, the blackened remains like a skullcap bobbing up and down with his head. "What comes next?"

"Oh you'll find out soon enough." The blacksuit grinned. "When you're tearing apart your little friends here."

Simon lashed out, slapping the blacksuit across his face. The guard spat out a mouthful of blood before turning back to me.

"You can't run from it," he said. "You can't hide. You've got berserker blood in you, it's swimming in those traitorous veins of yours. You can't even kill yourself, not anymore." He laughed, the sound filling the small space. "Because it'll bring you back, the nectar. It won't ever let you go."

He broke into a coughing fit, black-flecked spittle spraying upward.

"How is it doing this?" I asked, the anger building, fueled by my fear and confusion. "How can I be turning into one of them? It doesn't make any sense. The warden never said anything about this."

"The warden?" the blacksuit spat, his voice a wheezed laugh.

"No, that old waste of space doesn't know the half of it. Cross might think he's in control, but we answer to one man only, and it isn't him. What you're seeing now is something new, something that Furnace has been saving. You notice the difference? This nectar pumps red. It's a hundred times more powerful than the piss he lets Warden Cross play with. This nectar was designed with much more in mind than changing a bunch of pathetic cons into prison guards."

"We know. It's spreading a plague," said Zee.

The blacksuit looked up at him. "Oh, it's worse than that," he said. "It's so much worse than that." He turned his soulless smile to me. "Especially for you, Sawyer."

"What's so special about me?" I asked. "Why does Furnace want me to stay alive? Why haven't his berserkers tried to kill me?"

The blacksuit shrugged. "The only one who can tell you that is Furnace," he said. "He wants you for something, and trust me, it won't be something you'll like. If you ask me, it's because you got the better of Cross, and nobody's been able to do that before. You've made some powerful enemies." He coughed blood down the front of his suit. "For all I know, Furnace is keeping you just so he can slaughter you personally in his own sweet time."

I sat back, slamming the wall in frustration. If anything, the blacksuit's answers had made me even more confused.

Zee tried another tack. "It's not too late," he said to the blacksuit. "You can still be who you were, do something to end this. I know that inside you're just a kid, like us. I know what the warden did to you down in Furnace. Help us get out of here and we'll vouch for you. They'll grant you immunity. They might even reward you. You can get your old life back."

The blacksuit's eyes widened and he started laughing again, the chuckles descending into hacking coughs.

"You think I come from the prison?" he asked when he had recovered his breath. "*That* hole?"

I looked at Zee, then at Simon, both of them equally lost. The blacksuit saw our expressions and spat out another laugh.

"You really have no idea, do you? You're in so deep and you don't have a clue. The prison, that was only part of it. A side venture, something to keep Cross busy, to keep his meddling hands out of the way. Only scum come from there, the inferior specimens." He spat this last comment at me. "Us, we're purebloods, raised by Furnace himself. Only we are fit to wear the badge." His hand rose almost automatically to his arm, to the place where the band had been.

I sat there, my mouth hanging open, unable to believe what I was hearing. All this time I'd thought that the prison, Furnace Penitentiary, had been at the heart of Furnace's plans, and all this time it had been nothing more than a distraction.

"So where are you from?" I asked. "What were you?"

"What I was, was nothing," the blacksuit said. "What I *am* is a soldier of the new world. We will burn this country into ashes, and our fire will spread. When we are finished, there will be no more weakness in the world, only strength, only power."

The speech was one I'd heard before, from the warden back in the prison and from Furnace himself, hammered into my skull through the nectar in my veins.

"But where were you made?" I asked, stepping forward and angling my mutant hand toward his throat. "Where did they turn you?"

"The tower." The answer came from Simon rather than the

guard. "In the tower. Remember the vision? I'll bet you anything that's where this slimy creep was butchered."

"And that's where Furnace is," I added. "Right?"

The blacksuit merely smirked. It was all the confirmation I needed. I pictured the skyscraper I'd seen in my vision, the horrors I had watched through the windows, the way it had sat there in the middle of the burning city like a throne in the center of hell, and the beast that howled from the spire as it watched its new kingdom being born.

"It doesn't matter," the suit said. "You can't stop him, not now. Nothing can stop him."

"In that case, maybe you won't mind telling me something," I said.

I leaned in toward the blacksuit, pressed my razor fingers against his windpipe as I hissed:

"How do we get inside?"

BURGERS

"IF YOU GO to the tower, then you're dead," Zee said, long after the echo of my words had faded.

"I'm already dead," I replied, shaking my deformed arm at him. The virus inside me, if that's what it was, was spreading. I could feel it in my neck, the tendons expanding, something growing beneath the skin like a tumor, making it hard for me to turn my head to the right. "Look at me, Zee, *I'm already dead*. What else can I do?"

"Come with us," he replied. "Get out of the city, find the military intelligence post that Atilio was talking about. She said there were brains there, scientists. They'll be able to help you."

At this the blacksuit broke into another round of wheezed chuckles. I did my best to ignore him.

"And what if they can't?" I asked. And I didn't add, *Or what if they decide they want to cut me up, dissect me bit by bit to find out why I'm changing, to get their hands on the nectar?*

Zee shrugged. "It's better than giving yourself up to *him*. He can get inside your head from halfway across the city; what's he gonna do when you're right there next to him? How do you know you won't get to the tower and find yourself under his control?"

"Because I'm stronger than that," I replied, but I couldn't look him in the eye while I said it. That's what worried me more than anything. That I'd get to the tower and fall under Furnace's spell, that the gut-twisting sense of excitement I felt when I heard his voice—something that surely had to be due to the nectar, not me—would become too powerful. I shook my head to get rid of my fears. "It just won't happen. I'm going to find Furnace and kill him."

"Better men than you have tried," the blacksuit said. "You won't get anywhere near him."

"Yeah? Well, we'll see about that," I spat back, suddenly feeling more like a kid than ever. "Now tell us what we need to know. How do we get into the tower?"

"We?" mouthed Zee, looking at Simon. But I paid him no attention, focusing on the dull murmur of the blacksuit's laughter.

"You don't need anything from me," he said eventually. "You're one of us, you can come and go as you please. That tower is your home now; one of them, anyway. You want to know how to get in? Just walk through the front doors."

And maybe that was the real reason for what I almost did next. Not that we wanted information, not that we thought he was holding anything back, but because he spoke those last words with relish, that smug smile never leaving his lips, and I hated him for it.

I got as far as lighting up the grill and hauling the blacksuit into the tiny kitchen. And I almost did it, I came so close. It wasn't even the nectar this time, although it thrashed and surged at the thought of what was to come. No, every person on this planet has darkness inside them, buried so deep that you only know it's there when your world is coming to an end. Oh, but it's there. It's always there.

I didn't do it, though. I couldn't. If I had, if I'd pressed that suit's face against the sizzling metal, then it would have been over. I'd never have found my way back.

And in the end I didn't need to. He must have sensed the rage boiling in my system because he told us everything we needed to know.

Afterward he lay beside the smoking grill, slumped on the floor, no more smirks and no more laughter. The four of us sat on the chairs on the other side of the counter, listening to the sound of gunfire and chopper blades from across town.

"You think he's telling the truth?" Simon asked.

I nodded, recalling the way the blacksuit had screamed the words at us when we'd held him over the grill, the heat rising against the burns he'd received in the parking lot. According to him there were tunnels beneath the tower, designed for carrying equipment and specimens in and out without being seen. None of the tunnels went far—none went to the prison either, which was a relief—and most were linked to shops on nearby streets. He gave us the location of a direct link to the tower basements, a funeral parlor about a mile to the east.

Chances are he was right. I probably would have been able to walk right in through the front doors of that tower. Furnace had invited me, after all. He was expecting me. But that was the problem. If we stood any chance of winning this battle, then we had to surprise him. We had to get into the tower and bring it down before he even knew we were there.

"We have to try, anyway," I said. "We don't have a choice."

"We do have a choice," Lucy said, lifting her head from Zee's shoulder and glaring at me with those fierce eyes of hers. "We have a million choices."

I returned her gaze, but mine was full of sadness.

"Yeah," I whispered. "*You* have a choice. You and Zee. You're both normal, you can go back to your lives." I looked at Simon, his one arm still bulging but nowhere near as badly as mine. He could blame it on a freak accident, a childhood disease, and maybe one day he'd even come to believe it himself, if he was ever lucky enough to forget the truth. "You too," I went on. "You can get out of the city, get out of the country, and you'll be free. You've got all the choices in the world."

"If there's any world left," said Zee, wiping his eyes before meeting mine.

"Yeah," I said. "This isn't some terrorist attack. This isn't a day's worth of chaos, a month of mourning then back to normal. This is an invasion. It's war. It's happening, right now, out there on those streets. And it isn't going to end today. It might not end ever."

They all looked at me and I could just about read their minds: *But it's not our fight, let the army handle it, there's nothing we can do.* Nobody spoke them aloud, though. They didn't honestly believe it.

"And we've all seen what's happening," I said. "In the cathedral. You saw how quickly those people went from regular folk to stark raving out of their bloody minds. That sort of thing is going to happen everywhere. This city, this whole damn planet, is going to tear itself apart before *he* even gets a chance to."

I fumbled over my words, my speech running dry before it could really get started. More than ever I wished Donovan was here. He'd have been able to rally everybody with a couple of jokes and that smile of his. He'd have the whole city charging after him into the tower, flaming torches at the ready. But Donovan was dead.

"So what?" Simon asked. "You're going to march in there and just ask Furnace to come quietly?"

I stood up, running my good hand over my head. When I pulled it away I noticed clumps of hair trapped between my fingers, coming out as easily as dead grass. Thinking about Donovan had brought back bittersweet memories and I remembered that I'd left the grill on, the small restaurant now as hot as a sauna. I knew that only ten minutes ago I'd planned to use it for torture, but right now I had a better idea.

"Alex?" Simon shouted as I walked around the counter and into the kitchen. "Where are you going?"

"Just keeping a promise to a friend," I said.

THE BURGERS WERE IN THE FRIDGE, wrapped in greaseproof paper. I peeled off five, stepping over the blacksuit and slapping them down on the grill.

"You want one?" I asked him, but he didn't even look up. Not that he would have been able to eat solids. He was like me, full of nectar. Real food would only make him chunder. Immediately the smell of cooking meat sizzled through the air, and it must have hooked the others because after a couple of seconds they appeared in the kitchen door.

"You're *cooking*?" asked Zee. "How can you even be hungry?"

But he was licking his lips as he spoke, his words wet with saliva. I dug a spatula out of an empty mayonnaise jar beside the cooker and flipped each burger over, breathing in that smell as if it were oxygen.

"Can I take your orders?" I asked, flashing them a smile. "It might be our last supper."

"Why, because you're going to give us food poisoning?" asked Lucy, looking at my blood-encrusted right hand. I pulled a face at her.

"Anybody see any buns?" I asked, flipping the burgers again, the grill making short work of them. Zee stepped over with a bag of sesame-seed rolls, tearing it open and placing four on the counter. I nodded at him until he realized what I was getting at, taking out a fifth. "There's cheese too," I said. "In the fridge, if anyone wants it."

They did, and I carefully laid cheese slices over the blackening burgers, waiting for them to start to melt before lifting the burgers one by one from the metal and sliding them onto the buns.

"Voilà!" I said, and even if I had been able to eat I doubted I could have forced any food past the lump in my throat. I looked at the ceiling, but past it, up to where I hoped my old cellmate was, basking in sunlight. "These are for you, D. Man, I wish you were here to share them with us."

Zee and Simon both fell silent, their eyes glassy as I passed them the burgers. I offered one to Lucy and at first she shook her head.

"I'm vegetarian," she started. Then she grabbed it. "Oh, the hell with it, I'm starving. Who's D?"

"D was Donovan," I said. "*Is* Donovan, even though he isn't with us anymore. He's the reason we're out here, in one way or another. He's what kept us going." I lifted the fifth burger to the ceiling in a toast. There was no relish, no onions either, but I think he'd have liked it. "Yeah, this is for you." Then I placed it carefully on the counter. I wasn't really sure what else to do with it. I'd seen my dad toast dead friends by pouring whisky on the garden, but it seemed a little silly dropping a burger on the floor.

Zee, Simon, and Lucy repeated my toast, then we all tucked in. I can't tell you how good that burger tasted, and even though I promised myself I wouldn't swallow any of it I just couldn't help myself. I managed to get down three massive mouthfuls before my body reacted as I'd known it would and I ran to the sink, spewing up my guts.

"That's gross!" Lucy shouted. "What did you put in these burgers?"

Then we were laughing, so hard that I had to grip the edge of the sink to stop from sliding to the floor. That's kind of what I meant, though, when I said that Donovan was the reason we were out here. Just the thought of him kept me grinning.

"You guys are insane," Lucy said, and when I looked up I saw that she was smiling, more with her eyes than with her mouth but smiling all the same. Zee was giggling and eating at the same time, doing his best not to choke. He stuffed the last fragment of burger into his mouth then nodded at the one on the counter.

"You think Donovan would mind?" he asked hopefully. I nodded.

"I reckon he'd kick your ass," I said. "But after that he'd probably let you have it."

Zee whooped and snatched up the cheeseburger, taking just about the biggest bite I'd ever seen. I wrung out the last few drops of laughter and wiped my mouth.

"You know, if Donovan was here he'd know what to do," I said. "He'd take us right into that tower and kill Furnace single-handedly."

"Are you kidding?" Zee said through a mouthful of mush. "Donovan? He'd be out of the city in a flash, leaving everyone else to mop up the mess."

"Yeah, okay, he probably would," I conceded, and we were all laughing again, even Lucy. "But seriously, I think he'd know what to do. I think he'd do the right thing."

"Okay, okay," said Simon, watching enviously as Zee took another bite. "Congratulations, you've guilt-tripped us into listening to you." He looked back at me, suddenly serious. "So tell us, what's the plan?"

PARTING WAYS

I DIDN'T HAVE A PLAN. Of course I didn't, I wasn't a military general, I wasn't even that smart. I was just a kid with a vendetta. I wanted to kill Alfred Furnace. Alfred Furnace was in the tower. We needed to head for the tower. Bingo, there it was, my masterpiece.

It was met by three expressions that were about as far from impressed as it was possible to be. Zee shoved the last of Donovan's burger into his mouth, swallowing it without really chewing.

"You better make sure that blacksuit doesn't report back what you just said," he mumbled through the crumbs, wiping his lips with his sweatshirt. "Because it would be such a shame if that amazing plan was foiled."

Sarcasm. Just what we needed.

"Seriously, though," said Lucy. "If that's all you've got then I'm out of here. Talk about strolling into your own grave."

We fell quiet, the sizzle of meat scraps on the grill like white noise. I tried to get my thoughts in order, to come up with something better, but I just couldn't. It wasn't that they were too chaotic. If anything it was that they were too calm. I felt like a ship in the doldrums, stranded by absent wind and motionless waves, unable to build up any momentum. Every time I tried to put something together it just fell dead in the water.

"Okay," Lucy went on, seeing me struggle. She was toying with her medallion again, nervously flicking it back and forth along its chain. "I know this is none of my business. But hear me out. This is what I think you should do."

We all listened as she explained, leaning in closer and closer with each word. It took her the best part of a minute to spell things out. And I have to hand it to her, it was a better plan than mine.

"It means splitting up," Zee said when Lucy had finished. "Are you sure that's a good idea? I don't really fancy being out there on my own."

"You won't be on your own," Lucy replied.

Zee raised an apologetic hand. "Sorry, I meant without Alex and Simon. They've kind of saved my ass a few times now."

"No," I said. "Lucy's right. If we stay together and something happens then that's it, game over. At least this way even if one of us . . ." For some reason I couldn't bring myself to say it, although the pause seemed to carry more weight than the word itself. "Then we still stand a chance."

"A very, very, very small chance," Simon said. "I wouldn't bet on us."

I wouldn't either, but it didn't stop a strange sense of optimism filling the room. It sat in every twinkle of our eyes and every gentle smile.

"Just remember," I said to Zee and Lucy, looking at the clock on the kitchen wall. It was shaped like a chicken, two skinny legs swinging beneath it and a goggle-eyed head staring at us in alarm. The greasy dial on its breast told us that it was nearly midday. It seemed impossible, utterly and completely impossible, that just eight hours ago we'd been in Furnace Penitentiary. That just twenty-four hours before that I'd been a blacksuit about to take the warden's final test. They were snapshots from another age, another life. "Just remember, two o'clock."

"Two o'clock," Zee said. "You sure that will give you enough time?"

"If I'm not out of there by two then I'm already dead," I said. "Or worse."

Zee nodded. He looked unsure but he didn't say anything.

"So I guess this is it, then?" he said, his voice so heavy that it almost broke. He coughed, then held out his hand. I went to shake it, forgetting about my bladed fingers and almost poking his eye out. He switched his right hand for his left and I shook it, realizing that it was the first time I'd ever done so. His hand was small and warm, but strong. And I never wanted to let it go.

"We'll see each other again, on the other side," said Simon, putting his own mammoth hand over ours and squeezing. Lucy stood to the side watching us, and I think there was genuine affection in her eyes. She caught me looking and offered me a smile.

"On the other side of what?" I asked Simon, raising my eyebrow. "Death?"

"No," he blurted. "I didn't mean that. I meant on the other side of this, the other side of the plan."

We laughed together, softly this time, because we might not get another chance. We stared at our hands, still locked together between us, none of us making the break.

"All for one," said Zee. And that did it. Simon pulled his hand off, using it to wave us away.

"Oh god, don't start all that musketeer crap again," he said.

"Heard enough of it back in the prison. Come on, let's just get this over and done with."

I released my grip and Zee's hand tumbled out of mine, slapping against his hip. I noticed the bands of white against his skin where my fingers had dug in. I didn't realize quite how hard I'd been holding it.

"What about him? Those cords won't hold him when he gets his strength back," Simon said, nodding at the blacksuit. The man turned to us, a flicker of concern in his silver eyes.

"Forget him," I said. "Even if he does get out there's not much he can do. This will all be over in a couple of hours, one way or another."

"It will be over for you," the blacksuit growled without conviction.

"Yeah yeah," I said. "So you keep saying."

I turned my back on him and led the way out of the kitchen into the small, dark corridor that ended at the back door. Zee had piled up a bunch of crates in front of it and we set about pulling them out of the way. I opened the door a crack to reveal the courtyard we had entered through, still deserted. It stank of rotting food from the bins lined up against the wall, but even more overpowering than that was the constant burning reek of smoke. Back in the open the sounds of gunfire and helicopters reasserted themselves. It made what we were about to do feel real. Too real.

"Be safe," I said to Zee. "Stay off the main roads, and if you see anything moving that isn't dressed in beige and brown then—"

"I know, I know," he broke in. "We'll be fine, we'll find them."

"And no smooching along the way," added Simon. Zee's cheeks flared, and so did Lucy's. Her mouth fell open as if she was about to protest but she obviously thought better of it. I wondered whether they'd make it through this, whether it would bring them together. I pictured them in ten years' time, or twenty, married, living miles away from here. I wondered whether they'd tell their kids stories about me, about what happened here. I hoped so.

My vision was blurring, so I started off out of the courtyard. There were two alleyways, one going west and the other east.

"Be safe," I repeated. Zee nodded once, then he took Lucy's hand and they made their way toward the second passageway. They hadn't gone far before Lucy shook him free and ran toward me, her hands around the back of her neck. Something glinted as she pulled it free: the medallion. She held it out between us. I studied it as it spun hypnotically, seeing an image of one man carrying another on his shoulders.

"It's a St. Christopher," she said bashfully. "My dad gave it to me. He was a cop, I told you." She paused, staring into the middle distance as though she wasn't quite sure what she was doing. She seemed to pull the necklace away, then reached for my good hand and pushed the warm silver into my palm. She hung on to me as she talked, her fingers tiny against my own.

"He was one of the policemen who got killed during that summer, the Summer of Slaughter. They never caught the gang members who did it, or maybe they did, I don't know. Nobody ever went to court for it, anyway. That's why I . . . That's how come I've been acting the way I have." She squeezed my hand tighter. "I hated you all, so much. I hated every single inmate in that place. But I guess I shouldn't have. And I need to thank you for that."

"For what?" I asked, genuinely confused.

"I don't know," she said. "I really don't. I was just tired of hating." She let go of my hand, stepping back. "It's not a gift, it's a loan.

St. Christopher, he's the patron saint of travelers, so you should take him, take him with you."

I started to protest, as she must have known I would.

"It's not a gift," she repeated. "It means too much to me. Give it back when you've killed him, okay? Give it back to me when things are back to normal."

"I will."

"Promise me?" she asked gently. And I realized she was asking for a promise not just to return the necklace, but to make things normal again. It was a promise I doubted I could keep, but one I made anyway.

"I promise," I said. She nodded at me, then jogged back to Zee, the pair hurrying from the courtyard together. Zee had his head ducked down, making him look even smaller than he already was. Right then he didn't look as if he'd survive for more than a minute out there in Furnace's new playground. I almost set off after him, but Simon grabbed my arm, knowing me too well.

"It's a good plan," he said. "It will work."

It better had, I thought. I had no hope of clipping the medallion around my neck with my hands the way they were, so instead I tucked the chain into my pocket.

Then Zee was gone, and without another word Simon and I turned and jogged the other way.

IF THINGS OUTSIDE HAD BEEN BAD BEFORE, they were a million times worse now. At the end of the alley we had to pause, hiding in the shadows as a bunch of people walked past. There must have been thirty of them, a mix of men and women, young and old, and their clothes were tattered and stained. The two men who led the pack brandished iron bars, the metal stained with what might have been rust.

We could have stepped out. We were all on the same side, after all. But I saw the terror in their eyes, and the violence too, so fierce it was almost spilling out of them, and I knew they'd have beaten us into the concrete before we could even get a word out. There was no self-styled priest goading them on this time, but scared people were stupid people. We waited for them to reach the end of the street beyond before sloping out and heading in the opposite direction, toward the glinting upper floors of the distant skyscrapers.

All around us was the sound track of war, an endless cacophony of explosions, shots, screams, and worse carried on a warm wind that didn't seem to know where to turn. It gusted down the streets in every direction, carrying scraps of clothing and a fine pink mist that soon burnished our clothes and our skin, collecting in the hollows of our eyes and making us cry tears of other people's blood.

At one point, as we were crossing an intersection that led down the hill toward the center of the city, a jet screamed overhead, so low it felt as if I could reach up and touch it. I saw the missiles clustered underneath the wings, prayed that Zee would get where he was going, that he'd be able to complete his part of the plan.

Simon swore, drawing me from my thoughts in time to see an army truck up ahead. There were bodies in the back, but nothing that I could make much sense of. I heard Simon take a deep breath, holding it as he jumped onto the truck and carefully pulled a grenade belt off one of them. He grabbed another, taking three in all, before leaping back down to the ground.

"Might come in useful," he said as he strung the belts over his shoulder.

We continued in silence, and although I'm not a believer I mouthed a prayer as we passed that truck, the constant drip of blood from the tailgate like a ticking clock. I wasn't sure if that prayer was for the dead soldiers or for me, though.

The blacksuit had told us that the funeral parlor was off High Court Road and he hadn't been lying. We ran across the cracked tarmac of the main road, past the corpse of a berserker—a fat freak whose blubbery torso had been detonated over the street like so much pink and black custard—the shops flashing by one by one until we reached a building painted black. A. GOLDBURN AND SONS was written in faded bronze, the windows tinted so that we couldn't see inside.

We were much closer to the center now, and even though the buildings here were big the skyscrapers towered over them. I couldn't make out the one we were heading toward, but I could almost feel it, as if it was hiding behind the others waiting to pounce. I pictured the tunnel that burrowed beneath the streets, a wormhole that led into the heart of darkness, and wished that Zee had this job and I had his.

I couldn't see any way of getting around the back, and neither could Simon as with a strangled cry he charged at the front door, knocking it inward in a storm of splinters. We dashed inside, momentarily blinded by the gloom as we did our best to rest the broken door back on its hinges. There was an odd smell in here, a mix of chemicals and that unmistakable tang of death that hung in the back of my throat. It wasn't surprising, really, given what the place was used for. We stood by the door, not even breathing, listening for noise. But I knew it was empty. A year or two of breaking into houses had given me a knack for understanding stillness.

"Over here," said Simon once our eyes had sharpened. We

pushed past a heavily curtained door, through a pristine waiting room, and behind a mahogany counter. A set of stairs led down to the basement, and we stopped at the top of them, leaning against each other for support.

"Underground again," Simon said with a shudder. "Can you handle it?"

I nodded at him, trying to ignore the claustrophobia that pulled itself over my head like a lightless hood.

"One last time," I said, setting off down the stairs. "One last time."

TALKING TO THE DEAD

I'D BEEN IN A FUNERAL parlor once before, years ago when my gran died. But we'd never gone behind the scenes. Up top it's all thick carpet and patterned velvet and heavy quiet. Down below it was exactly the opposite, hard steel surfaces, white-tiled floors, and every step we made seemed to echo for far longer than it should have. More than anything else it reminded me of the surgery rooms beneath Furnace, which came as no shock, really, considering who owned this place.

"I still think he was full of crap," Simon said as we stepped into the basement. It was a big room, three massive steel tables taking up most of the space. Only one was occupied, the body covered with a pristine white sheet. "The blacksuit. I think he was just making up stuff; don't think any of it was true."

"I guess we'll find out soon enough," I replied, hearing my words murmured back at me from the bare walls. "Hurry up, this place is creeping the hell out of me."

We scurried across the room, heading for the only door. As we passed the corpse, though, I swore I saw the sheet move. I skidded to a halt, Simon speeding on ahead of me. I studied the sheet, now motionless again. Or was it? I took a step closer, convinced that the fabric was moving up and down, almost imperceptibly, as if whatever was underneath was breathing.

Fear held my chest in an iron grip but I couldn't stop myself. I reached out with my good hand, curling my fingers around the material. It felt cold and wet, and for an instant I wondered whether it had grabbed me, not the other way around.

Then I pulled.

The sheet was heavy, but it came away like silk, riding on the cool air and folding delicately over itself in soft, graceful loops until it met the floor. Underneath, the corpse lay still, not breathing at all. How could it be? Its chest was a basket of ribs, empty but for shadows. It was a boy's body, so emaciated it already resembled a skeleton. I looked at the skinny limbs, the scrawny neck, and by the time I reached the face I knew what I would see.

The corpse was me.

I barely recognized myself, the kid I'd been before the warden had started my procedure. I felt my legs grow weak, grabbed the table to stop myself falling.

"It can't be," I said, the words not quite finding their way out of my mouth. But the corpse heard them, because its eyes flicked open, pale and wet as they studied me.

And then its thin lips parted and it spoke in a voice that was also my own except a hundred times louder, so immense that I felt rather than heard it. It emerged like a shock wave, shattering the jars that lined the shelves, sending gleaming surgical tools flying, causing the ceiling to buckle, raining dust.

"Trying to hide from me is like trying to hide from yourself," it screamed, loud enough to crack the walls. "I know everything you know, because I live within you, I flow in your veins." The world shook, disintegrated, the floor falling away into a void of swirling smoke and raging fire. I felt like I'd been sucked up by a tornado. "You cannot hide from me, Alex, and you cannot hide from the truth. Once you have made your choice, there is no turning back."

And in a flash of madness I saw it again, the vision of the city, the tower rising above me, and *him*, the same creature standing triumphant on the roof—a hulking behemoth howling at his ruined kingdom, at his dismembered subjects.

"There is no turning back," my corpse told me.

I staggered away, vertigo making my head spin as the undertaker's basement suddenly snapped back into view—the walls in one piece, the glass jars resting where they had been when we arrived, and the steel tables empty. All of them. There were arms on me, Simon's, pulling me close to him as he tried to calm my thrashing limbs, the grenades clinking against each other.

I stopped, sliding down the wall onto my backside, my heart pumping so fast and so hard that it was almost one continuous beat. I swore under my breath, again and again, and each time it seemed to slow my pulse until it was drumming in time with my voice—still quick but not out of control.

"Wanna tell me what that was all about?" Simon asked, his face several shades paler than usual. "You just went mental."

I started to speak, realized I was talking gibberish, took a deep breath to compose myself, then started again.

"Furnace," I said. "I thought I saw . . ." I didn't bother continuing, the nightmare or hallucination or whatever it had been already disintegrating like a sculpture of sand in the top half of an hourglass. "He knows we're coming, I think."

"How?" Simon asked. "How can he possibly know that?"

I looked at my arm, flexing the weird strands of nectar that rose from the char-black flesh like sea plants hanging in the tide.

"It's the nectar," I said. "I don't know how; it's like he's part of me or something. Part of *us*. He knows what we're trying to do. He knows we're going to kill him." I paused, picturing the beast in my vision—a monstrosity that made even the biggest berserker look like a cuddly toy—perched on his tower, his throne, above a sea of fire. Was that really Furnace? If it was, if that's what was waiting for us, then we didn't stand a chance. "Going to *try* to kill him," I amended.

"You want to carry on?" Simon asked, holding out his hand. "It's not too late to turn back, we can still get out of the city."

I reached out and grabbed him, letting him help me to my feet. I cast a nervous glance at the table beside me, nothing on it but the distorted reflections in its polished surface. There wasn't even a sheet on the floor, and I wondered how Furnace could make his visions seem so real.

"It really isn't too late," Simon said. "We could be back out there and on the move in no time. If Zee keeps his side of the bargain then we don't even need to go to the tower."

I took another ragged breath then set off toward the door, the one that I hoped led to the tunnels. Simon was right: if Zee was successful then it didn't matter if our part of the plan was accomplished or not. But Furnace wasn't the only reason I needed to go there.

Maybe the tower was where we'd find answers, I thought to myself as I pushed open the door with my mutated arm, stepping through. More important, maybe it's where we'd find a cure.

BEYOND THE DOOR was a short corridor that led past an incinerator. It was smaller than the one in Furnace, but the sight of it—and the smell too, that unforgettable residue of ashes—didn't help the sickness churning in my guts. We walked past it, peeking inside a storeroom full of medical equipment, before reaching a large double door that barricaded the end of the hallway. Simon grabbed the handles and pulled, the heavy steel portals swinging open to reveal yet another staircase beyond, dropping into darkness.

There were switches on the walls but we didn't bother with the lights. Both Simon and I had warden-vision, our silver eyes dissecting the gloom as we traipsed downward, leaving the doors open behind us just in case we had to make a quick exit. The stairs cut back on themselves four times before we hit the bottom, the air cold and damp. We were in a long, straight corridor—just wide enough to wheel a stretcher through, I thought—and I was thankful that the walls were made of cinder block rather than stone. The lights were on, embedded in the ceiling and stretching off into the distance, so far that it reminded me of an upside-down runway.

"So they brought corpses down here?" Simon asked as we started walking again, his whispered words scouting the path ahead of us. "Sick bastards."

It made sense, I guess. If the tower was anything like the prison, if they really were doing experiments there as well, then they'd need somewhere to dispose of the bodies. A funeral parlor was perfect.

"You have any idea," Simon went on, "that they were doing this outside Furnace?" I shook my head, keeping my eyes peeled for the end of the tunnel that just wasn't coming. "What if the blacksuit was telling the truth?" Simon went on. "What if the prison was just part of it? What if there are places all over the country, all over the world, churning out rats and berserkers and blacksuits?"

"Then we're well and truly screwed," I replied.

Simon grunted, hoisting the grenade belts up over his shoulder.

There was a change of light up ahead, and as we drew near I saw that it was a junction. Our tunnel kept on going, another one branching off to the right. I stopped, closing my eyes and trying to get my bearings. It took a while to work out which way I was facing.

"That one should lead downtown," I said, pointing to the tunnel on the right.

"What about that one?" Simon asked.

"Probably goes to another one of their buildings," I guessed. "A gym or something."

"Or a suit shop," Simon said, breathing a laugh through his nose. "I bet they've got a few of them."

We turned right, trying to hear past the gentle tap of our feet to make out any sounds ahead. But there was a deathly silence down here, too deep to be marred by the deafening chaos on the streets over our heads. I wondered whether Furnace would have left a berserker for us, a trap or a test, especially as he knew we were coming. But there was no sign of life other than our own labored breathing.

We passed two more junctions, tunnels stretching off in all directions with no clue as to where they led. We carried on straight, imagining the city passing over our heads, doing our best to visualize where we were. I was pretty sure we were on course, though. The tunnel was sloping down, angling toward hell.

There was one final junction, just a single tunnel skewing off at a forty-five-degree angle to the main one, and less than two minutes after that we reached a door. It was unlocked, leading to a flight of concrete steps identical to the one beneath the funeral parlor.

"I don't like this," Simon said. "It's too quiet."

"Makes a nice change from Zee blabbing on nonstop, though, doesn't it?" I whispered back.

"That isn't what I meant," he said. "Well, here goes nothing, I guess." And his words brought back a memory, the day—or night—that we had tried to climb the steeple, back in Furnace. We'd only made it a fraction of the way before we hit a nest of rats and were forced to retrace our steps. And for some reason, right at that moment, I knew that if we both went up those stairs together then something similar would happen. I don't know how, call it instinct, or call it luck. Maybe just call it madness.

"Listen to me," I said to Simon. "I need you to keep going." He started to argue but I didn't let him. "If Zee doesn't make it then I need you to do his job. Use those grenades, find a way."

"Where are you going?" Simon barked back. "The pub?"

"No," I replied. I was about to explain but Simon got there first.

"He told you he was waiting for you, right?" he said. "In the underground station, when he spoke to you. He said he was waiting for you to make a choice."

I nodded, knowing that Simon had experienced the same vision back in Twofields.

"He told you that you could be his soldier, his right-hand man?" Again I nodded. He bit his lip, as if not sure he wanted to continue, but after a second or two he did. "Not me. I didn't hear that."

"What do you mean?" I asked, frowning.

"I mean Furnace didn't say he wanted me. He told me that it was too late for me, that I had no place in the future. He said that if I help you then I die." He paused for a moment before continuing. "Alex, he said that if I help you then sooner or later it will be *you* who kills me."

"Come on, Simon," I said. "You know that would never happen, not in a million years."

But we were both looking nervously at my arm, at that obsidian blade.

"He wants you here, Alex," Simon said. "That's all I'm saying. So be very, very careful. Tell me, where are you going?"

I leaned forward and gave Simon a hug, holding him tight for a second before letting him go. He didn't protest, just stood there, dumbfounded.

"I'm doing what Furnace wants me to," I said, heading back to the last junction. "I'm going in the front door."

THE TOWER

I LOOKED BACK ONCE, just before I turned into the angled tunnel. Simon was standing half in and half out of the door, the grenade belts hanging limply over his shoulder. I waved, but he didn't return it. He didn't do anything, just watched. I wondered whether he'd carry on or whether he'd just head back the way we'd come, back up through the undertaker's and onto the streets. I wouldn't blame him if he did.

The tunnel was a short one, but there was still plenty of time for the questions to build up. Why had I left Simon? Why the hell was I planning to give myself up at the front doors of the tower, ready to accept whatever Furnace and the warden threw at me?

Maybe Furnace was controlling my actions the same way he'd been controlling my visions. I mean, he could burrow right into the flesh of my thoughts, show me things that seemed real. Surely anyone with the power to do that could force someone to obey his will. But I doubted it. If that was the case then why hadn't he stopped us breaking out of Furnace? Why didn't he just make me kill my friends, and then kill myself?

No, what I was doing now was my choice, mine and nobody else's. And I guess that's why I wanted to be on my own. This way

I wasn't responsible for keeping anyone alive. It was just me and whatever crap destiny had to throw my way. I'd fight Furnace, I'd give everything I had. But when he killed me—and deep down I couldn't see any other conclusion—at least he wouldn't kill them too. It was a bleak way of thinking, but I don't know how else to explain it. What I wanted more than anything else was an end. One way or another, I wanted out.

The tunnel ended after a hundred meters or so at another double door. I tried the handle and it opened, swinging out toward a staircase. At the top was a small, cramped office basement, reams of photocopying paper stacked against moldering walls, furniture collecting dust in the corner. I pushed through the clutter, finding more stairs and heading up into an equally gloomy, equally abandoned corridor—more like somebody's house than an office. A short walk later and I was at the front door. I pressed the electronic lock and when I turned the handle it swung open.

The office was one of many on a small side street, facing a public square. I didn't know where I was, but a quick scan of the skyline made it painfully clear. There were skyscrapers in every direction in this part of the city, rising like tombstones. And *his* was the nearest. From down here it looked vast, puncturing the heavens with its black steeple. The walls were so dark that the glass resembled rock, the entire structure more like some ancient Stygian totem than a modern skyscraper.

Just like in my vision.

I stood on the curb for what seemed like forever, listening to the gunfire, so far away now that it could have been somebody popping bubble wrap. I wondered where Simon was, and it was that thought that shook me from my paralysis. I made my way down the street until I hit the nearest main road, a wide, tree-lined avenue that led right past the tower's front entrance.

There was no sign of life here, none at all, but I ran all the same, keeping to the shadowed side of the street. I only slowed when I reached the large, open plaza that surrounded the tower. A huge, hulking figure stood in the middle of the open space, in front of the doors, and it took me a moment to realize that it was a bronze statue.

Curiosity more than anything else made me approach. The sculpture was of a man, maybe in his forties or fifties, dressed in a suit and wearing glasses. He looked like an ordinary guy, a neatly trimmed mustache and beard, his hands clasped behind his back, if anything slightly weedy. There was no name, just a quote: FEAR SETS US FREE.

"Alfred Furnace," I said, my voice amplified against the quiet. The man looked nothing like the creature in my vision, but then again I looked nothing like the kid I'd once been. Nectar did that to you. I was tempted to tear the statue off its plinth and launch it over the street, but I didn't. The coast was clear, no guards or berserkers in sight, and there was nothing like the sound of rending metal to blow your cover. I settled for a threat, staring the man right in the eye and saying, "You can't have me."

The statue didn't reply and I walked away with an absurd sense of victory.

Ahead lay the doors of the tower, four of them lined up along the front of the building, all the size of a house. The one on the right was open. There were no blacksuits on guard duty, no berserkers tethered by the entrance ready to tear intruders to pieces, just that black portal that seemed to beckon me inside. I could feel eyes on me, though. I knew I was being watched by the way my skin crawled, the flesh of my back and arms creeping as though thick with insects. I shuddered as I walked up the small flight of steps that led to the doors, trying to keep the fear from my face.

Not that I could hide anything from Furnace. If he could see inside my head, then he knew that despite my calm exterior I was well and truly bricking it.

The doors seemed to get bigger as I got closer, and as I walked beneath the jutting bulk of the tower I could feel the immense weight of glass and concrete over my head. It cut out the sunlight and plunged the world into shadow. It was just like being underground again, the world on my shoulders, pinning me down.

And that wasn't the only thing that reminded me of Furnace Penitentiary. As I reached the doors—two massive bronze plates pulled back against the wall—I saw a plinth above them. At first I thought it said GUILTY, like the one over the entrance to the prison. But my mind was playing tricks on me. It said SAVED. I took a step back, staring at the other three plinths above the doors to my left.

"They—are—all—saved," I read aloud, the words reminding me of the desk in the warden's office, the pictures of the kids who had been torn apart and turned into freaks. "Saved, my ass," I muttered. I walked up to the door and even though it was open I couldn't really see what lay inside, as if by stepping over that threshold I was passing through a portal, entering another world. It was the nerves more than anything else that made me speak, my words muted by the sheer, overwhelming size of the building. "Come on, then, you sick freak. Let's do this."

I lifted my arm, fear forcing the nectar to churn, powering up like a jet engine, making my body sing. I flexed my fingers, the blades making a noise like scissors as they snapped open and closed. And those extra digits, the weird whips of nectar, danced back and forth as if they were excited.

They should be. What came next would be a battle to the death.

I didn't look back. I was too scared to. If I'd taken one last gaze at the sunlight, at the glorious day that sat at my back, then I might have lost my courage, I might have turned tail and bolted. I kept my head forward, my jaw clenched so tight it felt as though my teeth might snap, my arm held out like a sword, trembling as it sliced apart the shadows of the doorway, opening up the darkness as I stepped inside.

OUTSIDE THE TOWER the world had been deserted, as though somebody had turned it upside down and tipped everybody out.

Within the cool dusk of the interior it was a different story.

I heard the blacksuits before I saw them, that same deep, rolling laughter greeting me the moment I entered. My silver eyes burned, probing the shadows to make out a large, open lobby supported by pillars. Dead ahead was a reception desk, and behind it were three guards, all holding shotguns and all wearing the same red bands on their arms—those black Furnace logos against a white circle seemingly the brightest things in the room. These were Furnace's soldiers, not the warden's.

There were more figures to my left and right, standing by the pillars and aiming their weapons at me. I tensed, ready to fight, but they showed no sign of attacking. What had I expected? I was one of them, after all, as the blacksuit in the burger joint had told me.

"So," said one of the guards behind the desk. "You came."

"We knew you would," said another, their voices throbbing

around the lobby, reverberating off the marble floor and walls so much that they didn't sound real. The whole thing felt like a dream.

"We knew you'd choose this," said the first guard, and then they were all laughing again, that sound making the nectar inside me boil.

"I'm going to kill him," I shouted, but my own words carried no echo, falling dead at the blacksuits' feet and sounding strangely hollow. More laughter, then the first blacksuit lifted his gun, using it to point behind him.

"We know," he said. "He's up there, top floor. He's waiting for you. You won't be able to access the penthouse without an elevator key, so take it up to fifty and walk from there."

"Furnace?" I asked, wondering when the trap would be sprung, when the guards would start shooting. But they didn't even seem tense, leaning against the pillars or resting on the reception desk as if this was their day off. "You know they'll be coming for you," I spat, fear growing into anger. "The army. They know you guys are behind this now."

The blacksuit shrugged then shook his gun, gesturing toward the bank of elevators that sat behind the desk.

"He's waiting," he repeated. "Penthouse."

I began to walk, if only to get away from this burgeoning nightmare. I gave the desk a wide berth, still wary of the blacksuits, their eyes glinting. I felt like an antelope tiptoeing through a pride of lions, knowing that at any minute it will feel teeth in its throat. But still the attack didn't come.

There were six elevators here, three on either side of the lobby. And on the wall between them was another bronze sculpture—not a statue, this time, but a two-dimensional image fixed to the marble. It showed an army of marching blacksuits, all wearing armbands, row after row stretching back into a gleaming city. The lead soldier held a flag, that same emblem of three circles joined by lines, and his face was filled with such pride that once again I felt a spark of excitement burrow up from inside me.

I tore my eyes away from the sculpture, taking one look over my shoulder to see the blacksuits—the real ones—standing by the desk, all watching me. *They know,* I thought, seeing the recognition in their faces. *They know how I feel.*

I ran, almost stumbled, to the only elevator that was open, hitting the button to close the doors. But they didn't close quickly enough to mute the sweeping thunder of laughter that chased me, or the final words from a blacksuit that squeezed in just before they met. Words spoken sincerely. Words that I couldn't quite believe.

"Good luck, Alex."

THE PETRIFIED
ORCHARD

THERE WERE BUTTONS beside the door, brass circles labeled SB
at the bottom to P at the top with the floor numbers in between.
P must have stood for Penthouse, and there was a keyhole next to
it. I almost had my finger on 50 when I thought better of it, pressing 45 instead. I didn't honestly know what was waiting for me up
there. Maybe if I got out early I'd have a better idea of what lay
inside the tower, maybe I'd stand a better chance of taking Furnace by surprise.

I sensed a shape behind me, spinning around to see my reflection staring back from the elevator's mirrored wall.

My stomach lurched as the elevator began its journey, produc-
ing nothing more than a gentle hum as it soared up the backbone
of the tower. While it moved I studied myself, feeling the bile rise
once again as I tried to make sense of what was happening to me.
My right arm was as big as a leg, knotted with muscle and studded
with veins. It was still coated with nectar, shining black like a
beetle caught in the moonlight. When I swung it from side to side
it moved with undeniable power, my hand cutting the air with a
swish, making the elevator rock.

The infection had spread more than I'd let myself believe. My neck was now a mess of bruises and blisters, the skin pushed out into gross folds, reminding me of the fungus you sometimes see growing on tree trunks. The right side of my face was puffed up almost beyond recognition. Almost. Somewhere there, past the swelling, past the scars, past the silver, I could see myself, the boy I'd once been. But there was almost nothing of him left, outside or in.

There was a dial above the elevator doors and I glanced at its reflection, noticing that we were about halfway up and rising fast. I lifted my hoodie—the material so torn and burned that it almost crumbled away at my touch—and looked at what lay beneath. There was none of my own skin left over my stomach and chest, just a lumpy mass of blistered hide that looked as if it had been charbroiled. I tapped it with my good hand. It felt like kevlar.

I was gripped by panic, wanted more than anything else to tear off this impostor's skin, to flay the flesh from my bones just so I wouldn't have to feel its filthy touch. But I closed my eyes, gripped the handrail and tried to breathe—in, out; in, out—as deeply as I could, until the moment passed. I felt the elevator slow, a soft chime announcing that we'd reached the forty-fifth floor. I waited until I heard the doors part before opening my eyes and turning around, my heart thrumming in my throat as I gave up the safety of the elevator for the unknown tower beyond.

I found myself in a corridor, dimly lit and carpeted. It could have been any office block in any city except for the scars that covered the white walls, craters and canyons gouged into the plasterwork, and at one point a hole punched clean through. The floor was stained with black footprints. No two were exactly alike, and none were human.

I turned left, heading toward the hole in the wall. Sunlight peeked through it, pooling on the carpet in the corner almost ner-vously. Dust hung in the golden trail, specks of light that reminded me of the swirling galaxies in nectar—the warden's nectar, that was, the old nectar, nectar that felt familiar now, almost safe. I ran a hand through it, causing the particles to scatter. Then I put my face to the hole and peered through.

Cages. A huge room full of them. All empty.

I stood up, walking a little farther down to a door. It was solid steel, at least a foot thick, and hung off its hinges, reminding me of the vault door back in the bowels of Furnace. The metal was scratched and dented just like that one had been, and for the same reason too.

I replayed the events in my head: the cages being opened, the rats or berserkers or whatever the hell had been locked in here stampeding out, smashing through the door as though it was paper, storming down the hallways, down the stairs and out onto the streets beyond. How many of them? A hundred? A thousand? They'd been here all this time, waiting for Furnace's command, waiting for the war to begin.

No wonder the city had fallen so hard and so fast.

I paced the rest of the corridor, a dozen more rooms like this one, all empty. Eventually I found the door to the stairs, also ripped from its frame. Inside the stairwell there were bodies—rats, two of them, their necks stretched like they were plasticine figures, silver eyes open in a snapshot of their final moments. I guessed they'd toppled in the chaos, crushed beneath a thousand pounding feet. Even though they must have been dead for hours, I could still see the heat rising from them, turning the air to a dream-like haze that shimmered upward, pointing the way.

I leaped up the steps, swinging around the corner then doubling back on myself again until I reached the next level. A quick glance through the door told me all I needed to know—more rooms, more cages—and it was the same on 47, the mess up here even worse. I made my way up to the next floor, expecting to see the same thing, but when I pushed my way into the corridor I knew I shouldn't have let my guard down.

There was a wheezer standing there, less than three meters away. Only somehow it was different from the ones I'd seen in the prison. Its head was bald, its skin the color and texture of old porridge, the eyes like black pockmarks buried deep in the flesh of its face. But its gas mask wasn't sewn in place, the contraption shining like it was brand-new. Its clothes too showed no sign of age, as if it had been dressed only that morning. It wore the same armband as the blacksuits, the red and black insignia over its leather overcoat making the creep look like a Nazi Gestapo officer.

I noticed all this in less than a second, then terror took over. I might have been bigger than the wheezers now, stronger, but they still scared the living crap out of me. Just looking at the freak brought back the pain of surgery, the way they'd patched my body together while stripping my mind apart. I fell back through the doors and almost lost my balance at the top of the stairs before noticing that the wheezer was retreating too, staggering away down the corridor so fast that it was in danger of tripping over its own feet.

It's scared, I realized, the thought giving me a thrill of sadistic pleasure. *It's scared of me.*

I chased it, more from curiosity than anything else. I'd never seen a wheezer show any kind of emotion—except panic, the time that Zee and Simon and I had killed one in the infirmary. It flapped against the wall, taking those great big unsteady bird steps, its piggy eyes blinking, or trying to, anyway—its eyelids were like those of a burn victim, too shriveled to cover the bugling black pupils beneath.

It reached the first door and fell through it. Literally fell, crashing onto its back so hard that its booted feet bounced up. I laughed, I couldn't help it, the noise fueled not by humor but by disbelief and anger and the sickly sweet thought of revenge. I ran through the door, ready to put the monster out of its misery. And I was so intent on murder that I didn't notice the other figures until it was almost too late.

The door opened into a huge room, bigger than the infirmary back in Furnace although decked out in a similar way, lined with beds. The windows here had been tinted so heavily that barely any natural light found its way in. Red lamps swung from the ceiling, and in their hellish glow the room seemed to squirm and thrash and writhe.

Wheezers. Dozens of them.

The creature at my feet scrabbled away on its back, pushing itself into the folds of its brothers who lifted it up and cradled it. They all looked at me with those fearful insect eyes, the wheeze of their collective breathing almost deafening, a couple even uttering those gargled, screeching cries that I had come to fear so much in Furnace. What was worse, though, was the relentless flap of their eyes as they blinked at me, a noise so constant and so wet that it was like liquid. I backed out of the room, the confusion almost too much, making the tower spin around me, making the floor and the ceiling seem to switch places.

It didn't make any sense. None of it made any sense.

I retreated back to the stairs while I still could, but not before noticing the other doors that lined the corridor, red light splashing out from inside and the same awful, endless chorus of wheezes. I ran, climbing the steps as fast as I could, skipping the next level, and the next, only stopping when I saw PENTHOUSE stenciled by the door. I crashed against it, sucking in air that seemed to contain no oxygen, only the cold, dead exhalations of the wheezers.

What next? My mind screamed at me. *What next?*

I had no answers, and my frustration cycloned inside me, becoming anger, then rage, then a pure white fury that drove me through those doors and into the arms of Alfred Furnace.

I DON'T KNOW WHAT I'd been expecting to find up here, on the top floor of Furnace's tower, but it wasn't this.

There were no corridors, no warren of rooms and hallways packed with cages and wheezers. There was just one immense space covering almost the entire width and breadth of the building, the stairway and elevator shaft right in the middle of it. A bare oak floor stretched in every direction to walls of red glass that towered all the way to the ceiling ten meters or so overhead. Sunshine poured through those windows, turned into a bloodlight so thick and so rich it made me feel as if I could drown up here.

The tinted glass drenched the space in shadows, but I could make out shapes silhouetted against all four walls, dotted seemingly at random around the room. It took me a while to realize that they were trees, maybe fourteen or fifteen of them. I held my breath, listening for any sign of life, but other than my own racing heartbeat, there was silence.

I took a step forward, heading for the nearest tree, my arm held out in front of me, ready to strike at the first thing that moved. But those dark shapes remained motionless, as calm as if they had been carved in stone.

And that's exactly what they were, I realized when I was close enough to touch them, an orchard of rock. There was nothing else up here—at least nothing I could make out in the sulking red gloom—no furniture, no equipment, the floor dominated solely by these bizarre decorations.

I moved to the next tree, its gnarled and twisted trunk reminding me of the bodies of the berserkers. There were no leaves on these sculptures, just barren limbs raised like a forest of skinny arms, knotted with each other into a web of sinew and bone that almost completely covered the ceiling. I reached out and touched it, the rock as warm as human skin and pulsing almost as if it had a heartbeat. I knew it was my imagination, but it still creeped me out.

Not half as much, however, as what I saw next.

I crossed the room diagonally, reaching the next tree. I almost dismissed it, thinking it was the same as the others, until I caught sight of what was nailed to the trunk.

It was a body, a man's, stripped naked, his modesty preserved by an apron of coiled guts that spilled from his stomach. The bark of the tree was scarred and blackened, as if it had been on fire. And the man too seemed as though he had been burned. Yet his face was strangely serene, gazing out over the penthouse with the look of a loving father watching a sleeping child. I studied the figure. On closer examination I saw that he was much younger than I'd first thought, not much more than a kid, little older than me. But I'd seen that face before, an older version of it, on the bronze statue outside the tower. I knew who this person was.

Alfred Furnace.

"What are you?" I mouthed silently. The sculpture had been

carved with such painstaking detail that it was impossible to believe it was just stone. I expected the face to swivel down toward me, the mouth to open. And I wanted it to. Because maybe that's where the truth would be. Maybe that's where I'd find my cure. I don't know if I honestly believed that. I guess I did. Desperate men will believe anything.

And I was right. There were answers here. Just not in the way I'd been expecting.

"That was a long time ago."

The voice hadn't come from the sculpture, but from the blood-drenched shadows to my right. The shock was so great that I actually collapsed, dropping like a brick onto my backside. I reached out with my good hand, grabbing the tree, using it to pull myself to my feet.

A shape on the far side of the room, one that had been hidden by another tree, was moving. I peered into the gloom, trying to make sense of what I was seeing, but the light was too thick, too heavy.

"A long, long time ago," the voice went on, a familiar dry whisper that carried far more power than it had any right to. It was followed by a noise that was half growl, half purr. The shape seemed to curl upward, long, jagged limbs sprouting from it.

It was the creature from my vision, I knew it. The beast that howled from the tower. It was *him*.

"Furnace," I said, my voice unsteady but fierce. This was it, I thought, feeling the nectar begin to cloud my thoughts, knowing that this time I'd have to give myself over to it and damn the consequences.

There was a dull hiss of laughter, then two claps, and with a loud snap and an electrical whine the lights flickered on. I shielded my eyes from the glare, giving them a second to adjust before squinting at the scene ahead. The first thing I noticed was that the creature there was nothing like the one in my vision.

It was a berserker, bigger than any I'd ever seen. It stood three, maybe four meters tall, its body almost the same color as steel, ridged and rutted like something that had been put through a shredder and then stitched back together. An enormous hand rested on the tree beside it, bird-like talons embedded in the solid stone. Its head was too big for its bladed shoulders, so heavy that the creature didn't seem able to hold it upright. And the face that sat in the middle of that oversize knuckle of broken bone was a young child's, nectar streaming from its lips and splashing on the floor. Whatever this thing was, it wasn't Furnace.

And neither was the man who stood in front of it, whose eyes were unfathomable pits that seemed to suck the light from around him, pulling everything into the black hole of his heart. It wasn't Furnace at all.

It was the warden.

NEW BREED

"YOU," I SPAT, fury flaring at the fact that it was the warden who stood before me and not his master.

I scanned the room, looking for Alfred Furnace, but aside from the berserker the warden was the only living thing here. He was wearing the same pristine suit as always, his shoes polished, his hair immaculately brushed. His face was still crinkled leather pulled tight over the angular skull beneath, like a skeleton wearing a Halloween mask. And when I tried to look him in the eye I found that I couldn't.

"Where is he?" I demanded, although the huge space seemed to swallow my voice. "Where's Furnace?"

The warden's thin, wet lips pulled back over the tombstone teeth beneath and he uttered a sadistic hiss of laughter. The noise slithered into my ears, burrowing into my thoughts, and all of a sudden I found myself back inside the prison, back inside Furnace Penitentiary. The memories hit me like a punch to the gut—the first time I had seen the warden, that same shark's smile as he told us that to disobey his rules would make our lives a living hell; glaring down at us through the screen above the elevator, a constant threat of pain and punishment; his demonic face grinning as he watched the wheezers drag Donovan away.

And down in the tunnels beneath the cells, when he had tried to turn me into a blacksuit—the way he had almost become my new father, a patriarch of immense power and strength who had promised me the world.

I shook my head to try to clear the memories, feeling the room spin. I had fought the warden and I had defeated him. He was nothing, just an empty shell of what he had been in the prison, right? I hadn't expected to face him again, not really. And I'd figured that even if our paths crossed, then I'd crush him the same way I had before. But now that he stood before me, radiating that same undeniable aura of cold cruelty, his eyes black pools of hatred that swirled like vortexes in his head, I wasn't so sure. This was a man whose ability to butcher was as natural and as effortless as his ability to breathe.

And the worst thing was he could sense my growing panic.

He laughed, taking a step forward. The berserker started to follow him but jarred to a halt. I noticed that its hands and feet were bound with massive manacles. It let loose another guttural snarl that tailed up at the end into a whine, like a leashed dog calling for its owner. But its childlike face was staring down at those bonds with a heartbreakingly human expression of sadness and confusion.

"You will never meet Furnace," the warden answered, advancing at a leisurely prowl. "Why would a man as great as he deign to meet a cowardly, half-turned failure like you? He is nowhere near this place, he hasn't been for many years. No, he led you here for one reason, so that I could end your miserable life once and for all."

I felt my heart drum, the nectar powering up inside me. The warden glanced at the stone tree I was trying not to cower against, and for a second the expression on his face morphed from anger to awe.

"Did you recognize him, the boy in the carving?" the warden said, nodding at the sculpture by my side. "That was where it all began, so many years ago. A boy left to die in an orchard. A boy who didn't die. A boy who became a man called Alfred Furnace."

"Tell me where he is," I said, the nectar turning my words into the low, dangerous rumble of an approaching storm. The warden stopped walking, holding his ground midway between me and the berserker. I couldn't read his expression but there was emotion there, visible in the way he ground his teeth, in the way his tendons stretched like wire beneath the skin of his neck.

"I was just a boy too, when Dr. Furnace saved me," the warden went on. "When he pulled me from the mud and the blood of battle. But he saw something in me. He saw greatness. That is why he made me his general. Everything that we have done we have done together. I needed him, yes, but he needed me too. He still needs me. He will *always* need me."

The warden was spitting now. That mask of flesh was slipping, and I could see the rage beneath, red hot and lethal. He stretched out a long, bony finger, jabbing it toward me.

"We were going to declare this war together. I was going to be his right-hand man, we were going to trample this world as one. We were going to be gods."

"So what changed?" I said.

The warden took another jarring step forward, his anger growing by the second.

"You! You ruined it!" he almost screamed, that finger still

aimed at my heart, not quite close enough to grab. "I offered you salvation, but you decided to stab me in the back in a pathetic attempt at freedom. Now he thinks I'm a failure. You know what he told me? That a man who can't keep his house in order doesn't deserve a roof over his head. *A man who can't keep his house in order?* I watched over that prison for years. I designed that place, I had it built. It was *my* project. Without it, Furnace wouldn't even have his army."

"That's not what I heard," I replied, remembering what the black-suit had told us. "I heard you got stuck down there with the rest of us because he knew you were useless. I heard he gave you the prison because he wanted to get rid of you. Up here, that's where the real army was made. Down in Furnace," I looked at myself, my lopsided body, "you couldn't even make me a blacksuit. You couldn't even do that right."

The warden's jaw dropped, flecks of white foam resting on his lips. The darkness around his eyes seemed to dissipate for a moment, draining away like dirty bathwater, and those two weak, blue eyes just blinked at me, utterly flabbergasted. I don't know how old the warden was, how many years the nectar had kept him alive, but right then he looked like a child, like the boy pulled from the dirt.

"How dare you," he said eventually. His voice was quiet now, little more than a tremor. "You have no idea who I am, and what I can do."

"I know exactly who you are," I replied, as calmly as I was able. "You're a boy who made the mistake of thinking he was a man, a bully stupid enough to believe he was in charge, a coward whose army has deserted him. You're nothing, Cross. You're nobody. Alfred Furnace isn't here to help you; he's forgotten all about you."

I lifted my arm, the blade of my fingers pointing right at him. "And you're going to die, right now."

I lashed out, punching the tree beside me with as much power as I was able. My fingers pierced the stone with a crack that made my ears ring, the trunk exploding into dust and debris. With a groan the upper half toppled to the floor, heavy enough to blast a crater. The warden must have seen the nectar at work inside me, the murder in my eyes, because he staggered back, groping for the chains that held the berserker.

I didn't care. The nectar was singing now, its power coursing through me, undeniable. Let the warden unleash his pet. I'd killed berserkers before. I would deal with this one, then I'd turn my wrath on him.

But the warden didn't unfasten the creature's chains. Instead he pulled a knife from his suit jacket, a cruel, curved blade that glinted in the crimson light from the window.

"You were bitten, weren't you?" he said as he toyed with the knife, twisting it between his fingers. "That's why you're changing. One of the new breed got you."

"New breed?" I said. I felt the rush of nectar inside me begin to ebb, numbed by confusion. The warden smiled at me, his eyes once again shrouded, unreadable.

"Oh, you think you know so much, but you're lost just like the rest of them. You're right, Furnace was building an army outside the prison. Here, and elsewhere too. He was working on a new nectar, an improved design." I thought of the nectar I'd seen since escaping, the bloodred galaxies that spiraled within it and the way it could turn a human into a rat—or worse—in a matter of minutes. "He was using it to create the next generation of soldiers."

He tapped the knife against the arm of the berserker, its elbow at the same level as the warden's head. It made a *clink, clink* sound, like he had knocked the blade against a suit of armor.

"They are bigger, and stronger, than the ones we already had. But that's not what makes them special. What sets this generation apart is the fact that they spawn their own children. The new nectar, all it needs is to find its way inside a host and it will begin to work. No surgery, no endless hours of brainwashing, just a small bite and the army grows. You were bitten, Sawyer. But you weren't chosen."

"Chosen?" I repeated, feeling like an idiot but desperate to make any sense of the truth.

"The berserker only started your transition, it only set the ball rolling. It didn't fill you with nectar the way they are supposed to, otherwise you would already be one of them. No, it didn't choose you, and I wonder why."

I remembered the berserker that had feasted on the inmate, back in the underground, nectar gushing into the boy's wound, filling him with poison. It had bitten me too, but it hadn't injected me with its filth, only a mouthful of tainted saliva. Yet I'd drunk a whole load of nectar afterward, hadn't I, from the dead, beetle-black berserker?

"First generation," the warden explained, plucking my thoughts out of thin air. "Those berserkers were the last of the old guard, already redundant. Their veins beat with the original nectar, the same that flows in yours. Mere water compared with Dr. Furnace's new miracle." He stared up at the creature beside him, his face full of awe. "Everybody who is chosen joins the ranks of the new breed, a generation of soldiers that will grow and grow and grow until all are either members or lost."

"A plague," I said, remembering Zee's word. The warden cocked his head as if in thought.

"An interesting concept," he said, "but quite wrong. This isn't disease. It's evolution."

"The authorities will contain it," I spat back, feeling the grip of the nectar loosen even more, pried away by uncertainty. "It won't spread past the city."

The warden's grin twisted even more tightly toward the edges of his face.

"City? What city?" he said. "You only have to look out of the window to see how far the devastation has spread, and in a matter of hours. The world is crumbling, Sawyer. Nobody but us can put the pieces back together. And when we do there will be one Fatherland, and nothing but strength. And I will stand there as his right-hand man. Nobody else. You hear me? *Nobody else.*"

In a flash of pure understanding I realized why the warden was afraid. He had made a mistake, he had angered Alfred Furnace by allowing the prison break. Now he was in danger of losing his role as a god of the new world, he was in danger of being replaced at his master's right hand.

And with that knowledge came another revelation, one infinitely terrifying:

The warden believed he was in danger of being replaced *by me*.

It was insane, so much so that I spat out a startled grunt of laughter, but it was true. How could it not be? That's why I had been guided to the tower by Furnace's visions, why the blacksuits below hadn't stopped me, why the warden was facing me almost entirely alone, stripped of his army and his dogs. Because this was his only chance to prove that he could get his house back in order,

to show Furnace that he could be trusted. He had to kill me or
lose everything.

This knowledge drove me toward him, but the warden held the
knife out defensively. I stopped. I don't know why—instinct, I
suppose. I'd been in prison for so long that the sight of a shank was
enough to send me running. It was a survival mechanism, hard-
wired into me. Maybe if I hadn't flinched, maybe if I'd thrown
myself on him, things would have worked out differently. That's
the thing about life, I guess. You never know.

"The new nectar, it's clever," the warden said, reaching down
and popping the clasp of the manacles that held the berserker's
left claw. The chains fell to the floor and the creature bellowed
with relief. It lashed out with its free hand, catching the nearest
tree and sending a stone branch flying. The missile struck a window, cracking the thick glass and letting in a shard of brilliant
golden light. This far above street level the wind was fierce, and
the room was suddenly alive with its howl, as if there was an army
of demons outside tearing the world to pieces.

I guess that wasn't too far from the truth.

"Those red flecks add almost what you'd call intelligence," the
warden went on. "The nectar is not . . . alive, not in the sense that
you and I are. But it is aware. It senses everything it needs to know
about the host; it uses every resource available to it to ease the
transformation. It really is quite remarkable."

I took another step toward the warden but the berserker moved
between us, those childlike eyes never leaving mine. It flexed its
claws into fists, barbed talons glinting. The warden had walked
to the other side of it, releasing the final manacle. I waited for
the creature to charge but it stood there obediently, waiting for the
order.

An order that never came.

"If you are human then the new nectar will change you." The warden held up the knife, appeared to be studying his reflection in the polished steel. "You become feral, intent on nothing but destruction. But when you've already got the old nectar inside you. That's when it gets really interesting." He peered over the blade at me. "Take you, for instance. You had old nectar in your system from the prison, and you're changing. Slowly, yes, but inevitably. But your transformation was in its infancy. The bite you received, it carried a trace of new nectar into your system, like the vanguard of an invading force. It began to prepare your cells, to change you. With more of the new nectar the change would have been faster, and much more . . ." He paused, his eyes seeming to glaze over as if imagining something wondrous. "Much more *dramatic*. Yes, adding new nectar to the old is where the true power of Furnace's creation becomes apparent. And I can tell you this for a fact, Sawyer. There is nobody in the world, Dr. Furnace excluded, who has devoured more of the original nectar than me. I have consumed it since I was a boy."

"But you're—" I started.

"Still human?" he interrupted, his grin stretching even wider. "That is because I was weaned onto it in childhood. Dr. Furnace raised me like a son, not as one of his soldiers, one of his pets. I never had the surgery. I never needed it. The surgery is only a necessity when the transformation is required quickly. But with me, my adoptive father had years, decades. I may look human, but I am not." I thought about all the times I'd tried to look the warden in the eyes, and all the times my gaze had been pushed away. What he was saying didn't make any sense, but I knew it was true. "Nothing but nectar runs through me now—the original nectar—and it has been waiting for this day. All it needs is a dose of Dr. Furnace's new weapon."

The warden reached up, grabbing the berserker's chin and pulling its head toward him. It looked almost like a lover's embrace, as if the warden was about to kiss it. Instead, he guided the beast's drooling mouth toward his own neck.

With a shock, I realized what he was going to do, and what would happen when he did. This time the rush of nectar flooded my mind as if the very walls of my sanity had been breached, the poison driven there by my pounding heart, and the knowledge that I was in way over my head.

"Do it," he whispered, and I watched in horror as the creature opened its mouth and sank its blunt teeth into the flesh of the warden's throat. The man flinched, panicking for the briefest moment before the nectar flooded into the wound, and then he was laughing, howling as he held the berserker's head in place. Seconds later he pushed it away, the creature's jaws slipping free with the sucking grunt of a kitchen plunger.

"I am ready to take my place in the new kingdom," the warden shouted, speaking not to me but to the room. Bubbles of nectar popped from his lips with each word.

He clamped a hand to the wound, the skin already hardening there. Then he stabbed the knife into the side of the berserker— right in the fleshy socket of its armpit, ruby-flecked nectar cascading onto the floor. The berserker raised its head and bayed at the ceiling, but it didn't move, it didn't try to escape. It stood there as patiently as a mother feeding her cubs, the warden's face buried beneath its arm as he furiously gulped down the poison.

He was right. Nobody in the world had consumed more of

Furnace's poison than him. The new nectar would hit him hard, like an evolutionary sledgehammer, and his body was ready for it.

I charged toward him, knowing I had to get him away from the berserker before he began to change. But when he tore his face away from the wound, his mouth hanging open too wide and black veins bulging beneath his skin, I knew there was nothing I could do to stop him.

It was already too late.

VENDETTA

I THREW MYSELF at the warden, knowing that if I was quick then I could kill him while he was still changing, before he reached his full strength. The blade of my hand glinted in the crimson light as though it was already covered with blood, the strands of nectar flattened against my skin as I prepared to thrust the living weapon into the warden's chest.

The berserker was too quick. It saw me coming, using one hand to shove the warden out of the way and the other to grab my arm. It may have been half drained of the poison that fueled it, but it was still freakishly strong, gripping me so hard I thought my bones were going to snap. It studied me with those childlike eyes, cocking its head the way a five-year-old might before crushing a bug. Then it swung its body around, ripping me off the floor and sending me rolling across the room.

I dug my blade into the floor, grinding to a halt in time to see the berserker bounding toward me. I launched myself at the oncoming freak, meeting it head-on. Something cracked, although I wasn't sure if it was inside it or me. Its momentum was greater, and it shunted me back, crushing me against the wall of the elevator. One fist wrapped itself around my throat, the other firing at my head. I only just managed to weave out of the way, the hooked claw plowing right through plaster and concrete and denting the metal casing of the elevator beyond.

I lashed out with my mutated arm, aiming for the wound in its side. It saw what I was doing, letting go of me and batting my arm away hard enough to send me skittering over the floor into one of the trees. No sooner had I recovered my balance than it was on me again, spirals of black saliva trailing from its open mouth as it cannoned in for the kill.

The nectar inside me reacted, its cold intelligence steering my hands to the tree beside me and snapping off one of the man-sized branches. I don't know how much that slab of stone weighed and yet I swung it as easily as if it had been made of polystyrene, aiming at the berserker. The stone bat slammed into the creature's face, exploding into rubble and sending it somersaulting back the way it had come, flipping end over end half a dozen times before rolling to a halt.

It groaned feebly, gripping its head with one bony hand, its other arm broken and limp beneath it. It attempted to get up, its body wracked with tremors, but it never got the chance. In a heartbeat I was across the room, and with a cry of rage I thrust my mutated hand into the hole in its side.

It slid in like a knife through cooked chicken, buried to my elbow. I could feel the nectar at work in there, beating against my fingers as it rushed to patch up the berserker's ruptured organs, the torn muscle. Then those strands of flesh on my wrist began to spin, ever faster, turning like the blades inside a blender, until all that was left inside that creature's chest was soup.

Behind me, something began to clap. Big, heavy slaps that sounded more like pistol shots.

I didn't want to turn around. I didn't want to see what was waiting for me there. But I didn't have a choice. I got to my feet, shaking snaking ribbons of entrails from my arm, and turned to face the warden.

I don't really know what I'd been expecting. I thought he might have grown, his flesh ballooning out grotesquely like a berserker's, unrecognizable. But he didn't seem to have changed much at all.

Or had he? I was finding it difficult to focus on him, as though his body was surrounded by a dense cloud of fog. No, it was more as if light couldn't grip him properly, like it just slipped off, leaving a distorted, shifting mosaic of darkness, almost as if I was viewing him through patterned glass. I squinted, seeing the same suit, the same face, only they were different. His limbs seemed too long, his body strangely distended, like an evening shadow. My sense of perspective was shot—it was impossible to tell whether he was the same size and close, or much taller and farther away.

Pain fireballed in the middle of my head, white noise that could have been the warden's laughter. And suddenly he *was* right there in front of me, towering over me, his entire body flickering like he was being projected into the air. I could see the nectar pulsing beneath his skin, so much of it in his veins that it seemed as if he was crawling with flies, his entire body alive with them.

I thrust my bladed hand toward the warden's chest but his body seemed to blink out of the way. He was still laughing, that endless hiss. From his pocket of shimmering shadow I made out two eyes, black pennies that bored into me with such malevolent glee that it took my breath away.

"I pity you, boy," the warden said, each syllable a hammer blow. "You could have stood with us, helped usher in the Fatherland." Once again his shifting form seemed to balloon into the space before my eyes, and once again my clumsy strike swept through thin air. A knife-edge of fear cut through the nectar, carried on the warden's words. "But now, after everything, you *will* die."

I didn't see him move, and yet something crunched into my ribs and the world came apart. I soared, splintering a canopy of stone branches before hitting the wall of the elevator hard enough to crack it. I picked myself up from the floor, shaking off the plaster dust and preparing to retaliate. But the warden had vanished.

"Do you see?" His voice seemed to come from thin air, impossible to pinpoint. "Do you see now that I can keep my house in order?"

I swung around, my breath stuck in my throat, my heart pounding so hard it seemed as though the entire room was reverberating with its pulse. I couldn't see the warden anywhere.

"Do you see?" he repeated. I looked frantically to my side, trying to make sense of the shadows behind the trees. Had that been him? That shimmer of darkness?

"Do you see?" and this time the words were a whisper fed right into my ear. I turned too late, saw his grinning face so close it was almost pressed against my own, his breath a putrid cloth held over my mouth. Before I could react he had struck me again, blasting me across the room as though I'd been fired from a cannon. I rolled headfirst through another stone tree, leaving a trail of dust and debris, and this time, even through the roar of the nectar, there was pain.

I struggled up, spinning wildly, hoping my blade would catch him. But once again he seemed to have spirited into nothing. I willed the nectar to keep me strong, yet it seemed to be waning, as if even it was afraid of what the warden had become. I growled, more from fear than from anger, then started to run—if I could get to the stairs, then at least he'd have nowhere to hide.

"I don't think so." The warden flashed up before me, his sick smile seeming to hang like the yellow crescent of the moon. I felt a hand around my neck, lifting me off the floor, carrying me backward. I flailed against it but with no air in my lungs my strikes were pathetic, those of a child. "There is no running," the warden went on, spitting the words at me. His strides grew faster and faster, my body swinging from his fist like a rag doll. "Not anymore. Not for you."

I sensed the window behind me, instinct forcing me to tuck my head against my chest as best I could with the warden's hand there. He punched me right through it, glass detonating against my back, and suddenly I was suspended fifty-one stories above the ground, only his grip keeping me from spilling to the distant streets. Even though the wind howled in my ears I could still hear his laughter, relentless, unending. I tried to reach the wall with my feet but there was nothing to grip, tried to snatch in a breath but my windpipe was crushed. My brain fired off black sparks that scarred my vision, my whole body screaming.

The warden's face was framed in the broken glass of the window, still human and yet somehow not. His mouth was too large, his eyes too big, and the leathery flesh of his face seemed to be drooping, as if he was finally shedding the mask he had worn for so long. I saw my hands—the one that was my own and the obsidian blade, slapping powerlessly at the arm that held me. The warden just stared at me, wearing his nightmare smile, the one that had terrified me so much back in the prison, only now a million times worse.

I wondered how I ever thought I could have beaten him.

But you can beat him. The words cut through the wind, cut through the dry hiss of the warden's chuckles, so clear that I thought it had come from me. *You must.*

The warden's fingers squeezed ever tighter, compressing my throat. The vision in one of my eyes flickered like a broken television before snapping off completely. There was a ringing sound, like a machine whose gears have been jammed, so loud that it seemed to be coming from everywhere around me. Only I knew it was inside my head. It was the sound of me dying.

"To think, you actually believed you were stronger than me," the warden said. "But you're just a boy. You were always just a boy."

You're more than that, came the voice. My voice? One last-ditch attempt by my brain to keep me alive? *Look at you. Look at what you have become. At what you are still becoming. You are much more than the child you once were.*

The hallucination I'd seen in the funeral parlor flashed before my eyes, my body the way it had been before the wheezers took their knives to me—weak, pathetic. I *was* more than that, so much more.

"Any last words?" the warden asked. "Dr. Furnace is watching, you know. He's listening. Do you have anything to say for yourself?"

Even if there had been words, there was no air to fuel them. And yet somewhere inside my mind that voice spoke again.

Tell him, it said, a whisper as loud as a bomb. *Tell him his time is over.*

I opened my mouth, spitting blood onto the warden's sleeve, my lungs on fire. I stopped trying to fight him, letting my arms hang loosely by my sides. His grin seemed to widen even further, as though it had stretched right off the edges of his face.

"You . . ." I mouthed, the words carrying no sound. The warden cocked his head and I felt his grip relaxing, allowing a sliver of air into my lungs to fuel my final words—the warden's one last gift to me. "Your time . . ." I hissed, a lurching wheeze as I fought to finish, "is over."

His lips tightened, locking the lunatic smile away, but still those eyes burned.

"Who told you to say that?" he demanded. I didn't answer, even though I knew. That voice in my head was *his*. It was Alfred Furnace's. And I saw understanding blossom in the warden's expression even as it spoke again.

Now kill him.

The warden released his grip, my stomach lurching as gravity took me. I punched out, my bladed hand sliding into the warden's shoulder. I could feel those strands of nectar splay out like the prongs of a grappling hook, locking the limb in his flesh and bone, halting my descent. For a second I thought we were both going to fall, then the warden braced himself against the windowsill, his face warped from the effort of rooting us in place.

"No!" he screamed. "You can't do this to me!"

He reached out, punching me, but my hand was stuck fast. With a cry of rage he grabbed my head and pulled me back into the tower. The nectar responded, the strands flattening and allowing me to wrench my blade free. I thrust it forward again, feeling it burrow into the warden's stomach with a sound like scissors cutting meat. In a heartbeat I had stabbed him twice more, a river of red-flecked nectar spilling from each wound. His body was growing weaker, slower, as its life force drained away, no longer shimmering but becoming solid. It was becoming *human*.

"I won't let you," he said, the words gargled. I felt the pressure on my head grow, crushing it, forcing me to the floor. He slammed his body on top of me, a coil of guts hanging down from the wounds in his stomach, pulsing black. Then he was hitting me, again and again, his strikes impossibly fast, impossibly strong, pummeling me into the wood, all the while screaming those same words: "I won't let you! *I won't let you!*"

He threw himself off me for long enough to rip a stone branch from one of the trees. Before I could find the strength to get up he was towering over me, holding it above his head like a spear. He didn't pause to speak, just thrust it into my chest. I felt ribs snap, organs shunted to the side by the shaft of stone before it pierced the floor, pinning me like a bug.

I cried out, looking down to see the nectar pouring out of me—a pool of dark, gold-flecked liquid spreading under my back—like rats deserting a sinking ship.

I thrust my hand into the warden's arm, into his chest, into his face, but he didn't even flinch. I thrashed even harder, knowing that it was useless, knowing that I was about to die, that the last sound I would hear was the warden's guttural laughter.

"Alex!"

I wondered if I had imagined the call. My brain was sparking on and off, the penthouse replaced by images of my childhood, flashing scenes from the prison, seemingly random events from my life splashed over reality as the synapses in my brain misfired. But the warden obviously heard it too, for his mangled face snapped around, those too-wide eyes blinking furiously at a figure on the other side of the room.

Simon, red-faced and sweat-drenched from climbing the stairs.

I sliced my hand up again, catching the warden just below his throat. He teetered back, hands to his neck, and with another cry of pain I gripped the stone branch and pulled. It was embedded deep in the oak boards but I had just enough strength left to tear it free, sliding it out of my chest and using it like a crutch to help me to my feet.

"Alex, Jesus, you okay?" Simon said, rooted to the spot, his expression one of disbelief. I didn't blame him, the warden and I—mutated into freaks, beaten halfway into oblivion, leaking nectar everywhere—must have painted one hell of a picture.

The warden growled at Simon, the wound in his neck already sealed by a shining coat of nectar. Then he turned his attention back to me. But not before I'd seen Simon begin to run, the grenade belts around his shoulders clinking and one of the explosives gripped in his white-knuckled hand.

I started running too, both of us converging on the suited freak in the middle of the penthouse. He lashed out and I ducked under his arm, plunging my blade into his stomach once again, all the way up to my shoulder. I heard him gasp, felt his fingers on me as he fought to pull me loose. But he had bigger problems. I looked up, saw Simon clinging onto the warden's back, his arm swinging around like a basketballer's as he slam-dunked the grenade into the man's distended, gaping, blood-rimmed mouth.

The warden coughed, trying to spit the explosive loose. I pushed Simon away, as hard as I could, sending him sprawling over the floor. Then I pressed my good hand over the warden's lips, holding the grenade there, praying that it would be over quickly, praying that it would take us both.

The warden had time for a single, gargled roar. Then the grenade went off.

It ripped away one entire side of his face, his cheek and his eye blowing outward in a wet explosion. I had time to notice that my left arm was missing from the elbow down as the warden staggered backward, his hands held up to his ruined head, the remaining eyeball staring at me in disbelief.

But he wasn't dead. He wasn't even close.

I hobbled over the floor after him. The world was fading fast, like a computer game switched off mid-scene. I was dying. There were too many injuries for even the nectar to repair. The old nectar, that was. There was only one way to finish this. There was only one way to beat him, and only one way to save myself.

The warden hit the remains of a tree and toppled over. I reached him in a flash, throwing myself onto his chest.

His mouth was a mess, but I saw it there, the nectar. It sparkled up at me from the tattered remains of his throat, pumping from the arteries that were already beginning to mend themselves, tiny crimson eyes almost willing me to consume it. I didn't wait. I *couldn't* wait. I could feel the life draining out of me, spurting from the stump of my arm, from the matching holes in the front and back of my chest. If I didn't act, then the warden would recover, and he'd finish this. It had to be now.

I leaned forward, put my lips against the warden's ruined face.

Then I began to drink.

LOST

IT WAS LIKE SWALLOWING liquid fire. As though I was an engine that had been on the verge of guttering out but had suddenly been pumped full of fuel. The nectar splashed down my throat, quenching a thirst that had been raging unnoticed in every cell of my body. I didn't think about the horror of what I was doing, the fact that I was supping blood from the severed neck of the warden—blood that he, in turn, had drawn from a berserker. I just drank, letting the nectar fill me from head to toe; drank until it felt as if my entire body was burning, as if I could have brought down this tower with a single blow; drank until my vision sparked back on, picking out every single thing in immaculate detail; drank until my lungs were screaming for air and my stomach felt as though it was about to split.

The warden squirmed beneath me, and I stabbed my right arm through his shoulder to anchor him in place. His only reaction was a wet, feeble cry. He was done. I had drained him. He was finished. And he knew it too, his movements becoming less and less urgent as the life force leached out of his system.

"Alex, please stop."

I could hear the voice behind me, the boy called Simon, but I didn't care. I didn't care about anything other than feasting, feeling my body repair itself, strands of nectar bleeding from the veins and arteries in my severed arm, from the ragged holes in my torso, from the countless other wounds, knitting flesh back into existence. I had no idea power like this could even exist, no idea that I could possess such strength.

I was invincible, I was indestructible, I was immortal.

I ripped my head up, snatching in a raw, desperate breath that stank of blood and nectar. The warden's single eye blinked at me, full of fury and fear, and I grinned at him, the nectar storming up from my stomach and exploding from me in a guttural, unstoppable laugh. I heard the way it sounded, about as far from anything human as it was possible to be. And I loved it. Why be human when I could be so much more?

The warden must have sensed my power, because he made one final bid for freedom. He bucked his body, tipping me off. I rolled onto the floor and he started to throw himself around, trying to get up. I stood casually, looking at my left arm, which had been severed by the grenade. The nectar had formed a second, shorter blade that jutted out from my elbow like a spear carved from a burned stick. It was still working there, tiny black feelers stretching from the tip like plants, weaving together to make me a new limb.

It was working on the rest of my body too. My skin was shimmering the same way the warden's had, as if draped in shadows. And it was more than that. It felt as if the world was running in slow motion, and that every move I made was faster than time.

"Alex?" That childish voice behind me, Simon. "Come on, we don't have much time left. Zee, he'll be on his way, right now. Remember?"

I glanced over my shoulder to see the kid there, tapping his wrist as if he wore a watch, a kid I didn't want to waste my breath speaking to. He too had been under the influence of the nectar, one arm swollen and muscled by its touch. But it was *old* nectar, and it had abandoned him. He hadn't been worthy of it. I hissed at him, reveling in the way he staggered back, fear lighting up his face.

"What's happened?" he asked. "What have you done?"

I looked away, bored with him. With a grunt, the warden finally made it to his feet, teetering unsteadily as he turned to face me. I don't know how he managed to keep going, considering his head had practically been turned inside out. But somehow he lurched my way, gaining speed and momentum, his fist held back, ready to strike.

I held my ground, punching my right hand through the warden's shoulder again before jabbing my left into his ribs. Both sank in deep and he slapped at me in an effort to knock them loose. But without the nectar his blows possessed nowhere near the same strength they had before.

With another howl of laughter I twisted my body and slung my arms around, lifting the warden off the floor and launching him into the air. He swung slowly, almost lazily, toward the elevator shaft that punctured the middle of the penthouse, thumping into it with an explosion of plaster.

"Screw this," the boy called Simon said, retreating to the door that led to the stairs. "If you're in there, then you'd better snap out of it soon." He took another look at me, waiting for a second or two before shaking his head. "Goodbye, Alex," he said. Then he was gone, the clatter of his feet on the staircase gradually fading out of earshot.

I walked to the warden, his wiry body lying in a pool of black blood. He was still trying to push himself up but there just wasn't enough nectar inside him to patch his broken limbs, his split sides. He saw me coming and tried to spit at me, the weak gob of dirty saliva making it as far as his own ravaged chin.

This is for what you did to me, I wanted to say, only the words wouldn't come, nothing but a loose groan falling from my lips. Maybe it was because I knew the words were a lie. In truth I had the warden to thank for *everything.* He had made me this creature of pure fire, of absolute power. Without him I'd be just another pathetic kid trapped at the bottom of the world.

Or would I? I fought the black cloud that blanketed my mind, trying to snatch any thought that wasn't murder. But my memories had scattered like birds before a storm cloud, lost in the darkness.

I dug the blade of my hand into the warden's back, the fibers of nectar expanding inside his skin, acting like a hand. I dragged him around the elevator shaft toward the stairwell, kicking him down the steps, flight after flight, until he rolled to a halt against the stenciled wall that read "48."

He seemed to know what was on this level because he tried to crawl away, actually attempted to throw himself down the steps. I didn't let him, lifting him up like an eel on a hook and pushing him toward the door. He fell through, ripping it off its hinges and falling against the opposite wall.

Noise filled the corridor, a sound like thunder, rising fast then fading. Seconds later the entire tower seemed to shake, the floor splitting in two, one section dropping at least half a meter below the other, a network of cracks spreading over the walls and ceiling. I ignored it, pushing the warden onward until we reached the first door.

The room was still dark, drowned in red light. And it was still full. The wheezers backed off into a corner as the warden tumbled through the door, their breathing and their cries rising to a crescendo. The warden lost his balance, sprawling forward, knocking one of the infirmary beds away as he crashed onto the floor. A trolley of surgical equipment spun into the crowd, shedding metal as it went.

That noise again, the sky tearing. The building rocked, harder, the windows in the room shattering in time for me to see a jet blast past outside, arcing gracefully to its right and out of sight, its missile bays empty. In the depths of my memory I knew what was happening. I knew that the girl Lucy's plan had worked—that she and . . . Zee, that was his name; that they had found help, had explained what was going on—and that the tower was under attack.

Thanks to Captain Atilio the army already knew the black-suits were enemies, that Furnace was fighting against them, and it must have made Zee's story easier to swallow. I hadn't honestly believed the authorities would take down an entire building, but things out there were catastrophic enough to try the most drastic tactics. Needs must when the devil drives, as they say. And there was no doubt who was driving now.

But it was none of my concern, not anymore.

Somehow the warden managed to turn himself over, shuffling back against a bed and pulling his legs up defensively. He stared at me with that cyclops eye, then he seemed to notice the wheezers. They had seen him too. They were edging forward, their faces masked but somehow alive with curiosity. One stepped right up to the warden, a scalpel clenched in its gloved hand. The warden lashed out, knocking the creature over. But that seemed to use up the last of his energy and he crashed down onto his side, sucking in rasping gasps of air.

Slowly, but unrelentingly, the rest of the wheezers approached, dozens of them, some holding surgical blades, others gripping tools, and some just flexing their fingers as if they couldn't wait to start work.

And work is exactly what they did. I don't know whether they knew it was the warden, whether they were somehow getting revenge for the part he had played in their nightmare existence. Or maybe they just sensed his fear, his weakness, and it angered them. Whatever it was, they descended on him like flies on a corpse, their black coats flapping like wings, their fingers scuttling over his flesh, and that endless, buzzing wheeze filling the room.

The warden tried one last time to knock them away but there were too many of them. I saw his eye flick between his attackers, growing ever wider and ever wilder. And just before it disappeared altogether it settled on me, a look of pure, absolute horror.

Then, with a final, desperate scream, he disappeared beneath them.

I WATCHED FOR AS LONG AS I could bear it, until there were too many pieces to count, then I turned and walked from the room, back into the corridor. There was smoke here, hanging over the floor like mist, and an alarm was ringing too. I ran back to the stairwell, peering down between the railings to see a fire raging below.

With no other choice I headed upward, climbing all the way back to the penthouse. I wasn't scared, the nectar took care of that, but a slight tremor of panic was beginning to rise as I pictured myself trapped inside the tower. I started across the floor just as another plane tore past, so close that the rest of the glass up here shattered in its deafening wake, golden light flooding into the space.

The tower shook, uttering a groan so deep and so loud that it was almost subsonic, a feeling more than a sound. It reminded me of some vast sea creature calling out in the depths. There were no other stairs here, but there was the roof. Maybe there'd be a way out up there. And if not, at least I'd have a better idea of what was going on.

I ran for the nearest window, faltering when I heard the sound of another missile ripping into the tower farther down. The penthouse was already beginning to fill with smoke, the breeze from the windows doing little to clear it. Once again the floor seemed to lurch, dropping by a meter or more, the view outside shifting like the horizon in a stormy sea, so violently that my stomach flipped.

I grabbed a stone tree to steady myself as another jet screamed past right outside. Fire licked through the cracks in the floor, curling up toward the ceiling and taking hold there. I reached the window, the stone frames drooping as the foundations of the tower crumbled. I stuck my head out, the view of the ground blocked by curtains of pitch-black smoke that poured from the windows all the way up the tower, like nectar bleeding from a corpse. It clawed into my eyes, into my lungs, and I turned my head up to see the ledge of the roof over my head.

I had no hands to speak of, not anymore, but I jabbed my bladed fingers into the walls, swinging myself up. The slope was steep, and it was slippery, but I managed to perch there in the shade of the vast black spire that topped the building.

The plane was coming around again, glinting in the sunlight as it banked. When it had lined itself up, two white trails hissed from beneath its wings, slamming into the tower beneath me with such strength that I was almost jolted into the void. The rumble grew in volume as the plane burned past, more smoke churning upward.

I shuffled up the roof, feeling the heat through the stone. And it wasn't just the tower that was alight. All around me the city burned, fires devouring entire blocks, entire neighborhoods, stretching into the distance as far as I could see.

I peered down onto the streets to see shapes there, too far away to make out clearly, indistinct figures that bounded through the smoke, who clambered over the rubble. There were soldiers too, armies facing off on the avenues and squares of the city. I saw tanks and helicopters, men and women in camouflage firing at the marching ranks of blacksuits, all so far away and yet so clear.

You made your choice, said a voice in my head. His voice. *I knew you would. You have killed my general, a man who failed in his duty, and taken his place by my side. I know you will keep your house in order, you have proven that time and time again, my son.*

"I didn't choose this!" I yelled, my voice snatched by the wind, carried off over the city. "It's not what I wanted."

Isn't it? Furnace asked, his voice louder even than the crack of superheated stone. *Isn't this exactly what you wanted? I showed you your future, and yet you still came.*

"I didn't understand," I replied. "You tricked me!"

And yet the nectar raged; it looked upon the carnage at my feet and cried out to join in. I couldn't deny the way it made me feel.

This is your world, now, Furnace went on. *I am coming for you, and we shall celebrate together, we shall watch side by side as the new Fatherland rises. This is your choice, Alex. This is your destiny.*

It was all too much, a tornado of fear and excitement and anger stripping everything from my head. I sucked in a lungful of smoky air and then unleashed it as a howl that came from the very core of my being, one that seemed to rock the city to its knees. I saw myself as the people on the streets would, a creature of matchless strength, of immeasurable power.

I saw the beast in my vision.

I saw *myself.*

"This isn't over," I growled when my lungs had filled again. "I'll kill you. I promise you that. This isn't the end."

Oh, you're right about that, Furnace replied. *This isn't the end. This is only the beginning.*

"I'll kill you," I repeated. This time Furnace only laughed, a sound that reduced the inferno beneath me to a whisper. I felt my fury grow, lent strength by the nectar. And I made a promise, there and then.

I'd find Alfred Furnace, and I would kill him.

And if the world got in my way then God help it, because I'd tear it apart. I'd watch it burn.

No, it wasn't over. Not by a long shot.

My reign of terror was only just beginning.

GO FISH

QUESTIONS FOR THE AUTHOR

ALEXANDER GORDON SMITH

What did you want to be when you grew up?
As far back as I can remember, I've wanted to be a writer. I don't remember really ever wanting to be anything else when I was growing up (except the usual helicopter pilot/rock star/Green Beret combination). I used to be obsessed by stories, writing them and drawing pictures for them, then stapling them into actual little books that I would pretend were real. I vaguely remember taking one into a bookshop once, complete with a hand-drawn bar code, and telling the cashier that I wanted to buy it because I was the author! The first time I walked into a shop and saw my book there (an actual book, not a homemade one) was one of the best moments of my life, a real dream come true. The only other job I'd still like to do is be a truck driver, driving from coast to coast in the States. Sometimes I think I'll take a year off from writing and give it a go!

What's your most embarrassing childhood memory?
Crikey, that's tough. . . . There are so many of them! There are the usual suspects: calling my teacher "mum" whilst crying in front of the whole class, falling in a puddle at playtime and having a massive wet patch on my ass, wearing my under-

pants over my trousers one day because I thought it made me look like Superman (honestly!), being forced by my mum to wear sandals to secondary school, going up to my sister in the middle of a shop and wrestling her to the floor (as we often did) before realizing it wasn't my sister; the list is endless. Thanks for forcing me to relive those awkward moments! To be honest though, the memories that are most embarrassing, and most shameful, are when I was a teenager and I stole a load of books from my mum and sold them so I could have a bit of cash. Some of them were irreplaceable, and I felt so awful. The guilt that Alex in *Lockdown* feels for being a thief is partly my own guilt at doing something so terrible. It is a horrible, horrible feeling.

What's your favorite childhood memory?
I think quite a few of my favorite childhood memories made it into *Lockdown* as well. When Alex gets sent to Furnace, when he spends his first few nights buried alive at the bottom of the world, he tries to remember the good times in his life, and I used my own memories to make it as poignant as possible. I've always loved Christmas, and although I don't remember many years specifically from when I was young, I do remember the breathless excitement of Christmas morning, lying awake waiting for your parents, then going downstairs and seeing the presents under the tree. Nothing beats it! And summer, too. I have hazy memories of beaches and football, picnics and sunshine. Nothing specific, just pure childhood bliss.

As a young person, who did you look up to most?
My parents were my heroes when I was a kid. They still are, to be honest! Even though they got divorced when I was really young, they gave us a wonderful childhood. There were loads of reasons why I looked up to them, but one of

them was the fact that they were both creative; they both made up their own stories and told them to us at bedtime. I thought that was such an amazing thing, and it really did inspire me to tell stories of my own. I also looked up to writers. We never had an author visit at my school, but I remember seeing them on the television and their pictures on book jackets and being totally in awe. These guys wrote books, real books! To me, as a kid, writers were gods.

How did you get your first book published?

Getting published was an adventure in its own right! I've been writing since I was a kid, but other than the horror novel that ruined my A-Levels, I never sent anything off for publication. In the summer of 2005, my little brother Jamie (who was nine) and I decided that we were going to try and write a book together. We both loved reading and we wanted to see if we could write something really cool, a book that we'd both love to read. We came up with the idea of *The Inventors*—two young inventors who have to save the world from an evil genius—and set to work writing it. In the end though, we spent more time actually trying to build the inventions in the book than we did writing. We wanted to know exactly what it was like to be two inventors, so Jamie designed and built dozens of gadgets, machines, and traps and tested them on me (which was an interesting, if not entirely pleasant, experience—especially the rocket boots). Although we had plotted most of the novel and developed our characters and knew exactly what was going to happen, we only actually wrote about 13,000 words.

At the end of the holiday, Jamie spotted a competition being run by a national bookshop chain. All they wanted was the first three chapters and a synopsis, so we entered. After that, school began again and we kind of forgot about the novel. A few months later, I got a phone call telling me that our book had been shortlisted for the award. It was pretty much the best phone call I had ever received in my life, until they went on to say that they needed the full manuscript by the end of the next week. I told them that we had only written 13,000 words, and they answered that if we couldn't give them the manuscript, then we weren't eligible. "Can you do it?" they asked. I said no, thinking it was impossible. As soon as I put the phone down, though, I realized this was our chance to be published, this was our big break. If we didn't take it, or at least try to take it, we would regret it forever.

So we started writing, really writing. Like I said, we had the story in our heads, we knew what was going to happen, so it flowed beautifully. Seven days later, we had a total of 96,000 words and a finished book. The experience nearly killed me—11,000 words a day—but to be honest, the mad rush actually gave the book so much of its energy. I've written every book in the same white heat ever since. We got it to the post office about one minute before it closed the day of the deadline, then we kept our fingers crossed!

When you finish a book, who reads it first?
It's always my sister, my mum, and my girlfriend. I send them each chapter as it's written, and get angry e-mails from them if I don't send them over fast enough!

What do you value most in your friends?
Wow, tough question. I think the thing I value most in friendship is the ability to be totally and utterly relaxed with somebody. To feel like you don't have to make an effort to impress them or entertain them. My friends often just turn up at the door and stay all day, and we'll watch telly or play video games and chat and eat takeaway or BBQ and just have fun. I feel totally at ease with them, totally relaxed. We're equals, and we trust each other implicitly, and that's why we're friends.

What's your favorite thing about the Furnace books? Was there a particular scene or character you especially enjoyed writing?

That's a tough question because I loved the whole process, every scene and every character. It's impossible to separate the various events, even the individual books, because for me it's all one single story. I always enjoyed writing the funny bits, though—the scenes where the characters get to laugh. Alex and Donovan and Zee and Simon go through so much in the series, so many horrific ordeals and blood-drenched battles and terrifying chases and heartbreaking losses. It really is a nonstop nightmare, and those moments when they manage to catch their breath, to pause long enough to talk to each other and make themselves laugh, were so good to write—mainly because it gave me a chance to have a rest, too!

Friendship, that unbreakable bond Alex shares with Donovan and Zee and Simon, is the most important thing in the series, and it really shines through in those moments. By laughing in the face of horror and tragedy, they're proving to themselves—and to their enemies—that they are living a life worth fighting for. They're proving they are human. That's what lies at the heart of this series, past all the horror and gore and violence. It's a story about being human, about holding on to your humanity no matter how inhuman the world has become, and there's nothing more human than being able to laugh.

How has Alex changed throughout the series?

He has changed in ways I never could have predicted. He's gone from being a naive, unpleasant, selfish, cowardly kid to being something much, much more. I never set out to write a book about a bad kid who sees the error of his ways and turns good. I didn't want to tell that story because to me it doesn't seem believable. Yes, Alex is a criminal when the series starts, but he's not a killer. He only becomes a killer after he arrives in Furnace, and that's through necessity, so he can survive. The things he does inside Furnace are far worse than anything he ever would have done outside. But he does them for the right reasons, and doing a bad thing for a good reason is always better than doing a good thing for a bad reason. His heroism isn't clean cut—it's in a gray area morally—but he believes that his actions are just.

The biggest change in Alex, though, is his priorities. Before, everything he did was about himself, about making a quick buck. But he soon learns that life is nothing without friendship. That's what I love most about horror: it makes you realize what matters most to you. When things are at their worst, you really do see people at their best. When things turn bad, people fight tooth and nail for everything they believe in. They fight for their family, for their friends, for their loved ones. They fight for what is right, and what is just. They fight because they know they must. That's what Alex understands by the end—heroism isn't about defeating evil; it's about standing up for the people you love. It's not about being brave, either; it's about always having hope. It's something I learned, too, while writing these books. I've changed throughout the series as well.

How much planning did you do for the series? When you began writing *Lockdown*, did you have an idea of what would happen in *Execution*?
I did absolutely no planning! I didn't want to, because it felt like cheating. When I was writing *Lockdown*, the first book in the series, I just threw Alex inside Furnace without knowing how—or even if—he'd escape. I thought that if I had planned it in advance, if I knew how he was going to get out, then *Alex* would know how he was going to get out. And if he

knew, it would change his character, his personality, inside the story. No matter what happened, he'd always have a safety net, a way out, and that knowledge would infect the story. It would make the reading experience much less intense, and much less enjoyable.

I stuck to that philosophy for the whole series; I just followed Alex and let him lead. It was a much more natural way of writing, because often I'd have no idea what he was planning to do until the day he actually did it. I got quite panicky toward the end of the series because I was worried that I wouldn't be able to tie up all the strands, that I'd box myself into a corner and be unable to think of a way to end the story. But I trusted Alex and the other characters, and it all came together in an incredible finale that I never could have imagined when I started writing. That's the thing—if I'd planned it all, then I'd have stuck to the plan, whatever happened. I wouldn't have felt free to follow the characters, to explore the world. But in going with the flow, I had so much more freedom; the possibilities were endless. It was as big an adventure for me as it was for Alex!

What can we expect in the final Escape from Furnace book, *Execution*?

Expect the unexpected! Seriously, as I said before, I had no idea where the series was heading, so hopefully nobody will be able to predict what happens in the final installment. I almost couldn't believe it even as I was writing it! Old enemies become friends, new friends become enemies, there are twists and turns in every chapter—plus some of my favorite action scenes in the whole series. It never lets up, from the first page to the last; it's completely relentless. But it answers all the questions, too. You finally find out the truth about the nectar, about the prison, and about Alfred Furnace. I really hope readers enjoy it!

How do you feel about wrapping up the Escape from Furnace series?

It's a whole mix of emotions, ranging from relief and exhaustion and joy to sobbing like a baby! It's a strange experience. For five years now, Furnace has been my life—it's been more real than my *actual* life! The strange thing is that when I look back over the last few years, I don't remember much at all about my day-to-day existence. But I remember *everything* about the world of the story: every conversation that took place, every decision, every punch and kick and bite, every chase, every ache and pain, every meal, every trip to the toilet, every glance over my shoulder, every sickening moment of terror, every joke, *everything*! Alex's memories are *my* memories, as real to me as anything that might have actually happened, and certainly no different from any memory I have of real life. I sometimes wonder if I can always tell the difference between them.

That's one of the most amazing things about writing—that you live countless other lives alongside your own. It transforms you as much as it does your characters. So when it all comes to an end, it feels like part of your own life is over. Suddenly you have to say good-bye to the world, to the adventure, to the excitement, to the characters. It can be heartbreaking because these are your friends, your brothers and sisters. You've been through so much with them, and you know that you probably won't see them again. I'm not ashamed to say that I was an emotional wreck when I wrote the last few chapters of *Execution*. But that said, when you've been through an experience like this with people—even if those people are imaginary—you can't totally let go of them. I know Alex, Donovan, Zee, Simon, and Lucy will always be up there in my head, and that they'll say hi every now and again.

And maybe one day I'll start writing about the next chapter in their lives. . . .

What's your relationship with your fans? Do you meet many of them? Do you have any interesting fan stories?

I have the best fans in the world! Getting to know them has been one of the most amazing things about the whole process. I get letters and e-mails every day, 99.9% of them positive, with only the occasional ransom demand or death threat. . . . I recently discovered that there is also Furnace fan fiction out there—people actually writing their own stories in the Furnace universe. How cool is that?! I know some writers who don't approve of fan fiction, who like to keep their fictional worlds to themselves, which seems a bit selfish. When you write a book, you have to give it up. Every single person who reads the Furnace series will have his or her own images of the characters and the locations. They put as much into the creation of the story as I do. If young writers want to take that story and go somewhere new with it, that's great! I'm flattered!

Yes, I get to meet fans quite regularly now, at schools, libraries, bookstores, and festivals. It's so awesome! When I first started writing, I'd go to events and nobody would have a clue who I was. But now most people in the class or audience have read the books. What always amazes me is the devotion these fans have for books—and not just mine, obviously! They make the world of the story real in every way they can. I've been to events where people are dressed up as characters from Furnace, and where the shop or school has been decorated to look like the prison. I've been invited to Furnace role-play events, where groups act out scenes from the story. One fan even named her puppy after Zee from the books, which was amazing. The best thing, though, has to be when fans give me presents—everything from homemade Furnace props to mugs! I love when that happens (hint, hint).

Tell us about some of your other projects, like Fear Driven Films. What sort of films does Fear Driven Films produce? What other projects do you have besides your novels?

I set up Fear Driven Films with my sister, Kate Smith. We both love watching horror movies, and one day we decided to have a go at making our own! Our first movie is called *Stagnant*. It's a horror movie—obviously!—about a mutant bride who murders bachelor parties in her search for a perfect husband. It's now with a producer, and with any luck it will be reaching cinemas in 3-D soon. We've got a few more scripts on the go, too.

There's a huge difference between writing a book and making a movie. When you write a book, it's usually just you in a room typing away. But making a movie is a collaborative process. There are dozens, sometimes hundreds of people involved. I love working with my sister because it's great to have someone to bounce ideas off of. It does get complicated, though, when suddenly you've got a number of different people—directors, producers, sales reps, cinematographers, actors, etc.—all with their own ideas about how the movie should work. It's no wonder that it can take years for movies to get made. I love it, though.

The main thing I learned when setting up Fear Driven Films—the same thing I learned writing the books—is that if you have a dream, you need to go for it. Everyone has ambitions, but so many people ignore them, or say "I'll get around to it one day." Don't procrastinate, don't talk yourself out of it, just go for it! And never give up. No matter what happens. That's the most important thing: whatever you want to do, never, *ever* give up.

What do you like most about writing horror? What other genres do you write?

I adore writing horror because you have so much scope to work with. Horror is pretty much the only genre in writing where there are no rules. Anything can happen, and anything is possible. Horror works by breaking down the rules: of science, of psychology, of religion, of geography, everything! As a writer, it gives you unlimited creative freedom to write anything you like. For the duration of the story, people will be willing to suspend their disbelief, to believe that anything is possible.

It isn't just about the freedom to write, though. Horror also has a positive effect on your personality. It turns you into a kid again; it opens up your imagination, making everything possible. That's the real beauty of it, I think. It's like exercise for your brain. If you believe that monsters are real, even for a short time, then suddenly other impossible things become possible, too—maybe even things you never thought you could achieve. It makes you question your idea of reality, your own world, and your own potential. Suddenly you are no longer being told what's real; you create your own reality, your own boundaries. It stops being a case of, "That's impossible; I could never do that," and becomes instead, "Well, who says it's impossible?" That's the true magic of horror. If anything can be real, then anything can be possible. If anything is possible, then anything is doable. And if anything is doable, then do it! Horror makes that happen.

And as I said before, horror allows you to see the very best in people. I don't think you ever see heroism, humanity, and hope like you do in a horror story. People sometimes accuse horror books of "corrupting" young minds, but I believe the opposite. I believe that horror makes people aware of their own powers, their own strengths and abilities, their own priorities, too. In the same way that fairy tales unconsciously bolster the confidence of young children, horror teaches us that whatever challenges and obstacles we may meet, we can overcome them. It teaches us (without explicitly teaching us) that we have what it takes to survive. It teaches us about friendship, too—the kind of friendship that keeps you standing shoulder to shoulder with someone even when the world is falling apart around you. I honestly believe that horror makes better people of us; it makes heroes of us, even if that heroism is just facing up to our everyday lives. It gives us hope when things seem lost. It makes us human, and all the better for it.

Thanks for reading! ☺

ALEX leaves his underground NIGHTMARE, only
to discover the WHOLE WORLD has become a prison.
MONSTERS RULE THE STREETS, and only Alex
can stop Furnace—but Alex is a monster now,
AND HE MAY DESTROY EVERYTHING.

Find out the fate of the world in

EXECUTION.

HOOKED

THE GATES OF HELL had opened. Monsters stalked the streets, beasts of unimaginable fury who turned life to death.

And I was their new prince.

I sat on my burning throne and watched as anger devoured the world. Perched on the spire of that tower I saw the horror spill across the smoking ground, gripping the city in a fist of molten rage. Ranks of blacksuits trod the bones of soldiers into the tarmac, too fast and too powerful for those poor mortals in camouflage. I saw their victims flee into the alleyways only to find far worse things there, nightmares made flesh. Beasts that had once been children but which now stalked the shadows with hatred in their blood and murder in their eyes.

And more creatures howled from the rooftops, beasts of impossible size and strength, their bodies warped and their minds broken. The berserkers earned their name well, pouncing on those terrified humans like demons greeting the damned at the gates of the underworld—rending, tearing, devouring.

It was an army the likes of which the world had never seen, and commanding it was a man whose laughter rang in my ears, a man whose dark presence drove every single one of the freaks below, a man whose vision of the world was nothing but fury.

Alfred Furnace.

He was the person I had come here to kill, the creature I thought I had seen in my visions—a beast who sat on the peak of his kingdom and watched the old world purged by the new dawn. But that creature hadn't been Furnace, it had been *me*—changed beyond recognition by the battles that had torn me apart, and the nectar that patched me back together. I understood now why I'd had to come here, why I'd had to fight the warden, why I'd had to change.

Because it was the only way I could ever hope to beat Furnace.

Far below, something exploded, the detonation causing the entire roof of the building to shake. The enormous radio antenna fixed to the peak of the tower snapped free with a whip crack, slicing through the air as it cartwheeled earthward, vanishing into a pillar of smoke. There was a second blast, followed by a third, louder than the first two put together, and this time a section of the spire caved inward, swallowed up by an inferno that raged just under the roof. I backed off to the edge, trying to snatch in clean air, trying to work out a way to escape.

But there was none. The spire was circled by a wall of fire, hot enough to melt the reinforced steel skeleton of the tower. The skyscrapers around me were too far away to reach, even with my newfound strength and speed. There was only one way out, and although I had the nectar inside me—the new nectar, a million times more powerful than the old—I wouldn't survive a fifty-story fall, no way.

Panic was beginning to claw its way through the rush, the sting of the fire on my warped skin making it all too clear how painful it would be to die up here. I used what remained of my left arm—the short blade that jutted from my elbow still growing as the nectar worked on it—to wave the smoke away from my face, the sword-like right to feel my way along the sloped side of the spire.

The jets that had attacked the tower were long gone, their job done. There were other things in the sky, though: black helicopters that hovered like falcons, shaded windshields all facing this way, watching as I was condemned to the flames. It brought back a distant memory of standing in front of a jury, being judged guilty of a crime I didn't commit, and sentenced to a living death. It was another life, another *person's* life. I wasn't that boy any longer. I was something so much more.

I stood, ignoring the vertigo that made the city spin beneath me, and I held up the blade of my right hand, spitting out another choked roar of hatred.

"You can't kill me!" I screamed when my breath had recovered, knowing that nobody in the helicopters would be able to hear me. "I won't let you!"

Another explosion, this time out in the city. Black smoke churned upward from a gas station, so dark and so dense that it looked like a granite mountain pushing its way out of the earth. Two of the choppers broke away, banking gracefully. I caught a glimpse of shadowed faces behind the tinted glass, and through the open door of one of the birds was a cannon. They continued to rise, heading this way, heading for me.

I backed off, using the smoke from the tower to shield myself. But as I did so I heard that voice in my mind, a whisper that was at the same time a shout, louder even than the howl of the wind and the thunder of the flames.

Let them take you, said Alfred Furnace, speaking through the nectar. I slapped my ruined left arm against my head, trying to knock his tainted voice away. He'd had his filthy fingers inside my skull right from the start, from the moment we first made our break from the tunnels beneath the prison, taunting me, manipulating me, controlling me with the ease of a puppet master pulling the strings of a marionette.

I still didn't know why he had taken such an interest in me, why he had led me to the tower just to fight the warden, why he had given me those last, vital words of encouragement that had enabled me to defeat his general, and why he wanted me to stand at his right hand as he ushered in his new kingdom. It didn't make any sense.

"No," I growled, speaking to him this time. "I won't listen to you. I'm going to find you, and end you."

You're going to die, the voice replied, a bone-rattling hiss. *And all our work will be for nothing. Let them take you, and I promise you will find answers to the last of your questions.*

The two choppers were approaching fast. They reached the level of the tower and held their position twenty meters or so away from me, their blades causing the smoke to dance in sweeping, majestic plumes. I wondered what I looked like to the people inside—more nightmare than human, two asymmetric jagged blades for arms and eyes like churning vortexes. I knew the terror that my new body must have inspired, and it made me feel good, made me feel powerful, made me feel like I could crush those soldiers, all of them, and take control of the world.

I could hear Furnace's laughter, but even the knowledge that I was acting the way he wanted me to didn't dull the sharp edge of excitement that wormed through my thoughts.

One of the choppers swung around, the open side hatch facing me. Through the burning air it took on a shimmering, surreal quality, but I could still make out the machine gun inside, pointing right this way.

"Come on," I bellowed. I'd been shot before and survived. There was nothing they could do that could kill me. Let them try, and I'd show them what true power was. "Come on!"

By the time the cannon opened fire I was already on the move, throwing myself farther up the spire, a cloak of smoke draped over me. I waited for the hammer of bullets against the roof, the storm of shrapnel, but all I heard was a dull clank. I turned as the chopper was rising again, using its rotors to blow away my cover. And I was just in time to see the gunner cut loose a rope and load in another.

It wasn't a cannon at all, it was a grappling gun.

He fired, catching me off guard. I tried to jump out of the way but a sliver of steel punched through my gut, dragging a black rope after it. It pinged off the concrete spire, opening like an umbrella. I grabbed at the rope, but with blades for hands I couldn't get purchase. The grappling hook that had sliced through me slammed into my back, the prongs holding it there, and before I even knew what was happening I was wrenched off the tower.

The universe came apart, the sky and the ground becoming one endless blur as I spun through the air, my stomach lurching so hard that for a second I thought it had left my body completely. I realized I was screaming, or at least as much of a scream as my air-starved lungs could manage. Then the line went taut, the grappling claw fixed into my flesh, and I swung beneath that chopper like a fish on a hook.

They began to reel me in and I was powerless to stop them. The only thing I could do was try to cut the line, but that would mean falling to my death. The other chopper was too far away to reach, arcing away as I watched, heading for the ground. The bird above me did the same, the world tilting sickeningly once again as we plummeted earthward. The tower flashed by beside me, every window hemorrhaging smoke, massive craters in its side where the missiles had hit, the entire building groaning like a mythical beast brought down by spears and arrows.

I'd wait, bide my time until they pulled me close enough. Then I'd strike, too fast and too strong for them to stop. I ran my eyes up the black cord that rose from my stomach, then focused on the bottom of the chopper, the bird getting bigger as I drew close. I'd be there in seconds.

A shape appeared from the hatch, a soldier leaning out over me, a harness holding him in place. He had a gun in his hands, and he aimed down the sights for no more than a second before pulling the trigger.

Something thudded into my arm, no more painful than a nettle sting. I glanced at it, a growl already spilling from between my lips. It wasn't a bullet. It looked more like a feather, a red plume sticking out just below my shoulder. The soldier fired again, and again, and again, a crimson forest sprouting over my torso and my neck.

Smoke began to cloud my vision. Except I knew it wasn't smoke. It wasn't nectar either. It was something else, a creeping darkness that cut off the relentless glow of the sun, that blotted out the city, that left only the grinning face of the soldier as he was pulled back inside the helicopter.

Let them take you, Furnace's voice again, and even this was muted by the unbelievable, inescapable tiredness that had settled into my thoughts, into my bones. *You will have your chance for revenge, I promise you that.*

Then the last scraps of daylight sputtered out like candles, and the world was no more.

WATCHING

MY DREAMS LED ME TO A PLACE OF INFINITE QUIET.

I stood in a forest, nothing but trees in every direction. Their gnarled trunks grew into fingerlike branches that twisted and entwined overhead, so many of them that they almost blotted out the twilight sky above. Only a sliver of cold moonlight made it through, and by its silver touch I saw piles of rotting fruit on the damp ground. Apples, thousands, black-eyed crows picking at them as if they were corpses, worms wriggling through the decomposing flesh.

Not a forest, then. An orchard.

I knew this place. I had seen it before; not like this, but carved from stone. It was the orchard that had been replicated at the top of Furnace's tower block, the one I had just been pulled from. Except back in that penthouse there had been a sculpture of a boy nailed to a trunk, the young Alfred Furnace, his stomach cut open. I scanned the trees before me—stretching off like an army of skeletons—but could see no sign of him.

I tried to turn around but my head was locked, my body paralyzed, as so often happens in dreams. Panic rose from my stomach like vomit, but I forced myself to swallow it back down. *It's only a dream,* I told myself, even though I knew it was something more than that.

The blanket of silence that cradled the orchard was so immense that it was almost a sound in its own right, a mute roar that I could feel against my ears as though I were deep underwater. The leafless branches swayed in the breeze, the birds fought and flapped between their feastings, but they made no noise. I couldn't even hear my own breath, or feel my pulse.

It was the fire that alerted me to their presence. The deep velvet shadows between the trees began to flicker gently, a ghostly dance of light and dark against the bark. Those forms gradually solidified into shapes that marched through the orchard, a procession of men and women, all holding flaming torches. Their clothes were like something from an old movie, the sort of thing peasants might have worn hundreds of years ago. Their faces were contorted with emotion—maybe fear, maybe anger, maybe both. And they held those torches against the encroaching night as if they were the only thing that stood between them and the devil.

They marched before me, from right to left, and it was only when they were directly in front of me that I noticed two other figures in the crowd. Both were being carried—one on a wooden board, a wreath on his motionless stomach, the other struggling and screaming between two hulking men, his hands and feet bound. I recognized the second kid immediately, even though his grief-filled face was the exact opposite of the calm expression worn by the carving in the penthouse.

It was Alfred Furnace, and he was no older than me.

Several of the mob seemed to scour the area before settling on a large tree to my left. They ran toward it, planting their torches in the wet soil and ushering the rest of the group forward. The two men threw Furnace down and the boy tried to squirm away, burrowing into the ground as if he could tunnel his way to safety. One of the women used a knife to cut open the twine around his wrists and ankles, but before he could make a run for it the men had hoisted him up again. They spun him around and one of them lashed out, slapping him across the cheek. There was still no sound, but my imagination was happy to provide one.

I wanted to step out, to try to stop what was happening. I knew the boy was Furnace, but the way he cried for help, tears streaming down his filthy cheeks, his skinny arms held out toward a nonexistent savior—those weren't the actions of a crazed psychopath, they were those of a terrified child. My body was still locked tight, however. I might as well have been one of the trees in the orchard, rooted to the ground and held fast by the branches of my brothers.

The biggest of the men lifted the boy against the tree, pinning him there while more of the crowd surged forward. Two women grabbed one of Furnace's arms, bending it back around the trunk, while another put a huge iron nail against his palm. All I could do as they struck the first blow was close my eyes.

When I dared look again I saw the crowd step back, leaving Furnace suspended from the bark, crucified. He hung there in agony, his legs scrabbling for purchase, unable to find the ground, blood streaming down his arms, pattering on the crushed fruit of the orchard ground.

The men and women gently laid the corpse of the other boy down between them and the tree. The dead boy was younger than Furnace, maybe nine or ten, but their faces were similar enough for me to know that they must have been brothers. One woman knelt by his side, howling into the boy's chest, and when she looked up at Alfred Furnace her expression was so warped it was almost inhuman. She hissed at him, the way a cat hisses at an enemy, and even though I couldn't hear her, or understand the word her lips formed, the dream interpreted it for me.

Murderer.

The emotion in the crowd swelled, two dozen people all shouting the same accusation. Somebody threw something at Furnace, the missile bouncing off his shoulder and leaving a mushy stain there. Seconds later the air was full of rotten fruit, a storm of apples that pelted the boy across every inch of his body. He sobbed, sniveled, begged, but his words were as silent to the crowd as they were to me.

I don't know how long the assault went on. Time has no meaning in dreams. But when the men and women grew tired the mountain of fruit was piled almost as high as the boy's feet. It had knocked the last of the fight from him, and he slumped motionlessly against the tree, his skin darkening with bruises, only the lazy blinks of his eyes letting me know he was still conscious.

A man stepped forward, dressed in black and holding a leatherbound book. He placed a comforting hand on the woman's head as he addressed the young Alfred Furnace.

You have committed a crime of unthinkable hatred and malice, he said, the words playing voicelessly in my head. *The slaying of thine own flesh and blood is the gravest sin, and you have been found guilty.* The man opened up the book—the Bible, I realized—and began to read. *"Where is Abel, thy brother?" And he said, "I know not: am I my brother's keeper?" And he said, "What hast thou done? The voice of thy brother's blood crieth unto me from the ground."* The priest, if that's what he was, snapped the book shut. *And now art thou cursed from the earth, which hath opened her mouth to receive thy brother's blood from thy hand.*

I could see the crowd murmuring, nodding their heads, some spitting onto the soil. The priest walked slowly to the tree, placing a finger under the boy's chin and lifting his head until their eyes met.

The Lord placed a mark on Cain to ensure he would not die. For his punishment was to wander the world tormented by the knowledge of his sin. But you shall not be allowed to wander. Your fate lies here, in this wood. Your punishment shall be death. Do you have anything more to say?

Alfred Furnace opened his mouth, a worm of blood slithering over his chin. His face was swelling, his eyes watery blue pools in his head. Even in the time I had spent in Furnace, among those kids who cried and wailed and groaned every hour of every day, I had never seen somebody look so weak, or so scared. His lips shaped a word, maybe two or three, but I couldn't make them out. The priest let the boy's head drop and stepped away, holding his hands out to the crowd.

He makes no protest, he said. *Justice has been done, let us leave him to the wolves.*

Seemingly satisfied, the crowd began to shuffle away, retreating into the woods with their torches. The last few to go carefully lifted the dead boy back onto their shoulders, disappearing between the trees until the only people to remain were Furnace and the woman. She stood before him, her shoulders lurching up and down as she mourned. The boy somehow found the strength to look up at her, and once again he shaped those same words, words I could make no sense of.

Her reaction was as shocking as it was brutal. She pulled a knife from the hem of her skirt, a wicked blade that caught the moonlight, and in a flash of silver and red she dragged it across the boy's stomach, side to side. The boy looked down at the wound, more in shock than in pain, and when he spoke I heard the word all too clearly.

Mother?

The woman threw the knife to the ground, staggering back as though she couldn't believe what she had done. She crossed her fingers over her chest, then turned and bolted.

As impossible as it was, the orchard seemed even quieter than it had been to begin with, as still and as silent as if it were a photograph. Except I could see the blood gushing to the ground, the steam rising into the cold air, could see the pulse in the boy's neck grow weaker. I don't know how he found the strength to do it, but he managed to lift his head once again, and this time he looked right at me.

I didn't do it, he said, the words crystal clear even though I knew it wasn't my language he spoke. Those pale blue eyes caught the light from the remaining torches, burning with a raging fire despite the fact he must have been right on the edge of death. I wanted to go to him, to hold out my hand to him, to cradle him, but it was hopeless. The only thing I could do was listen to his voiceless denials, to believe him. I could do that, I *would* do that.

"I know," I said, the words only in my head. And I *did* know. The kid, Alfred Furnace, was telling the truth. He seemed to manage a smile, nothing more than a tremor of his thin, blue lips, two final words tumbling out alongside his dying breaths.

Thank you.

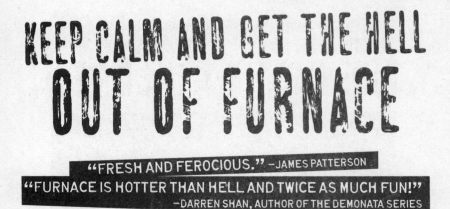